FEA

KT-426-062

WITHDRAWN

B000 000 007 3492

ABERDEEN LIBRARIES

The Shadow of Treason

The Shadow of Treason

Edward Taylor

ROBERT HALE · LONDON

© Edward Taylor 2012
First published in Great Britain 2012

ISBN 978-0-7090-9966-6

Robert Hale Limited
Clerkenwell House
Clerkenwell Green
London EC1R 0HT

www.halebooks.com

The right of Edward Taylor to be identified as author
of this work has been asserted by him in accordance with the
Copyright, Designs and Patents Act 1988

2 4 6 8 10 9 7 5 3 1

Typeset in 11/14.5pt Palatino
Printed in the UK by the MPG Books Group

'The shadow of treason creeps across this land,
Like some foul mist, corrupting many a man,
And bringing murder, lust, and treacherye....'

Thomas Smithson, *The Wanton Nobleman*, circa 1580

For Sue

AUTHOR'S NOTE

The *Shadow of Treason* is a work of fiction … I think. All the characters in the story are certainly fictitious.

1

WITH GREAT CARE Jefferson laid the sticky paper against the window pane, smoothed it flat, then hit it with the small jemmy he'd carried in his pocket.

Removing the paper with the broken glass attached was an intricate job. Jefferson took his time. He knew the floor inside was carpeted but glass falling outside on the concrete would be heard half a mile away. The night was still and there was no sound, except an occasional hoot from the neighbourhood owl and the spasmodic moan of foghorns on the estuary. Over the water a night mist was beginning to thicken.

When he'd made a big enough hole in the pane, Jefferson reached inside with his gloved hand. He knew where the catches were, and he opened the lower one easily. For the upper one he had to stretch, and a shard of glass fell quietly inwards.

He pulled the window open, hoisted himself onto the ledge, gently moved the blackout curtains apart, and climbed inside. In the darkness he stumbled against a chair, but he caught it before it toppled over and the noise was minimal.

Carefully, Jefferson eased the curtains together again. In the autumn of 1944, few German aircraft flew over Britain: at least, few that carried human beings, who might see lights on the ground below. Nevertheless, blackout curtains or blackened windows were still required by law. And ARP wardens continued to regard any chink of light as high treason. The curtains drawn, Jefferson switched on his powerful torch and crossed the room to the big desk. There he hesitated a moment before deciding to turn on the reading lamp.

The right side of the desk housed a stack of drawers. These were locked, of course, but yielded swiftly to his jemmy. In the bottom drawer was a metal cash box. Jefferson forced it open, scooped up a bunch of pound notes and a handful of coins, and put them in his trouser pocket. This had to look like a routine burglary.

The drawer above held a stopwatch and a number of papers, which Jefferson skimmed through swiftly but carefully. It was routine stuff: reports, accounts, a training manual and some local maps, plus other odds and ends. And then, underneath all that, he found something else: a blue notebook, its pages full of careful handwriting. A brief scrutiny under the lamp told him it was important, and he slid it into the deep pocket of his duffle coat.

He was moving on to search the next drawer up, when his luck ran out, and events moved too quickly for him.

If he'd had five seconds' warning, he'd have been across the room and out through the window. But it took only an instant for the key to turn, the door to open, and the overhead light to go on.

Three men came in, two young and well built, thuggish-looking, one with wild fair hair and a scar on his face that might have come from a razor-slash, the other dark, with a moustache. The third man was smaller and older, but hard. It was he who spoke.

'Nixon! What the hell are you doing in here?'

For a moment, Jefferson thought of saying he was retrieving something he'd forgotten. But standing there holding a torch and a jemmy, with all the desk drawers open, excuses seemed futile.

'I'm sorry, sir,' he said. 'I'm short of money. I knew there was cash in the desk. I'm sorry. I'll put it back.'

The short man stared at him with contemptuous disbelief.

'You bloody liar!' he said. 'Come away from there!'

Jefferson moved away, in the direction of the window. The short man went to the desk and began checking the drawers.

Then he looked angrily at Jefferson. 'You've taken a notebook!' he said.

'Notebook? Why should I take a notebook?'

The short man spoke to his henchmen. 'He's got it. And he knows what it is. Take him!'

The blond man's hand was coming out of his pocket, carrying something hard. But Jefferson already had his torch in his fist. He slammed it into the man's face and pushed him against the dark man, who was advancing. Then he took three swift paces, wrenched the curtains aside, and dived out through the open window.

The blond man, dazed, lumbered out after him, cutting his hand on jagged glass as he went. The dark man was about to follow but the boss stopped him.

'No! There's only one way he can get out of the playground! You go through the front door and cut him off!' Then he picked up the phone and dialled a single digit. 'Emergency! There's an intruder escaping through the playground! Make sure he doesn't get out on the sea side! But no shooting!'

Jefferson turned the corner swiftly and silently, mentally cursing the full moon that lit up the scene. He'd dealt with the blond man who'd followed him through the window, felling him as he landed, before he'd got his balance. But he knew there were at least three others after him. He'd got out of the playground before the dark man could intercept, but the man had seen him and was not far behind.

Jefferson had turned left towards the sea, but then he'd noticed the two figures waiting. He'd known at once that they weren't out for an evening stroll, and he'd turned about just in time. But the men had seen him and joined the pursuit.

He'd given them the slip briefly by vaulting a garden wall and then quickly jumping out the other side before they could see him do so. He'd gained a few yards while they looked in the garden. But now they were after him again, and not far behind. There was no shouting; they were very professional.

But Jefferson could hear quiet, urgent voices and crisp instructions.

Now came the shock. He was already well into the quiet little road when he saw the sign 'Leigh Gardens. Cul-de-sac'. He thought of turning back. But the road he'd left had no trees and no cover. With that moon, they'd see him like a bomber caught in a searchlight. He'd have to press on, and hope to take his chance through a front garden and down a side passage.

He began to feel the odds were against him: it would not be a good idea to be caught carrying the notebook. He saw a pillar box ahead, and remembered an envelope in his pocket: today's post, picked up in haste earlier. It was an advertising circular, but the packet-sized envelope bore his name and address. He slipped the notebook in, beside the circular. His mouth was dry, but he found just enough saliva to moisten the flap and stick it down. Then he darted to the pillar box and posted the package, before hurrying back into the shadows.

His pursuers were turning into Leigh Gardens: they'd guessed the way he had to go, and they knew it was a cul-de-sac. He could see three of them. One began moving slowly down his side of the road, looking carefully about him. A second did the same on the other side. The third stayed at the entrance to the road, cutting off his escape.

Jefferson was creeping past a large detached house, set back from the road; and at the side of the building he could see a wooden door, which should lead to a passage and a back garden. It seemed the best option, so he stepped quietly over the low front wall and swiftly and silently crossed the lawn.

As he reached the side door and raised the latch, Jefferson was praying to a God he'd never believed in. Not surprisingly, his prayers were unanswered. The gate was locked. Jefferson thought briefly of using his jemmy, but then he realized that the noise could betray him. Besides, the door was bathed in moonlight. The only course now was to hide, and he squeezed himself into the loose hedge that ran alongside the garden wall.

It was poor cover. The foliage stopped six inches from the

ground, leaving his feet exposed, and he was glad he was wearing dark shoes and trousers. Luckily, the hedge was shaded by trees. He had a chance.

The man searching his side of the road was halting in front of each house to peer into the front garden. In the blackout, of course, he couldn't use a torch without attracting attention, but he stayed long enough to scan each area thoroughly in the moonlight. Within moments he reached the garden where Jefferson was hiding, and his eyes raked the scene.

Jefferson held his breath and stayed very still. The suspense and the silence were almost tangible. But at last it seemed that the hunter had failed to see his prey and was about to walk on.

Then the silence was broken by a violent flutter of wings, and a small agonized squeaking. A mouse had tried to cross the lawn, close to where Jefferson was crouching, and the neighbourhood owl had pounced. The sound caused the man to stop and stare at the source of the noise, and this time he saw the feet.

His reaction was cool and efficient. There was no exclamation, just a low whistle, which brought the man's two companions to his side, and told Jefferson that the chase was over. Now there was nowhere to run, and Jefferson could only curse his luck. The office should have been empty tonight.

He straightened up and prepared to confront the men who were crossing the grass. He managed to land a punch on one of them but then a fierce blow with an iron bar cracked his skull. After that, he didn't feel any of the other blows that overwhelmed him.

Back in his tree, the neighbourhood owl swallowed the last of his mouse and began looking round for new victims.

2

SEVERAL PEOPLE FROM the Cavendish boarding house attended the inquest: Adam Webber, Jane Hart, Maurice Cooper and, of course, Emily Hart, the owner. She was a key witness, and wore her best hat.

She told the coroner that Mark Jefferson had been staying at the Cavendish for ten weeks, that he seemed a decent young man, though he didn't keep regular hours, and that he'd described himself as a freelance journalist. He'd paid his rent regularly and didn't appear to be short of money. She confirmed that she'd reported him missing when he'd been absent from the Cavendish for twenty-four hours. She'd done so at the insistence of her daughter, who was friendly with Jefferson and had been expecting to meet him.

It was as a result of Mrs Hart's report that the police had been able to identify the body found on the main Fleet Road. A police doctor told the coroner that the corpse had multiple injuries, consistent with having been hit by a heavy vehicle. He added that there were tyre marks on the body, and that there was whisky in the dead man's throat and gullet. A police inspector said that the vehicle involved had not yet been traced. Enquiries were continuing.

No next of kin had been found, and local people knew little about Jefferson. He'd joined the Home Guard on his arrival in the district, and the local commander, Captain Brigden, was called to give evidence. He confirmed that Jefferson had spent two evenings a week training with his unit, but said he'd not been there on the night of the accident. Brigden described him as a loner, and said he often had whisky on his breath, though he'd never actually been drunk on duty. He'd learned little of Jefferson's background, except that he said he'd been a merchant seaman, and that this had exempted him from call-up for military service.

It was no surprise when the coroner brought in a verdict of manslaughter by a person or persons unknown. He added that everyone should be aware of the dangers of excessive alcohol, especially before going out in the blackout.

All those leaving the inquest wore suitably sad faces. But perhaps the only one truly grieving was Jane Hart. She'd grown genuinely fond of Jefferson during his stay at the Cavendish. She missed him and she was in sombre mood as she emerged into the street. Adam Webber hurried to catch up with her.

'A sad business,' he said, walking along beside her.

'Very sad,' said Jane. 'And very odd, too. They didn't make much effort to get to the bottom of it, did they?'

'Well, if he was hit by a truck, I suppose there's not much more to be said.'

'I think there was. Anyway, he was a decent bloke, and they wrote him off in an hour. As if no one cared.'

'You were quite close, weren't you?'

'Yes, we were. I liked him.'

'D'you fancy a cup of coffee? It'll be a bit bleak back at the Cavendish.'

Adam had been staying there for six weeks, and normally found it quite congenial. But, after a brief hubbub of excitement following the accident, the place had been gloomy.

Jane brightened. 'Yes. Thanks. Good idea.'

From Adam's point of view, Jane Hart was the best thing about the Cavendish. Understandably serious since Jefferson's death, she was usually a lively, bubbly, young woman. They'd exchanged friendly words, on the stairs or in the breakfast room. And, like all the other male guests, Adam found the land-lady's daughter extremely attractive. But she'd had eyes only for Jefferson.

Jane was something of a local celebrity because she was a dancer at the famous Windmill – the little theatre in London's West End, which had stayed open throughout the Blitz, bringing feminine glamour to tired businessmen and war-weary troops. The place was unique, providing non-stop performances from 1 till 10.30 every day. This was achieved by two different companies doing the same show on alternate days. Jane's job was the first thing Adam had heard about her: news imparted by a fellow guest with a grin and a wink. Now Adam smiled at her across a cafe table, with a red-and-white chequered tablecloth, on which stood two cups of coffee and a plate of biscuits.

'You weren't working today?' he asked.

'I should have been. But I swapped with a girl from the other company so I could come to the inquest.'

'Oh, you can do that?'

'Not usually. It needs to be something special. I told Mr Van Damm I had to be here to give evidence.'

'Why did you say the inquest was odd?'

'All sorts of reasons. No one wanted to query anything. That Home Guard chap, for a start.'

'Home Guard chap?'

'The local commanding officer, Captain Whatshisname. He was talking nonsense, but no one challenged him.'

'What was there to challenge?'

'He said Mark was a heavy drinker. Often had whisky on his breath. In fact, Mark didn't drink much. And, when he did, it was beer not whisky. A half of bitter at the pub.'

'Maybe he didn't want you to know he had a taste for the hard stuff.'

'I don't believe that. And what was he doing on foot out on the Fleet Road, in the middle of the night?'

'I don't know. I don't know anything about him really. What was his job? Why was he here?'

'Like Mum said, he told us he was a writer. On my days off we went to the pub or the pictures. Or just for a walk by the river.'

'He always had plenty of free time then?'

'Not always. He never missed Home Guard duty.'

'Funny that. You wouldn't think they'd have much to do these days.'

'Wouldn't you?'

'I mean, they were formed in 1940, weren't they? When it looked like the Nazis were going to invade us.'

'I suppose so. I don't remember the date.'

'Start of the war. The German army was just across the Channel. The Home Guard had to be ready, in case they decided to come over here. But Hitler's not going to invade now, is he? He's on the run.'

'That doesn't discourage the Home Guard. They still turn out, to do their drill and bang away on the firing range. Mark took it quite seriously.'

'What else did he do?'

'Well, he was writing a series of articles about the Thames in wartime. Sometimes he had to go and talk to people about that.'

'Strange no one mentioned that at the inquest.'

'Yes. That's what I mean. They hadn't tried to find out anything about his life. And how was it no one found any next of kin? I mean, everyone has a mum and dad, don't they?'

'Well, they do to start with. But they don't always keep in touch. Did Mark ever mention his family? Did he tell you anything about his life?'

'Not much. He said he came from up north, but he didn't have an accent, did he? He'd lost touch with his parents, like you said can happen. It seems he didn't get on with his dad. But that doesn't mean they don't exist. Someone should have found them.'

'Captain Brigden said Mark had been discharged from the merchant navy. Did he ever mention that?'

'Yes. Sometimes we'd hear people making snide remarks about him not being in the Forces. In the pub and so on. Then he'd start talking about being chucked off the boats on medical grounds. Something to do with his heart.'

'His heart? Really?'

Jane smiled. 'I expect you get that problem, don't you, being in civvies? Busybodies asking why you're not in uniform?'

'Yes, of course. And you're wondering the same thing.'

'Well … Since you mention it….'

'All right, I'll tell you. More coffee?'

'Are you having another one?'

'Yes, I think I will. It's not brilliant, but it's better than the stuff at—' Adam suddenly remembered who he was talking to. Jane laughed, for the first time in weeks. 'At the Cavendish, right? It's OK, Mum wouldn't disagree. Caterers are rationed like everyone else, you know. A boarding house gets less coffee than a cafe does. Mum has to make a little go a long way.'

'She's a nice lady.'

'Of course she is, she's my mum. You don't want to get the wrong side of her, though. She can be tough when she wants to be. Anyway, yes, I will have another coffee, please.'

Adam looked round for the waitress. And, as he did so, he was aware of a sudden movement at the next table. A middle-aged man in a dark suit was sitting there, with a tightly-rolled umbrella hooked over a spare chair. As Adam turned, he'd hastily raised his newspaper, and was now studying it intently. It didn't seem important at the time. The coffee ordered, Adam looked back at Jane. 'I've been asking all the questions. I guess it's time I did some answering.'

Jane recalled the phrase she'd heard so often in police dramas on the radio and in films. 'You don't have to say anything that could be used in evidence against you.'

'I'm afraid I've nothing to hide. I'm rather boring really. The reason I'm not in the army is I'm in a reserved occupation. They think I'm more useful doing my normal job than marching round a barrack square.'

'Gosh. So what's your job then?'

'I'm a marine scientist. Working at the Marine Research Centre at Southend.'

'Marine research! Does that help the war effort?'

'They hope so. We study the effect of salt on different metals … ways of converting sea water for drinking … all sorts of things.'

'You're a boffin!'

'A very junior one. I only finished college this year.'

'So where's your home?'

'I haven't got one at present. I was brought up in Bristol, but my parents sold the house and moved to Canada at the start of the war.'

'Canada? They'll be all right over there.'

'That was the idea. My stepmother has trouble with her nerves, and Dad wanted to get her away from the bombing. He has a brother in Toronto.'

'Well, well. You're another loner, like Mark.'

'I suppose you could say that. In a boarding house you probably get quite a lot of loners.'

'Yes, we've had a few. Some nice, some not so nice. We've got a pretty poisonous one at the moment.'

'You must be thinking of Maurice Cooper.'

'How did you guess?'

'He's not very pleasant, is he? Always finds something to complain about. And he should change his socks more often.'

'He gives me the creeps. He keeps leering at me, and trying to get his hands on my body. Just because I'm a dancer, he thinks I'm fair game.'

'I believe he fancies himself as a bit of a Casanova.'

'God help us! He's revolting! And he's old enough to be my dad. Thank heavens he isn't!'

'He's too old for the call-up, of course. Commercial traveller, isn't he?'

'Yes, he goes round all the shops in Essex.'

'What's he flogging?'

'Household goods, he says. But I bet he does black market stuff as well.'

'Black market' meant illicit goods, illegally acquired, often by theft and violence, and sold at inflated prices. German attacks on British shipping had created shortages. Essentials like food, clothing and petrol were safeguarded by rationing. Luxuries like spirits, tobacco, and nylon stockings became rare. This was where black marketeers made their money.

'Well,' said Adam, 'I must say he looks slimy enough.'

Jane was contemptuous. 'Slimy's the word,' she agreed. 'He's always hinting that he can get me nylons if I'm nice to him. Eugh! Fat chance!'

'Look, if he gives you any trouble, let me know. I'll deal with him.'

'Thanks. But I can usually cope with creeps like that. I've had practice.'

The coffee arrived, and Jane changed the subject.

'Adam … is it all right if I call you Adam?'

'Of course.'

'Adam, there is something I'd like your help with.'

'Then you'll have it.'

'Mark's stuff is still in his room. The police wouldn't allow anything to be touched until after the inquest. But now Mum needs to let the room. So someone has to clear it out.'

'And, because you were his friend, she thinks it's a job for you.'

'Right. And I don't fancy doing it on my own.'

'That's understandable. I'll be glad to help.'

'Oh, thanks! That's a great relief. Mark didn't have many belongings. There's a few spare clothes and things that can go to the Salvation Army. But we'll have to go through the pockets. And there are a few personal bits and pieces we'll have to think about.'

'Don't worry. We'll sort it out.'

'It won't be so depressing with two of us. Oh, and there are some bits of post that arrived since Mark's death. We'll have to go through those.'

'Yes, I saw some stuff for him in the hall.'

'I put it in his room for safety. The thing is, Mum wants the place cleared by the end of the week. But I can't do tomorrow, I'm at the theatre.'

'And I can't do Thursday or Friday – we've got a major experiment on. Look, I'm off to work now, but I'll be back at the Cavendish by nine. We can make a start this evening, if you like. If we reach some decisions, I can take things to the Sally Army in Southend tomorrow.'

'Right. That's really good of you, Adam. I'll be waiting in the lounge at nine o'clock. Gosh, you've really cheered me up.'

Adam called for the bill. This time there was no movement from the man with the newspaper. He was totally absorbed in his reading.

Emily Hart hadn't intended to be a businesswoman. As a child, she'd hoped for a theatrical career. There'd been singing and dancing lessons, and bits in school plays and concerts. She'd even appeared briefly on the professional stage, as one of the fairies in *Where the Rainbow Ends*, a Christmas attraction at a theatre near her London home. But family money was tight and, when no further offers came along, she'd had to settle for an office job.

Then came marriage, the birth of her daughter, and the move to a semi-detached house in Essex, thought to be a healthier environment for Jane to grow up in. After a few years her husband Fred tired of commuting to London to work every day, and they took out another mortgage, bought the adjoining house, built an extension, and converted the whole into the Cavendish. Fred and Emily were hard workers, and the business prospered. By the time Fred died, in 1938, the mortgages were paid off, and Emily had some staff to help her.

The Cavendish had ten rooms available for guests, and offered a modest serve-yourself breakfast. Cereal packets, bread, margarine, toaster, electric kettle, teapot and other attendant necessities stood on the sideboard each day until 9.30 a.m. Cold supper could be provided, if ordered in advance. But, on the whole, Emily encouraged her guests to be independent.

A key member of Emily's staff was George Fowler, handyman and general helper. And it was he who answered the doorbell when it rang that afternoon. There was a conversation in the hall, and then George returned to the kitchen.

'Bloke asking if there's a room to let,' he announced. 'Number six will be coming vacant, won't it? D'you want me to show him?'

Emily knocked back the last of her tea. 'No, I'll deal with it. You get on with fixing that tap in the scullery.'

The visitor was a dark-haired young man, neatly dressed, with a moustache. Probably a business type. He looked like a suitable Cavendish resident. Emily had never quite lost her theatrical abilities and, recognizing a good potential customer, she put on her most winning smile and a warm but business-like voice.

'Good afternoon,' she proclaimed. 'You're enquiring about a room?'

'Yes,' said the man. 'I'll be working in this area for the next few weeks. War work, you know. I saw your advert in the local paper.'

'We're always pleased to accommodate people on war work,' said Emily. 'But I'm afraid there's nothing available at the moment. There's a very nice room coming free next Monday though.'

'That might do. Can I see it?'

'By all means. There's no one in there at present. But there's some clearing up to be done.'

She led him to the staircase, where the upright at the foot of the banisters was topped by an electric lamp in the shape of a flaming torch. The young man seemed affable, and made conversation as they walked up two flights of stairs.

'Nice spot, here by the river.'

'Yes indeed,' purred Emily. 'We get very good air.'

'I read in the paper that some chap who was staying here got killed. Road accident or something.'

'Yes. Poor Mr Jefferson. That was a great tragedy. Actually, it's his room that's becoming available. We rarely have vacancies at this time of the year.'

'Oh.' The young man looked slightly uneasy. 'Dead man's shoes, eh?'

Emily hurried to reassure him. 'I don't think the bad luck will rub off. I'm afraid it seems that Mr Jefferson had been drinking.' She sighed. 'The police have only just given us permission to clear his room.'

'That's all right. It'll be cleared by Monday, will it?'

'Oh, certainly. It'll be emptied and cleaned over the weekend. Here we are.'

She unlocked a door at a corner of the second floor and opened it. 'This is one of our best rooms. You have windows on two sides.'

'That's good,' said the man. 'I like a lot of light.'

He crossed the room and opened the windows in turn, peering out of each with interest. 'Nice view from this one.'

'Oh yes. On a clear day you can see right across the river into Kent. And there are always lots of ships out there.'

'I'll bring my binoculars.'

'As you can see, there are plenty of drawers and cupboards. If you need more room, there's extra storage space allocated in the basement.'

The man seemed interested. 'Oh. Did the other chap use that?'

'No, he didn't. Why do you ask?'

'Er … well, I've got a lot of stuff. So I may need that basement bit. I … er … I was going to ask you to check it was clear before I moved in.'

Emily gave a small deprecating laugh. 'We wouldn't need reminding. I have a very efficient staff here.'

'Yeah, of course, sorry.' As an afterthought, the man went and sat on the bed. 'Nice comfy mattress.'

'I think you'll find everything in good order here, Mr … er …'

'Mason. My name's Mason. What's the charge?'

'Twenty-five shillings a week, payable in advance. We

provide breakfast. And we need seven days' notice when you leave. Otherwise we have to charge for the full week.'

'Fair enough,' said the man. 'Right. I'll let you know in the next couple of days. I've got to see if there's somewhere to stay for the rest of this week. Or I might keep travelling from London.'

Emily held the door open. 'Don't leave it too long, Mr Mason. Other people may be after this room. And you'll need our phone number, won't you? Here's my card.'

Thanks.' The young man looked out of the window again. Then Emily accompanied him downstairs, closing the door behind them.

From the landing above, Maurice Cooper watched them go.

The Cavendish lounge was spacious, the only common room available to all residents. By the door was the sideboard, on which breakfast things stood in the morning. At the window end there were some armchairs, low tables and a bookcase. Here, tilted at various angles, rested a random collection of books, left behind by past residents. These ranged from paperback thrillers and Westerns to a crossword book with most of the puzzles filled in, and a guide to body building, abandoned by a guest, who'd given up after pulling a muscle.

On the mantelpiece stood a radio, the front of its shiny wooden frame built to look like the rays of the sun. From this came the closing signature tune of *It's That Man Again, ITMA* for short, the phenomenal comedy series which had delighted and united the British since the start of the war. It was estimated that sixty per cent of Britain's population heard the show each week. Tonight three Cavendish residents had shared the communal experience. One of them now tapped out his pipe in a large glass ashtray, and rose to his feet. 'Well, that'll do for me,' he said.

'Not staying for the nine o'clock news, Jack?' asked his neighbour.

'No,' said Jack. 'I need to stretch my legs. I think I'll pop down to the White Horse for a nightcap. Care to join me?'

'Well … yes, I don't mind if I do,' said the other. 'You got your torch?'

'In the hall,' said Jack, and the two men set out to brave the blackout.

Left alone, Jane Hart switched off the radio and picked up a copy of *Illustrated Weekly*, noting with pleasure that it was only a month old. But before she could start reading, Adam came in, still wearing his raincoat and carrying his hat.

'Hi there,' said Adam. 'Ready for action?'

'I certainly am. Excellent timing, Adam. *ITMA* just finished.'

'Good one tonight?'

'OK. Not as funny as our new comic at the Windmill.'

'Did you get the house key to Mark's room?'

'No, I have my own. Mark had his key copied, and gave me the spare. Don't tell Mum. Copies are against the rules.'

'Right. I'll just take my hat and coat upstairs, and freshen up a bit. I'll join you in number six in five minutes.'

Two surprises awaited Jane at Jefferson's room. First, the door was unlocked. And then, when she opened it, she found the light was on. She entered warily. A man was bending over, rummaging through drawers and, as he straightened up, she saw it was Maurice Cooper. The exertion had brought little beads of sweat to his blotchy face. Close by, a cupboard door stood open. Jane was incensed. 'Mr Cooper! What are you doing in here?'

Cooper licked his lips uneasily. 'I'm thinking of changing rooms when this one's free. It's bigger than mine.'

'How did you get in?'

'Very easily, my dear. Your mum lent me the key, so I could look around.'

'I'm not your dear, Mr Cooper. And looking around shouldn't involve poking about in drawers.'

'I'm entitled to see what space I'd have, aren't I? I got a lot of things to put away.'

'You can see what cupboards and drawers you've got

without opening them. And when did my mother lend you the key?'

Cooper had regained his confidence. 'That's between me and her – none of your business! She runs this place, not you! You stick to flaunting your tits on stage, and don't start interfering here!'

Jane flushed. 'You pig! How dare you talk to me like that?'

'I'll talk to you how I like, girl! I'm not taking cheek from a tart like you!'

Cooper kicked the door shut and grabbed Jane's arm. 'It strikes me you need a lesson!'

'Get your hands off me!' Jane slapped Cooper's face with her free hand and tried to shake off his grip. But, in spite of his flabby body and pasty features, Cooper was strong.

He was pulling Jane towards the bed when the door opened and Adam came in. He took in the scene instantly, and punched Cooper hard. The man lost his grasp, fell backwards, and landed in a heap on the floor.

Adam was anxious. 'You OK, Jane?'

Jane breathed deeply. 'Yes, I'm all right. I found this oaf in here, going through Mark's things. When I told him off he grabbed me. Once my mum hears about this, he'll be out on his ear.'

'And the sooner the better,' said Adam.

Cooper was getting unsteadily to his feet, showing no inclination to fight. Adam seized the lapels of his shabby suit. 'Listen to me, you bastard,' he said. 'If I ever catch you troubling this lady again, I'll knock your block off!' Cooper slouched towards the door. 'Yeah, you would, wouldn't you? You're young and strong. Why aren't you in the bloody army, fighting for your country, instead of thumping older men?'

'Get out!' said Adam.

'I'm going,' said Cooper. 'But you watch your step. I've got some friends who'll sort you out.' And with that he was gone. Adam glared after him.

'Shouldn't you tell your mother straightaway, and get him slung out?'

'No, it can wait till the morning. She'll have to give him a week's notice, so one day won't make much difference. Right now, I'd rather get on with clearing this room.'

Jefferson had left few belongings. His clothes and toilet kit went easily into the holdall they found in the cupboard. In the top drawer of the dressing table were three envelopes, a railway timetable, a fountain pen, a blank notepad and a wallet. The latter contained some postage stamps, cards from a taxi firm and a London restaurant, and a faded photo of two elderly people, smiling faintly at the camera. The money section was empty.

'He certainly believed in travelling light,' Adam observed.

Jane was looking at the photo. 'And yet somewhere, sometime, he must have had a life. Family, friends and so on. I suppose these are his parents.'

'Probably.'

'D'you think someone could trace them from this?'

'I doubt if anyone would make the effort. Not in wartime. Still, you could give it to the police and see if they're interested.'

'Yes. I expect they'll be round again. What about the other bits and pieces?'

'There's not much, is there? Perhaps you could hang on to them for a few months, in case anyone claims them. After that, you can take them for your own use.' Adam smiled wryly. 'Make sure you use the stamps before the postage goes up.'

'That seems fair enough. I'd like to have Mark's fountain pen as a keepsake.'

'I'll take the clothes and stuff to the Sally Army, like I said.'

'Thanks. That just leaves these letters I brought up.'

Jane took the three envelopes from the drawer, and opened the first. 'It's a charity appeal. The Red Rose Society for Children.'

'Strange,' said Adam. 'I've never heard of that one. Anyway, I'm afraid that's for the waste-paper bin. Mark won't be contributing this year. Let's see the others.'

'This one's addressed by hand,' Jane observed as she slit open the second one with her thumb. 'This might tell us something about him.' She took out a card and studied it. 'Oh no, it's just a dental appointment.'

'Dental records could be useful.'

'No, this is recent. I remember Mark went to the dentist in Tilfleet last month, and he was expecting a follow-up. In fact, he was dreading it.'

'Oh well, at least he's been spared that. I'll ring tomorrow and cancel.'

'Too late. This appointment was last week. Still, I'll phone up and explain. I wouldn't want them to think he funked it. Now here's a puzzle.'

Jane was looking at the third envelope, which was rumpled and larger than the others. 'There was postage due on this one.'

'That's odd. Someone must have paid it.'

'George Fowler. See, the envelope's been reused, but without a new stamp. George was moaning because he had to give the postman tuppence ha'penny.'

'He could have rejected it.'

'George? He wouldn't turn down a letter; he's too nosey. Anyway, he made a profit. I gave him a threepenny bit, which is what Mark would have done.'

Then Adam saw the slogan stamped on the envelope. 'Let Memory Magic change your life!' he read aloud. 'So it's just advertising anyway. Some scheme for improving your memory. I had one of these a couple of weeks ago. It's only paper. You can chuck this in the bin too.'

'It doesn't feel like just paper. There's something solid inside here.'

The flap was only loosely stuck down. Jane pulled it open, took out a blue notebook with a hard cover, and opened it. 'This isn't advertising,' she reported. 'It's full of handwriting.'

Adam watched as Jane turned the pages. They both peered at lines of figures and letters, neatly written in black ink, and all totally incomprehensible.

'It's weird,' said Jane. 'All so carefully set out, but it makes no sense.'

'It's got to mean something to someone. And they must have expected Mark to understand it, or they wouldn't have sent it to him.'

'I suppose so. But why did it come in this Memory Magic envelope?'

'Economy, I suppose. We're always being told to reuse envelopes and things, aren't we? To save paper. Also, this already had Mark's name and address on it. Did George hand this to you?'

'No. It was in the hall, with everyone else's post. You know, George takes in all the letters and puts them in people's pigeon-holes. It was when I saw him later that he complained about the postage due.'

'Can you remember when it arrived?'

'It was the day after Mark disappeared. I brought his letters up here for safety.' She smiled sadly. 'I thought he'd be coming back.'

Adam had been studying the pages closely. 'This is in code. You can see sequences recurring, as in ordinary writing. Was Mark interested in codes?'

'Not that I know of. He just wrote ordinary stuff.'

'This is intriguing,' said Adam. 'There's a chap at the research centre who's good on codes – it's his hobby. D'you mind if I take this and show it to him?'

'Go ahead,' said Jane. 'I'd be grateful for anything that might tell us more about poor Mark.'

Adam returned the notebook to its envelope, and slid it into his side pocket. 'Well, I think that's all we can do. What time are you up in the morning?'

'About 9.30. On working days, Mum does me some breakfast. Then I catch the 10.45. First show starts at one.'

Adam grinned ruefully. 'I'm in the wrong business. I'm up before six and out before seven. So I shan't see you. I'll take Mark's holdall to my room, and get rid of the stuff tomorrow.'

Jane smiled and moved closer to him. 'Adam, you're a saint. I'm very grateful. I really hated the thought of doing this job on my own.'

'Most things are better when there's two of you.'

'Yes, I guess they are. Now if you'd like to come down to the kitchen, I'll make us some hot drinks.'.

The men came at one in the morning.

They'd worked out that Jefferson's home was the most likely place to find the notebook. It hadn't been on his body when they searched it. And they'd unsuccessfully scoured the surrounding area. Then the short man had noticed the pillar box and guessed that, somehow, the fleeing man had posted it: probably to himself. But of course, until the inquest, they hadn't known the address, or even the real name, of the man they'd known as George Nixon. Now they knew both and, thanks to Clark's visit, they knew the location of his room and how to get into it. They used the drainpipe Clark had spotted at the back of the building. For professionals, the climb across two ledges was no problem: nor was the window of number six. Cregan and Clark were extremely professional.

Their entry was swift and totally silent. Once in the room, they closed the blackout curtains, put the light on and began their search. It was annoying that drawers and cupboards had already been emptied. The landlady had seemed to say it would wait for the weekend. But they were interested in more devious hiding places. Obviously, Jefferson wouldn't have been there to conceal the book, but an associate might have done. Quickly and methodically they got down to the business of raising carpets and ripping open pillows.

Where money was concerned, Maurice Cooper didn't give up easily. Through many years of living on his wits he'd found that eavesdropping on quiet conversations and peering through half-closed doors could often lead to the acquisition of cash, or the means to raise it. And one sighting of Mark Jefferson had stayed with him for weeks. It was a glimpse of Jefferson stuffing a large wad of five-pound notes into an envelope, and hastily pushing it under his mattress as the chambermaid came in.

It hadn't been under the mattress when Cooper searched earlier. But he was undeterred. There'd been something mysterious about Jefferson. Cooper had seen him with a fistful of notes on other occasions. He could well have hidden money in places where Webber and the girl wouldn't have looked. Now, at 1.15 in the morning, Cooper was ready to try again. The house was quiet and in darkness, and Cooper still had the key to number six. He'd borrowed it at teatime and, by carefully avoiding Mrs Hart, he'd been able to escape returning it.

He moved silently down a flight of stairs and along the landing to the end room. A little moonlight came in through the staircase window, but Cooper knew his way by heart.

A floorboard creaked as he approached number six, and Cooper froze for a moment. But there was no reaction anywhere in the building, and he resumed his stealthy approach. Reaching the door, he used both hands to guide the key noiselessly into the lock, and gently turned it.

The creaking floorboard had been enough to alert the intruders. By the time Cooper entered the room, the light was off and the two men flattened against the wall on either side of the door.

Cooper closed the door behind him and switched on the light. As he did so, a large hand came from behind him and covered his mouth. Clark spoke quietly but clearly in his ear. 'If you make a sound, you're dead! Understand? If you've got that, put your hands up.'

Cooper raised trembling arms above his head, and the hand was removed from his mouth. His terrified eyes took in two men in balaclava masks and dark clothing. One was pointing a hand-gun. The other, having withdrawn his hand, stood back to look at the new arrival. He reacted with surprise.

'Gawd, it's Creeper Cooper! The sod who sold us that dodgy Scotch!'

'Shut it!' said Cregan. 'You're talking too much.' He snarled at Cooper. 'You live here, do you?'

Cooper tried to sound calm. 'Yeah. I've got a room upstairs.'

'Friend of that bastard Jefferson, were you?'

'No, no. Not a friend. I hated him.'

'So what are you doing in here in the middle of the night?'

Cooper moved a dry tongue across parched lips.

'Jefferson always had a lot of cash. I reckon he might have kept some hidden away.' He glanced at a ripped mattress and torn pillows. 'Looks like you boys had the same idea.'

'Why did you leave it till now? Jefferson snuffed it weeks ago.'

'The room was locked. They wouldn't let anyone in here till today. I only just got the key.'

'And why did you wait till one in the morning?'

'I was here earlier, but this couple came in. They wanted to do their own search. And this bloke was bigger than me. Younger too, so I cleared out.'

'A bloke was here searching? With a bird?'

'Yeah.'

'Did you know the bloke?'

Into Cooper's mean little mind came an unexpected chance of revenge. Clearly these men were hostile to Jefferson and there-fore, probably, to his associates. 'Yeah. His name's Webber. Adam Webber. Room ten on the top floor. He was a mate of Jefferson's. Very close, they were.'

'Webber. Room ten. What's he look like?'

'Tall. Fair hair. About twenty. Cocky.'

'What does he do?'

'I think he works on Southend Pier. Marine Research, someone said.'

'And the girl. D'you know her?'

'Yeah. She lives here too. Landlady's daughter. Dancer at the Windmill. Stuck-up bitch, throws her weight about. But quite a glamour-puss.' Cooper looked round the room. 'Those two took a lot of stuff from here.'

'How d'you know?'

'I saw them.'

'You said they threw you out.'

'Yeah, but I was watching from upstairs, wasn't I? I saw them come out of here an hour later. He had a holdall, she had a carrier bag.'

Cregan stared hard at Cooper. 'Listen, Creeper, you'd better get this right. You were searching this room before those two got here, OK?'

'Yeah. I hadn't got very far. Just done a few drawers. Nothing worth lifting.'

'Think hard. Did you see a blue notebook anywhere?'

Cooper responded eagerly: he'd been given a chance to get on the right side of these hard men. 'Yeah. I did. In one of the drawers. A blue notebook. Hard covers. Sort of like a logbook.'

'Are you sure?'

'Yeah. I remember, cos it was a big disappointment. It was in an envelope, see, and I thought it might be cash. But when I opened it, there was just this bleeding notebook. I left it there.'

'Well, it wasn't there when we looked. So those two chancers nicked it.'

'I reckon they nicked a lot of stuff.'

'Which is what you were aiming to do. Right, Creeper. This bloke scared you off, so they could clear the place.'

'Like I said, he was bigger than me.'

'OK. But now you've come back. Why?'

'I could tell those two weren't pros. I reckoned they wouldn't know all the smart places to look for money. Loose floorboards and that. I thought there might still be something here for me. I thought I'd look again.'

While Dave Clark listened to this interrogation, he'd been recalling the foul taste of Cooper's bootleg whisky. As Cregan paused, he felt he was entitled to intervene. 'That was a bad idea, Cooper. We don't like slimy bastards who flog us bad booze for good money.'

Cooper had started to relax. He thought he'd convinced them they were all on the same side. Now the fear came flooding back. 'Look, if I flogged you some dodgy Scotch, it was a mistake.'

'You bet it was.'

'I mean, it wasn't my fault. I've been having to use a new supplier. A Yank. Says he gets it from army stores.'

'You lying toe-rag! You told us you had a mate in a Scottish distillery! Quality stuff, you said. And it turned out to be cat's piss!'

'I must have got confused. Look, I'll give you your money back.' And then Cooper made his big mistake. With a rancid smile and an attempt at mateyness, he added, 'You must be the two blokes I met at the Bull.'

For a moment there was silence.

Then Cregan sighed, and growled at Clark. 'See? I told you to keep your mouth shut. Now we got to croak him.' Changing his grip on the revolver, he smashed the butt viciously into Cooper's head.

Jane had gone back to sleep, when a worried Adam returned to her room. He bent over and kissed her, and then shook her shoulder gently.

'Darling! Jane! Sorry to wake you. Something weird's happened.'

Jane opened bewildered eyes. 'What? Weird? What d'you mean?'

'My room. Someone's been in there. It's a shambles! Everything's ripped apart … drawers pulled out … it's chaos!'

'Good God! Anything valuable gone?'

'I haven't got anything valuable. And I don't think anything's missing.'

'Thank God for that.'

'It's unbelievable! Why would anyone want to burgle my place?'

'We'll have to call the police.'

'But that's a problem! They're going to ask why I wasn't in my room.'

'Oh my God!' Jane was wide awake now, and sitting bolt upright.

'Exactly. We don't really want your mum to know I spent the night with you, do we?'

'Too right we don't!'

'I mean, it's OK for me. The worst she can do is chuck me out. It's you I'm worried about.'

'We won't tell her.'

'Then how do I explain my mattress and pillows ripped open? And two drawers smashed? Mark's holdall's all pulled apart, by the way. Someone must have been looking for something – God knows what!'

Jane was trembling. Mrs Hart belonged to a generation with very strict views. Jane loved her mother dearly, and was appalled at the impending embarrassment. 'What the hell are we going to do?'

'It'll have to look like it happened this morning. After I'd gone to work.'

'Would anyone believe that? What's the time?'

'Six o'clock, and still dark. I'll get out quick and catch the 6.40 train. But I'll say I got the 5.15. This house sleeps till seven. That's three hours when the break-in could have happened.'

'The police can check what time you got to work.'

'They won't bother. The police won't be interested in a burgled room, with nothing taken. Your mum must report it, of course, to get her insurance. But no one's going to follow it up.'

'So what do I do?'

'Nothing. Just act normally. Get up and go to work at your regular time, everything as usual. I'll find my room's been wrecked when I return tonight.'

'D'you think this'll work?'

'Who's going to argue? No one's likely to think I wrecked my own room. And, whatever happens, you're not involved. You haven't seen me since we cleared Mark's room last night. You won't know anything about this till you get home from the theatre. Now go back to sleep.'

'Not much chance of that.'

'Then read a book or something. You mustn't get up any earlier than usual. Don't do anything different. Now the sooner I get out, the better. I'll see you when you get back from your show tonight.'

Adam went swiftly, leaving Jane staring uneasily into the darkness.

'You killed a man at the boarding house?' The short man spoke with controlled fury.

'We had to, guv,' said the man with the scar. 'He knew who we were.'

'Don't "guv" me, Cregan!' The short man's eyes bored into Cregan's face. 'It's "sir" to you. Always.'

'Yeah. Sorry, sir.'

'You were wearing masks?'

'Yeah, of course … sir.'

'So how did he know who you were?'

Clark's stomach churned. But his accomplice didn't let him down.

'I reckon it was our voices. We done a lot of business with this sod, couple of months ago. Shifting Scotch and stuff.'

'Well, you can't make this one look like a road accident.'

Clark felt it was his turn to speak. 'It's all right, sir, we're in the clear. We was wearing gloves. Frank finished him off with his cosh, and we've scrubbed that clean. No one saw us go in or out. They won't trace us.'

'They'd better not. And then you went to this other man's room?'

Cregan was spokesman again. 'Yeah. This bloke Webber that Creeper told us about. We took his room apart. But there was no notebook there either.'

'But you still believe he had it?'

'According to Creeper. And he was too scared to lie. He saw it in a drawer early on. When we looked it was gone.'

'So Webber must have took it,' Clark added helpfully.

'God knows how it got to the Cavendish,' said Cregan. 'But it was there!'

'I told you, the man could have posted it. Or maybe his friend

34

Webber was waiting outside when Jefferson took it. Either way, they must have been working together.'

'Creeper said they was best mates.'

'What do you know about this Webber?'

'He works on Southend Pier. Marine Research or something.'

'You said he had a girl with him?'

'Landlady's daughter, according to Creeper. Dancer at the Windmill.' Cregan grinned. 'You want us to grab her, persuade her to talk?'

'Don't be flippant!' snapped the short man. 'You go after this man Webber.'

The gleam remained in Cregan's eyes. 'We go down to Southend Pier and sort him out, right?'

'Yes! And quick! Whatever's going on, we have to stop it!'

'So we top him?'

'Eventually. But first we have to find out how much he knows, and who else is in on this. And he has to tell us where the bloody notebook is. Get him to the hut on the marshes and ask him some questions.'

'Right.' The gleam in Cregan's eyes brightened.

'But don't keep mixing business with pleasure, Cregan. Keep it professional.'

'Yeah, of course.'

'Southend Pier's closed to civilians,' said the short man. 'It's now a naval base. I'll have to get you permits to enter. They'll be ready in an hour.'

'In Belgium, British troops have been consolidating their positions in and around the town of Liège, which they captured yesterday. Isolated pockets of resistance remain, but all enemy supply routes have been cut. Further south, American troops are advancing on a broad front—'

Mrs Hart switched off the radio as her daughter came through the door. She was pleased to see Jane looking brighter again, after the depression of the last few weeks. Her cheeks were a healthy pink.

'Morning, Mum.' Jane kissed her mother, and sat down at the kitchen table.

'Good morning, dear. Ready for a cup of tea?'

'Not half.'

Mrs Hart poured her tea in a blue-and-white striped mug. 'Porridge is waiting. And I've got a bit of dried egg left. Shall I scramble it for you?'

'No thanks, just porridge and toast for me, please.'

'Sleep well?'

'Yes, thanks. Like a log.'

'It's good to see you with a bit of colour in your cheeks again. Let's hope we can all get back to normal, now that dreadful inquest's over.'

Mrs Hart put a bowl of porridge in front of Jane. Then she poured herself a mug of tea, sat down beside her, and reported the morning's news.

'Jerry's on the run again. Our lads are on top in Belgium.'

'Yes. Mr Van Damm says the war will be over next year.'

'Please God. How are things at the 'Mill?'

'Fine. We're still packing them in. We've got a brilliant new comic, Vic Dudley. He's going to be a star.'

'Oh yes, I've heard him on the radio. A bit like Ted Ray.'

'All the girls think he's hilarious. He does a lot of topical stuff.'

'I hope he makes it.' Mrs Hart sipped her tea. 'Jane, dear, I don't want to press you, but when d'you think you might start clearing those bits and pieces from Mr Jefferson's room? I've already got a gentleman interested in it.'

Jane smiled triumphantly. 'It's already done. Adam Webber helped me with the job last night.'

'Oh, that was quick. Thank you, dear.'

'He put all Mark's clothes in a holdall, and he's going to take them to the Sally Army. I've got a few personal things Adam felt I'm entitled to keep.'

'Well done! And it's "Adam" now, is it?'

'Oh yes, he's a real friend. He was ever so helpful.'

'Good. He seems a nice young man. Though I don't know why he's not in the army.'

'He's doing war work. Scientific research. Anyway, I was very glad he came to help last night. When I got to the room that awful Cooper man was there.'

'Oh yes, I gave him the key, so he could look it over. He's thinking of changing rooms.'

'He wasn't just looking at the room, he was prying into drawers and cupboards. When I questioned him, he turned very nasty. Grabbed my arm and threatened me!'

Mrs Hart was shocked. 'Did he? Right! Then he's not moving anywhere except out. I can't say I ever liked him. Damn cheek!'

'I don't think he'll give any more trouble. Adam hit him.'

'He hit him?'

'And he told him he'd get worse if he ever touched me again.'

'Well, I don't want that sort of thing in my house! I'll give him notice today!'

'Thanks, Mum. The place will feel better without him hanging around.'

'He'll be gone within the week. Anyway, dear, I'm glad you got that room cleared. Millie and I can go in this morning and start giving it a good clean.'

'Well, don't overdo it. Gosh, is that the time? I'll have to hurry.'

Jane finished her breakfast swiftly, and was gone by 10.15. Mrs Hart had a third cup of tea, and then did some accounts. Room six could wait till after elevenses.

3

In Robert Westley's Hampstead house, six men sat round a highly polished table. There were none of the formalities of a committee meeting but clearly important business was being discussed, and Westley himself was presiding. He turned to the gaunt man on his left.

'Gerald, perhaps you'd bring us up to date on numbers.'

Gerald Collis had been polishing his glasses with his tie. Now he put them on, and studied the papers in front of him. 'We have dominance in sixty-five locations,' he pronounced. 'Another thirty might be taken over, given time.'

'Of which we have very little,' said Westley. 'We must leave might-bes out of the equation.'

Ernest Cox, the bald man on Westley's right, spoke impatiently. His manner was as bullish as his appearance. 'Sixty-five's enough. Especially as we have strong support in London and the Home Counties. Am I right?'

Collis nodded. 'Yes, forty per cent support in the London area. And since the other sixty per cent are likely to prove ineffectual, forty should suffice.'

'So we're still on course for the first of the month,' said Alfred Jupp, sitting at the end of the table.

Westley managed a dry little smile. 'I see no reason to amend our timetable. Assuming, of course, that things in Europe proceed as we expect.'

Colllis looked up. 'Bob, there's a rather important point I have to raise.'

'Go ahead,' said Westley.

'Senior management. We're all agreed, aren't we, on the importance of having one or two of our people in every key area.'

'Of course. It's essential. Are you going to say there's a gap somewhere?'

'I think we might be under strength in Joint Service Planning.'

'Really? But Neville Straker has been with us from the start.'

'Yes. And I'm sure he still is. But he's rather junior, isn't he? Also, I hear he's developed a drink problem, which could impair his efficiency.'

Jupp chimed in. 'I know what Gerald means. I'm told Straker was pissed at a liaison meeting. Apparently, he got quite abusive.'

Westley's eyebrows rose slightly. 'Oh dear. You don't think he'd rat on us?'

'Oh no,' said Collis. 'Nothing like that. But I fear he might fall short on the day. I believe we need someone else there as well. Someone senior.'

'Have you anyone in mind?'

'Yes. Martin Hunter. I'd have proposed him in the first place, but he was in Australia. Now he's back, and he's right at the centre of things.'

'So I gather. I hear he's on the Executive Council.'

'Yes,' Collis continued. 'I was at college with Martin. I know his views. I'm sure at heart he's one of us.'

'I know Hunter,' said Jupp. 'He's the sort who should be on our side.'

'Don't bank on it,' growled Cox. 'He's a bit too comfortable these days.'

'That's superficial,' said Collis. 'He's still committed to the cause.'

Westley pondered. 'It could be dangerous to bring in someone new at this late stage.'

'Obviously we'd have to go very carefully,' Collis conceded.

'I'm due to lunch with Martin this week. Would you approve of my sounding him out?'

Charles Bell stopped doodling, and looked dubious. 'There's not much time for taking soundings, is there? You'd have to tell him what we're planning. And then, if he didn't want to go along with us, we'd be in trouble.'

'Not half so much trouble as Hunter,' said Cox. 'He'd be dead. Like that fool Miller.'

Westley made his decision. 'All right, Gerald. Go ahead. Don't tell him more than the basic idea. No details, no dates.'

'Are you sure about this?' asked Bell.

'I think we'll be safe enough,' said Westley. 'I'll have a twenty-four-hour tap on his phone. Besides, if he decided to blow the whistle, the first person he'd call would probably be me.'

'You say you definitely heard this man Webber threaten Mr Cooper?' The inspector's words were firm and emphatic.

George Fowler had no doubts. 'Yeah, he hit him, see? And he said if Cooper made any more trouble, he'd get it worse. And he meant it. He was shaking his fist in Cooper's face. Like that.' Fowler waved a bony fist in the air. 'I was just outside the door, see?'

The discovery of Cooper's body had, understandably, brought extreme reactions from Cavendish personnel. Worst affected were Mrs Hart and Millie, who had opened the door on the grisly sight at midday. There was a lot of blood. Millie had fainted. Mrs Hart, in deep shock, had retained her wits long enough to catch the girl and guide her to a chair. Then she'd shouted for help, before herself subsiding, clutching hastily fetched smelling salts.

On the other hand, George Fowler – a keen reader of detective stories – had responded with what could almost be called enthusiasm. It was he who calmed the ladies, phoned the police, made the emergency pot of tea, and insisted that no one should intrude on the murder scene until the police got there. This injunction was scarcely necessary, since all the Cavendish residents were out, going about their daily business. But when Inspector Jessett and Sergeant Monk arrived, Fowler was able to assure them that nothing had been touched. And now he had taken on the role of star witness.

'Where would Mr Webber be now?' continued the inspector.

'He'll be at work, won't he?' said Fowler. 'Unless he's done a runner.'

Mrs Hart, at last recovered, was not to be left out of the dialogue any longer. 'Mr Webber often goes off to work very early in the morning. George, would you go to his room and check? He might be home by now.'

George was briefly reluctant to leave the heart of the action. But then he moved off quickly, to ensure he got back without missing anything.

'Mr Webber seems to do shift work,' explained Mrs Hart. 'Sometimes early, sometimes late. At the research place on Southend Pier.'

'Who might have seen him last?' The inspector was clearly interested in Adam Webber.

'It was probably my daughter. As George told you, he was helping her clear Mr Jefferson's room yesterday evening. That's the room where ... where you saw Mr Cooper's body.'

'And that was where Mr Webber threatened him. Yes, of course. And where is your daughter to be found, Mrs Hart?'

'She's a dancer. She's in the show at the Windmill Theatre. In London.'

'Ah yes,' said Jessett. 'I think we all know where the Windmill Theatre is.'

Sergeant Monk looked up from his notepad. 'Do you want me to go there and talk to her, sir?'

Mrs Hart was alarmed. 'I hope you won't send anyone to the theatre, Superintendent. This is Jane's first job. Being interviewed by the police won't make a good impression.'

Jessett was reassuring. 'We'll have to talk to her, of course. But it's not urgent.' And then, as Monk shot a glance at him, he added, 'And it's not superintendent, I'm afraid. Just inspector. When will your daughter be here?'

'She gets back around midnight. And she'll be here all day tomorrow. They do alternate days, you know. It's very tiring work.'

'Of course. Well, tomorrow should be soon enough. We've got a lot to do before we chase more witnesses. Our doctor should be here in a minute. When he's done his examination, the body will be removed.'

It was then that George Fowler burst through the door with more sensational news. 'Mr Webber's not there! And his room's been done over! It looks like it was hit by a cyclone!'

Mrs Hart gasped. 'My God! Whatever's going on? What d'you mean "done over"?'

'Come and see for yourself!' said Fowler, who'd never had so much excitement in his life. 'Someone's turned everything upside-down!'

'Excuse me, Inspector. I'd better find out what's happened.' Mrs Hart moved swiftly off, with George Fowler in the lead, eager to show her the damage.

In the silence that followed, Sergeant Monk ventured a theory. 'What d'you think, sir? Sounds like Cooper smashed up Webber's room, in retaliation for being thumped. And then Webber went back and roughed him up again. This time a bit too thoroughly. He may not even know he finished him off.'

Inspector Jessett nodded. 'It has to be a possibility. Anyway, the sooner we talk to Webber the better. Phone Southend and have them send someone to this research place on the pier. Bring him in for questioning.'

'I'll ring right away, sir.'

'On second thoughts, tell them to send two men. This Webber sounds a tough character.'

Southend Pier is the longest in Britain, more than a mile of timber and ironwork, stretching out into the Thames Estuary. Here, in peacetime, thousands of holidaymakers had swarmed:

most of them on day trips from London, taking in fresh salt air, to drive out the city's smoke. Southend has always been known as 'London's Lung'.

Most of the entertainments were sited at the seaward end, where the pier broadens out into a large double-decker platform. Here food, drink, music, fun and more drink rewarded patrons at the end of the one-mile walk. And, for those who didn't fancy such strenuous exercise, an electric railway was installed, running the length of the pier. It was modelled on London's underground train service, with neat coaches entered through remote-controlled sliding doors. Before the war, the carriages had been painted a merry mixture of green and cream. But now they were a sombre grey and, instead of happy families with ice creams and paper hats, they carried naval personnel and research workers with serious faces. The restaurant at the pier-head, now much partitioned, had been turned into naval offices. A scanner turned slowly atop a radar station, where once the band had played. And, tied up alongside, where pleasure steamers used to pick up passengers, a grim-looking naval corvette rose and fell with the waves.

The passes Cregan and Clark carried appeared legitimate. The men passed through security at the entrance to the pier, and took the train to the pier-head. They knew, though, that the hastily forged War Office ID cards would not bear close scrutiny, so they kept a low profile. There was a certain amount of activity out there on that wooden island in the middle of the sea. Sailors from the corvette, naval staff and civilian workers scurried purposefully about and were glad to get back indoors out of the chilly breeze. No one took any notice of the two men who left the train and strolled out onto the open deck, apparently deep in private conversation: but actually looking shrewdly around them.

They located the Marine Research Centre, a cluster of prefabricated cabins on the west side of the pier-head, and then they leaned against the railings that lined the edge of the pier, and waited. Eventually, a small middle-aged woman, with close-cropped grey hair, bustled out on her way from one cabin to another. She was wearing a white overall and a stern expression, and she looked displeased when Cregan accosted her.

'Excuse me,' he said. 'Can you tell me where Adam Webber works?'

'Who are you?' snapped the woman. 'And why do you want to know?'

'Security,' said Cregan, briefly flaunting his membership card for a snooker club. 'There are gaps in Mr Webber's file we need to fill in. Just routine.'

The woman snorted. 'Paperwork! Pah! It's all paperwork these days!' Having got that off her chest, she remembered that she'd been asked a question. She pointed at the cabin from which she'd emerged. 'He's in there. But you'll have to wait till he has a break. We're in the middle of an experiment.' And with that she disappeared through the opposite door.

Cregan and Clark resumed leaning against the railings, with their backs to the sea. They watched as the woman returned to her original cabin. The weather had got a lot gloomier and, now the lights were on, the men could look through the window and observe the researchers at work. The middle-aged woman and two men were studying instruments and making notes.

It was easy to identify their quarry. One man was short and bespectacled. The other, tall and well built, fitted the description Cooper had given them.

It was an hour later when Adam's boss put down her clipboard. 'That's all we can do for now,' she announced. 'Webber, you may take the first tea break, if you wish. Newman and I will begin the report.'

Adam did wish to take the first tea break: it had been a long day already, following an active night, and an early-morning shock. He removed his white overall, put on his coat, left the cabin, and headed for the canteen. Halfway there, as he crossed a deserted area of the deck, the two men came up behind him, one on each side.

44

'Adam Webber?' said Cregan.

Adam was surprised. 'Yes, that's me.'

'We're War Office investigators. We need to talk to you.' As he spoke, Cregan's hand was on Adam's arm, subtly moving him into a dark corner.

'Really?' Adam decided to be affable. 'I'm on my way to the canteen. You can buy me a cup of tea. But I've only got ten minutes.'

'It'll take longer than that,' said Cregan. 'We got a lot of questions to ask.'

'Then I'm afraid you'll have to wait. I'm in the middle of a job.'

'This can't wait. Urgent government business. You're coming with us. Now.'

'Coming with you? Where to?'

'We've orders to take you to London. There's a car waiting on the sea front.'

'That's ridiculous. I have to work here till five. Have you spoken to my manager?'

'Yeah,' said Cregan. 'It's official.'

'Then why didn't she tell me? You'd better show me some authorization.'

'My mate will show you something better than that, son,' said Cregan. His large hand now had a firm hold on Adam's arm.

Clark undid his coat and held it open with one hand. The other hand rested on the handle of a six-inch knife in a sheath on his belt.

'Just do as we say,' said Cregan, 'or he'll shove that in your guts before you can blink. And don't shout, or he'll shove it in your guts and twist it. Then you'll be into the sea and we'll be gone. Understand?'

Adam understood. The men weren't War Office investigators. And they'd given up pretending to be. It didn't actually make any difference, of course. If they had been genuine government officials, Adam would still have had his own reasons for not going with them. But that knife, one quick thrust away from his chest, was not to be argued with.

'Yes,' he said. 'That seems straightforward enough.'

'Our guv'nor wants you alive best,' added Cregan. 'But dead would do.'

Adam let the men lead him towards the pier railway.

Suddenly Clark was excited. 'Hey, look!' he said. 'In his side pocket!'

Cregan looked, and then he smiled. He could see the top of a blue cover just protruding. There was relief mixed with triumph in his voice. 'Well, well. We'll take that, son, in case you were making plans to chuck it in the sea.'

Adam shrugged. 'I've often felt like it. But they'd only issue another one. It's a summary of pier safety regulations. We have to carry it at all times.'

Cregan had grabbed the booklet and opened it. Now his voice was bitter. 'He's right, sod him!' He threw the book down in disgust. 'Well, you'll just have to tell us where to find the real thing, won't you?'

'I don't know what you're talking about,' said Adam.

'You will, son. You will.'

After that, the three walked on in silence.

They waited in gathering gloom at the pier-head station. In spite of the wind, dark clouds hung low overhead, and drizzle had begun to mix with the salt spray on their faces. There was no one else on the platform. It was a quiet time of day. When the train arrived from the shore, it too was almost deserted. Two seamen got out and made for the exit gate. Adam's captors obviously thought he might cry out for help: they stood between him and the passing men, Clark's hand firmly on his knife. But Adam made no sound.

Now the train was empty, and Cregan's grip guided Adam into the coach furthest from the gate. There would be a short wait before the train began its return journey, and Cregan hoped that last-minute passengers would choose the nearer coaches.

The two men sat either side of Adam. Nothing was said. The driver ambled along the platform from what was now the rear end of the train to what was now the front. With no room to turn, the trains had controls at both ends.

Adam's mind was racing. He'd no way of knowing who these men were but he sensed they must be connected with Jefferson's brutal death and the violent attack on his own room. And he realized that once they got him in a car, he'd be helpless. He had to get away in the next fifteen minutes. But the men were watching him like birds of prey, and Adam was convinced they were ready to use the knife. Indeed, it seemed that Clark could scarcely wait.

A few passengers got into the rear coaches, but it seemed no one was coming to theirs. And then, just as the train was due to leave, a middle-aged man in a dark suit came strolling along the platform, swinging a rolled-up umbrella. He entered their carriage and took a seat close by, but not quite opposite them. As the newcomer sat down, the doors closed, the engine began to hum, and the train moved slowly off on its seven-minute journey to the shore.

By now, Adam had made his plan. Having done this trip many times, he knew that, two thirds of the way along, the train always lurched, as it changed tracks at a fairly rough junction. At times when the train was full, and there were people standing, he'd seen some of them thrown off balance as it jolted. The men wouldn't be expecting that. Adam would. And he knew where the emergency button was, to stop the train and open the doors. This would be his chance: a slim one, but the only chance he was likely to get.

While he waited for the train to reach the junction, Adam studied their fellow passenger. He felt that he'd seen him before, but he couldn't remember where or when. Perhaps it was his imagination. The greying hair, the unremarkable features, the white shirt, sober tie and polished shoes would have had the man cast as a senior civil servant in one of the

British films of the time. Maybe that's what he was. Top-level people often visited the pier for naval business or research.

Adam looked round to see if there was anything to help his escape bid. And there was. His gaze fell on a twelve-inch red cylinder fixed to one of the carriage uprights. It was the standard small fire extinguisher. The big moment was approaching, and now the train was travelling at speed. Outwardly, Adam seemed cowed: inwardly, he was bracing himself for action.

And then they hit the junction. There were two loud clunks, the coach rocked, and Clark was unprepared. With one hand on his knife and the other on the front of his coat, he had no upright support and was thrown sideways towards Adam. As he swayed, Adam landed a rabbit-punch behind his ear, sprang to his feet, and snatched the fire extinguisher. Taken by surprise, Cregan was a fraction slow getting up and, as he rose, Adam brought the heavy cylinder hard down on his head. Then he pressed the emergency button.

Cregan and Clark were only briefly stunned, and both were now trying to grab their prisoner. Adam stepped back, pulled the lever on the fire extinguisher, and fired a jet of foam, first into Clark's face, and then into Cregan's. Again the respite was brief, but now the doors were open. Adam threw himself through the space and began running along the walkway beside the track. By the time the men got out, Adam was five yards away, and going fast. 'Croak him!' yelled Clark. 'Use the gun!'

Cregan had the gun out of his pocket already. He steadied himself and took careful aim. Twelve yards away, Adam was an easy target.

But the man in the dark suit had also got off the train. And he'd flicked a switch in his umbrella and drawn out a sword-stick. As Cregan's finger tightened on the trigger, the man thrust the blade deep into his back, between the shoulder blades. The trigger remained unpulled, and Cregan slumped to the deck.

Clark watched with astonishment and terror as the man withdrew the sword from Cregan's body and turned towards him. His knife would be no match for that long blade. He'd always enjoyed administering cold steel, but he had no enthusiasm for receiving it. Quickly deciding that a ducking would be preferable, he vaulted over the railings at the side of the pier. He'd miscalculated. At the pier-head, the sea was fathoms deep. But the train had brought them close to the shore, and the tide was out. Clark fell thirty yards onto hard sand, and lay there in a crumpled heap.

The man in the dark suit wiped his sword-stick on Cregan's jacket, removing the blood. Then he replaced it in the umbrella, and began walking briskly back towards the pier-head.

Running at full tilt into a strong wind, Adam was unaware of the drama taking place behind him. It was strangely noiseless, the accuracy of the sword-thrust giving Cregan no chance to cry out. Adam didn't look back. Escape was his sole concern.

He found himself running towards the shore, that being the direction in which he'd tumbled from the train. The thought raced through his mind that perhaps he should be running back to the research centre, to don his white coat and apologize for a prolonged tea break. But in his heart he knew that life could never return to the normality he'd enjoyed in the last six weeks. He didn't know the fatal outcome of the scuffle outside the carriage. But he realized that the stopping of the train and the struggle in the coach would be reported. There'd be an investigation and his guilty secret was likely to be discovered.

So he ran on. His immediate need was to get off the pier and away from the thugs. He was now approaching the pier entrance. The turnstiles which had admitted holidaymakers in peace-time had been replaced by a naval checkpoint, with a guard-room and a barrier. As Adam got close, he risked glancing back. No one was following. Relieved, he slowed down to a walking pace, striving to regain his breath and a calmer appearance.

At the barrier, two men in dark blue raincoats had shown their passes and were talking to the guard, who seemed to be giving them directions. Then he saw Adam approaching. 'That's Mr Webber now,' he told the men helpfully. As the men moved forward to meet him, Adam's mind reeled under another blow. These burly individuals were obviously two more members of the gang from whom he'd just escaped. Was the whole world out to get him?

'Ah, Mr Webber,' said the detective sergeant genially. 'We'd like a word with you, please.'

Adam hit him as hard as he could, pushed the other man aside, vaulted the barrier, and resumed running.

'My uncle's a very clever man,' said Vic Dudley. 'He's crossed a sheep with a kangaroo. That's right, a sheep and a kangaroo. So he gets woolly jumpers. And another thing ...' He paused. There was mild laughter from the Windmill audience. They hadn't come to hear jokes: they'd come to see the girls. But Dudley had a pleasant personality. They'd tolerate him, as long as he didn't go on too long.

'Thanks for the titter,' said Dudley. 'We're always glad of titters here. And another thing. He crossed a carrier pigeon with a woodpecker. Very clever. He's got a bird that carries messages and knocks on the door when it gets there.'

In the wings, Jane and two other girls, dressed in fishnet tights and not much else, were watching. Dudley was not only personable but also rather good-looking. Jane felt a hand on her shoulder, and turned to find Andy, one of the stagehands. 'Message from Bert,' he said quietly. 'Your mum rang. She wants you to phone back as soon as you can.'

Bert was the stage-door man, and keeper of the backstage telephone. Jane was alarmed. Her mum had never rung her at the theatre before. But she'd given her the number in case of emergency. This must be an emergency. She thought quickly. Vic Dudley had only just started his routine: he had a way to go. Then there'd be the accordion act. She had fifteen minutes before she was needed for the Montmartre scene. She hurried towards the stage door.

*

Mrs Hart was almost incoherent with alarm, emotion, and the sheer amount of news she had to tell. As soon as Jane said hello, it all came tumbling out.

'Jane, dear, the most dreadful things have been happening here! Mr Cooper's been murdered!'

'Murdered?' Jane was aghast. This was Britain in the 1940s. Murders were rare. '*Murdered?!*'

'Someone knocked him about so badly he died! Millie and I found him this morning. In a pool of blood,' she added, to fill in the picture.

'My God, how awful! How did it happen?'

'That's even worse! The police think Mr Webber did it!'

'Adam Webber? That's impossible!'

'It's true, dear. After they had that quarrel, when you were clearing number six, Mr Cooper smashed up Mr Webber's room! And they think Mr Webber went back and beat him up!'

'But he couldn't have, he was with … I mean, he's not that kind of man.'

'You don't know the half of it, dear. The police went to arrest him on Southend Pier, and he attacked them and got away!'

'Attacked the police? That I don't believe!'

'And there was a fight, and two men got killed!'

'What?!'

'It's true! It was on the nine o'clock news! The police are searching for Adam Webber. Anyone who sees him has to ring Scotland Yard. Whitehall 1212.'

'Mum, I've got to go. What am I supposed to do about all this?'

'There's nothing you can do. I just thought you ought to know. I didn't want you having too much of a shock when you get home. There's a policeman on duty in the hall.'

'Just as well, with all this going on! But I'm sure Adam's done nothing wrong!'

'Then why's he run away, dear? You're too trusting, you are. If he comes near you, make sure you call the police.'

Jane could hear The Accordion Aces going into their last

number. 'I've got to go, Mum. I'm on in two minutes. See you later. Take care.'

She hung up, and raced back to the wings, ready to take her place for 'One Night In Paris'. But her mind wasn't in France. It was in turmoil.

There were another fifty minutes and four routines to get through, which Jane did on automatic pilot. The Windmill girls were well drilled, and she made only one mistake, turning left instead of right in the seascape ballet, and nearly bending Neptune's cardboard trident. But at last the final curtain fell, and the cast dispersed to their dressing rooms. There were six girls sharing Jane's room, and the chair next to her was occupied by her friend, Maggie. Maggie took a good look at her.

'Are you all right, Janie?' she asked. 'You've gone all tense. I thought you were going to fall over in that last number.'

Jane was hurrying to remove her stage make-up and get away. Her reply was terse, and obviously false. 'Yes, I'm OK, thanks. But I've got to rush.'

'Come off it, you've been wobbling like a jelly. Something's the matter!'

'All right, yes, it is. But I haven't got time to explain. I'll tell you on Friday, when things are a bit clearer.'

'OK. But listen, if you're in trouble, if you need help, you let me know, right? I mean it.'

'Thanks, Maggie.' Jane knew she meant it. Maggie's heart was as big as Tower Bridge, near which she'd been born. But now the need was to get home and see what was happening. And she had to sort out her thoughts. She'd only known Adam casually for a few weeks, and intimately for twenty-four hours. But last night was enough to tell her there was something special between them, and she'd have sworn he was a good man. Had she got it wrong? She knew, of course, that he hadn't murdered Maurice Cooper. But what was this about attacking police, and men being killed on the pier?

Jane finished dressing, said a quick good night to the girls, and hurried away. At the stage-door, Bert looked up from his evening paper. 'Oi, Jane, did you see? There's been a nasty murder in Tilfleet. That's where you live, innit?'

'Yes,' said Jane. 'I want to get home and see my mum's all right.'

'Well, mind how you go, there's some funny people about,' said Bert, adding as an afterthought, 'Pity that bloke Dudley's not one of them.'

As Jane stepped out into the alley behind the theatre, a figure moved forward from the shadows.

'Jane,' said Adam. 'Can we talk?'

Jane was shaken, but she knew at once that she was glad to see him. She managed to blurt out, 'My God, it's you!' She'd been about to speak his name, but then remembered he was a wanted man. She moved close to him, and he put his arms around her. He smelled of salt spray, but he also smelled of Adam, which was comforting. 'What the hell's been going on?' she asked.

'I don't know,' said Adam. 'But I can tell you what's happened to me, if you've got time. Is there somewhere we can have coffee?'

'Solly's Salt-Beef Bar,' said Jane. 'You must be starving.'

So, for the second day running, the two of them sat at a cafe table drinking coffee. But now the dainty biscuits had been replaced by huge hot salt-beef sandwiches, which Adam was wolfing down. Only thirty hours had elapsed since the red-and-white tablecloths of Tilfleet's Crescent Tea Rooms. And now they were in a different world – a bare wooden table in a crowded little Soho nosh-bar, amid a haze of cigarette smoke, and the babble of London voices. And events had changed their lives for ever.

It took Adam ten minutes to tell Jane all he'd been through since they parted that morning: a tale punctuated by her exclamations of surprise and alarm. In turn, she was expecting to amaze him with the news of Cooper's death, but it turned out he'd already read about it in the evening paper and vented his astonishment and disbelief hours ago. And then, when they'd shared all the day's astonishing stories, and expressed their mutual bewilderment, there was a pause. And Jane had to ask the inevitable question.

'Adam, I know for a fact that you didn't kill Maurice Cooper. And it's not your fault these men attacked you. So you'd done nothing wrong.'

'No. Nothing.'

'And when you came off the pier, you didn't know you were wanted for questioning.'

'No, I didn't.'

'So why didn't you go straight to the police and tell them these men had tried to kidnap you?'

Adam munched his salt-beef for a moment. Then he said, 'I bought an evening paper. The Stop Press column said the police were looking for Adam Webber. In connection with a murder in Tilfleet.'

Jane frowned. 'No, Adam, that won't do. You knew I could tell them you didn't kill Cooper.'

'Then your mum and everyone else would know we'd spent the night together.'

'There might be ways round that. And, anyway, a little embarrassment's not as bad as a murder charge. There's something else, isn't there?'

'Something else?'

'You thought you had two thugs chasing you … trying to kill you! You wouldn't have stopped to buy a newspaper. You'd be looking for help.' Jane's eyes locked onto Adam's. 'Why didn't you go to the police, Adam?'

Adam sighed. 'All right, Jane, I suppose I'll have to tell you.' He cleared his throat. 'I reckoned that, once the police began questioning me about the trouble on the pier and the damage to my room, they'd start checking on my background. And then they'd find out I'm not Adam Webber.'

Jane spilled some coffee from her cup. Then she steadied herself, and put it carefully down on her saucer.

'Excuse me, did you just say you're not Adam Webber?'

'I'm the Adam Webber who's been working on the pier for the last six weeks. But no, I'm not the original Adam Webber.'

'Perhaps you'd better explain.'

Adam thought for a moment. A juke-box was blaring, and the other customers were deep in their own conversations. He wouldn't be overheard. So he said, 'Yes, perhaps I should.'

'This had better be good.'

'I can't say it's good. But it'll be the truth.'

'I certainly hope so.'

'All the stuff I told you, about Bristol and my parents in Canada and so on, that's all true. Right up to my last day at London University. I was sharing digs in Bloomsbury with another student. Adam Webber.'

'So there really is an Adam Webber.'

'Was, unfortunately. We were friends, both studying marine biology. He was another loner, like me. Even more so, actually: his parents were killed in the Blitz.'

Adam stopped. Harry James' 'Carnival In Venice' had finished, and the juke-box was silent.

'Go on,' said Jane.

'Let's wait for a little more background music, shall we?'

A coin dropped. Bing Crosby and the Andrews Sisters burst into song, and Adam resumed.

'Webber was more clever than me. He passed his final exams and was grabbed for the research centre at Southend. I failed mine, so bang went my exemption from call-up. I was due to join the army. But Hitler had it in for the Webber family. On our last night in London a flying bomb hit our digs. I'd gone out to buy cigarettes. When I got back, the place was smashed in. Everyone killed.'

'My God, that's terrible!'

'Part of the house was still standing, including the room we shared on the ground floor. I went in, to see if I could help. Adam was undoubtedly dead, no pulse, some falling masonry had crushed his head.'

Jane was horrified. 'Oh dear. I think I know what you're about to tell me. And I don't think I'm going to like it.'

'I'm not proud of it myself. It was an impulse, Jane. But, looking back, I can't think it did anyone any harm. And I'm damn sure my friend Adam Webber would approve. He had a great sense of humour.'

'You did a switch!'

'Yes. It was only a matter of taking his identity card from his pocket and replacing it with mine.'

'Just that?'

'Well, there were a few other things to change over; neither of us had many possessions. Next day I reported for duty on Southend Pier. They didn't know what Adam Webber was going to look like. And I honestly believe I'm doing a better job for Britain in Marine Research than I could do square-bashing in some army camp.'

'I don't know how you thought you'd get away with it.'

'This is wartime, Jane. Hundreds of people get killed by bombs every day. Records get destroyed. People are busy, everyone's on the move. So I have got away with it. And I still would, if the sky hadn't fallen in today. Now I can't face questions. So I realized I had to run.'

'With the result that, instead of charges of false identity and so on, you're wanted for three murders and assaulting the police!'

'What?! What d'you mean, three murders?'

'It was on the news this evening. Two men died in a struggle on Southend Pier. They're linking your name with that.'

'Jane, I didn't kill anyone! All I did was run away, like I told you! Honestly!'

'All right. I believe you, I'm not sure why. But will anyone else? And it seems the man you hit as you charged off the pier was a policeman.'

'Oh. Well, I wasn't to know that, was I? He was in plain clothes.' Adam finished his coffee. 'I suppose I've been a silly boy.'

'Yes. And what did you do after you came off the pier?'

'I caught the train to Tilfleet. I was going to collect my things from the Cavendish, and leave a note for you, to say I'd be in touch.'

'Well, after last night, I'm glad to hear that bit.'

'But when I approached the place it was swarming with coppers, so I didn't go in. I bought the *Evening News,* to try and find out what was going on. The Tilfleet murder was in the Stop Press column, and it said police wanted to talk to Adam Webber. So I knew I had to disappear.'

'How are you going to do that?'

'I don't know. Try and get out of the country, I suppose. Go to Canada or somewhere. I have to have time to think, Jane. That's why I came to you. I need a friend.'

Jane hesitated no more than a moment. Then she moved her hand across the table and rested it on his. 'You've got one. You've been a bloody fool, but I don't believe you'd hurt anyone who didn't deserve it. I think I trust you, Adam.'

Adam grinned and said, 'Now who's being a bloody fool?'

'Just a minute. You're not Adam, are you? So what do I call you now?'

'The same. My real name is Adam John Carr. With a C.'

'Two Adams in the same digs! That's extraordinary!'

'And lucky. It made the transition much easier. I still answer to the name I grew up with.'

'But what a coincidence!'

'Well, there is a possible explanation. Webber and I used to laugh about it. We were both born in the twenties, when there was an early film star called Adam Finch. Very good-looking. What they used to call a "matinee idol". We reckoned both our mothers fancied him.'

'Anyway, that's a relief. I'm glad I don't have to learn a new name.'

'And I'm sticking to "Adam Webber" for now. As Adam Webber I haven't actually done anything wrong. It was Adam Carr who stole the ID card.' Now Adam was holding her hand. 'Jane, did last night mean as much to you as it did to me?'

'Yes. I wouldn't be sitting here if it didn't. But I don't think we'd better discuss that now. We've got to decide what to do with you.'

'Look, I'll work that out. When I said I needed a friend, I didn't mean I was dumping myself on you. Mainly I need someone to talk to. Also, pretty soon I'll have to borrow some money. All I've got are the clothes I'm wearing, and seven pounds in my wallet. Anything I borrow I'll pay back, I swear it.'

'Don't worry about cash, I've got savings in the post office. There are more urgent problems than that. Like where are you going to sleep tonight?'

'It's a dry night. I'll sleep on a park bench.'

'Don't be daft – pneumonia won't help. Besides, if you start sleeping rough you could get nicked by a policeman. We'll have to stay with my friend Maggie.'

'We?'

'You don't think I'll let you out of my sight again, do you? God knows what you'd get up to next time. I've lost one good man in the last month, I don't want to lose another. Maggie's got a little flat in Maida Vale, I've stayed there before. She just said that if I'm in trouble, she'll help.'

'You're not in trouble, it's me. You don't have to do this.'

'For God's sake, think! Did the research centre have your picture?'

'Yes. They took one for my security pass. And they'll have kept a copy.'

'Right. So tomorrow that picture will be in all the newspapers. You won't be able to go out! You're going to need someone to look after you!' She glanced at her watch. 'Maggie always goes for a drink after the last show. In the pub opposite. But they'll be chucking out in five minutes. We need to be quick.'

4

Now IT WAS the short man's turn to take a tongue-lashing. The midnight voice on the phone was furious.

'I suppose those clowns who got killed at Southend were your men?'

'It looks like it, I'm afraid. They haven't returned from the job.'

'Bloody incompetence! I thought you were employing professionals!'

'So did I. Of course, the police haven't released names. They probably haven't identified them yet.'

'You'd better hope to God it takes them a long time. Because, when they do identify them, they're going to wonder how two low-life thugs got passes to enter a high-security zone. Aren't they? Aren't they, you bungling bastard?'

The short man held the phone slightly away from his ear.

The voice stormed on. 'They might be able to trace those passes. Right?'

'Not necessarily to you. There are plenty of forgers around these days.'

'But these had a lot that was official about them. The police may come sniffing round my office.'

'Then you just deny everything.'

'Don't tell me my business! Listen, if this blunder wrecks everything, you're going to suffer!'

'I'm suffering already. I don't like things going wrong any more than you do. But accidents happen.'

'There'll be a nasty accident coming your way, if you don't sort out this mess! The notebook's still missing, obviously.'

'Yes. But we're sure we know who's got it. We'll catch him before long.'

'You'd better! Get your finger out and get this dealt with! Find out who's trying to sabotage our operation! Ring me tomorrow with a progress report!'

The phone was slammed down at the other end. The short man sighed and replaced the receiver.

Then he began making phone calls himself.

'This is great!' Adam's words were filtered through a mouthful of breakfast. 'You do wonders with dried egg.'

Jane smiled. 'For scrambling, I think it's better than the real thing. Maggie's aunt in Australia sends her packets of the stuff. And it piles up, as she doesn't eat breakfast.'

'Shouldn't she at least be getting some toast? And a cup of tea in bed?'

'You stay away from Maggie's bed. She sleeps in till noon on days she isn't working.'

'Hm. It's a great life for some. And Windmill money must be better than I thought. This flat must cost a few bob.'

'It doesn't cost Maggie anything. This place belongs to her gentleman friend. Maggie lives here free.'

'Ah, a gentleman friend. So where is he today?'

'He lives with his wife and family most of the time. He gets here when he can.'

'I see. And he doesn't mind Maggie having overnight guests?'

'No, Maggie can do what she likes. The man's crazy about her. I've stayed here before.'

'He might feel different about blokes.'

'We'll cross that bridge when we come to it. Maggie says he gives her plenty of notice when he's going to arrive. And she says he's up north this week.'

'Good. Well, that explains the razor and shaving soap in the bathroom.'

'I hope you didn't use them.'

'No. I thought that might be stretching hospitality a bit too far.'

'You were right. I'll buy some stuff for you this morning.'

'Thanks. Any chance of a new shirt and underwear?'

'Sorry, not today, I've got no clothing coupons with me. I might borrow some clean things from one of the boys at the 'Mill tomorrow. More tea?'

'Thanks. You know, I think I'd like to go on sharing breakfasts with you.'

'That might be fun. If you could learn to stop talking with your mouth full.'

'I'll try. But I mean it, Jane, I think we could have a future together.'

'We might. If things were different. But I can't spend my life with someone on the run.'

Adam's smile faded. 'No, I suppose I couldn't ask that. You've done enough for me already.'

'And I'll do a lot more. I shan't desert you. But I'm not running away to Canada, hiding in the hold of a banana boat.'

'Banana boats come the other way.'

'Yes, but they have to go back, don't they? Probably carrying exports and people fleeing the country. Is that still what you're planning to do?'

'Well, the police are after me, some people seem to want me dead, my cover's blown – what else can I do?'

'Give yourself up to the authorities.'

'What?'

'I can tell them you didn't murder Maurice Cooper. I don't care if people know we spent the night together. And now we know there are witnesses to say you didn't kill those men on the pier. We didn't know that last night.'

The morning paper Jane had fetched was full of war news, of course. But the Tilfleet death, and the drama on Southend Pier, were sensational enough to rate two columns on the front page. As expected, there was a picture of Adam, who linked the two stories, and whom the police wanted to interview. But there were reports from the train driver and another passenger that the man who wielded the fire extinguisher had run away. And they'd seen another man do the killing on the walkway.

'As far as I can see,' continued Jane, 'all you're guilty of is turning up at the research centre pretending to be someone else. That can't be too serious, especially if you've been doing a good job there.'

'Well, I've certainly put in the hours.'

'If they jail you, I'll be waiting when you come out. Go to the police and get your life straight.'

Adam sighed. 'It's not as simple as that. Once the police know we're lovers, they may not take your word on the Cooper alibi. Also, the two thugs who collared me yesterday talked about their boss wanting me dead or alive. There's still someone out there who wants to get me.'

'But you'd be safe with the police.'

'Would I? How did those two get on the pier? There's tight security; they must have had passes. If they could reach me in a naval base, they could reach me in a police station.'

'That's a nasty thought.'

'But it's true, isn't it? I don't want to show my face until I know who's trying to kill me, and why.'

'I've just remembered. After you hit Cooper, he threatened you, didn't he? He said he'd got some friends who'd sort you out.'

'That's right, he did. So if they thought I'd bumped him off, they might well come after me. But the thugs were talking about their boss. Would that fit in?'

'Yes. Cooper could have been part of a gang. Probably black marketeers.'

'Right. Jane, you may be on to something. How can I find out more?'

'You can't; you've got to stay out of sight. I have to go down to Tilfleet this afternoon. I'll have a word with George Fowler. He knows a bit about the local underworld. He might tell me who's big in the Tilfleet black market.'

'Thanks.' Adam downed his third cup of tea. 'You're going to Tilfleet?'

'I have to. I rang Mum last night, to tell her I was staying in town for a morning rehearsal. I said I'd be with a friend. I didn't say who or where. Mum said the police want to talk to me. Just routine, she said.'

'That's tricky.'

'Well, I think I'd better go down and see them, don't you? Rather than wait for them to come to London, looking for me?'

'I suppose so.' Adam spread margarine on another slice of toast. Jane was thoughtful. 'Adam, something's been niggling me.'

'Oh dear. My snoring?'

'No, seriously. Your parents in Canada. They'll have been told you're dead. They'll be grieving.'

'Yes, I hate that. But it's not as bad as you think. My mum died when I was eight. I scarcely know my stepmother. Or my father, come to that. He was always travelling. I was at boarding school or staying with aunts.'

'Have you got brothers or sisters?'

'No, but Dad has a second family with Diana. They're with him in Canada.'

'Oh well, that's a relief.'

'I'll give Dad a nice surprise after the war. If he remembers who I am. Listen, is there anything useful I can do while you're down in Tilfleet?'

'You lie low. Try and recall anything you can about those men on the pier, any details that might help us. If anything occurs to you, write it down.'

'Right. Good idea.'

'Maggie will be up about twelve. If she offers to show you her birthmark, don't let her. Wait and see it on stage.'

St James's Park was bathed in gentle sunshine, as the two men walked beside the lake. Swans cruised serenely past, while ducks and geese competed for bits of bread, thrown from the bridge by a boy and his mother. Not all the bread reached them. Seagulls from the Thames had invaded the park and swooped to catch the titbits in mid-air. A group of flamingos remained aloof, standing in elegant postures, waiting to be admired. The war seemed a long way off.

'Beautiful, isn't it?' said Hunter. 'London at its best. I walk here after lunch every day. Unless it's raining, of course.'

Hunter was feeling mellow. There had been little sign of wartime austerity at his club. They'd enjoyed a good meal, with an unusual amount of reminiscing. The two men were in the habit of lunching together occasionally but the talk was usually of a general nature, mainly topics of the day, plus the latest rude jokes circulating in Whitehall.

Today, though, they'd been remembering student years, prompted by Collis having recently run into a mutual friend from the old days. His report of that had led them back to Cambridge in the twenties, when they'd both been members of the Socialist Action Group. Today, over poached salmon with an agreeable wine, they'd recalled fiery debates in the Union, disruptive raids on Tory meetings, writing provocative pamphlets, and hurling eggs at a visiting Cabinet minister on the hustings. After university, they'd found themselves side by side on the picket lines in the General Strike. Then their paths had diverged, as Collis took his left-wing views noisily into politics, while Hunter took his quietly into the Civil Service.

Today's conversation had been stimulating and amusing, full of anecdotes, some remembered triumphs, and a few regrets. Of course, Collis had been probing his old friend's current views, to see if he retained his Socialist zeal. At Cambridge, Hunter had been the firebrand, organizing street protests against capitalism, and trying to galvanize college staff into striking for more pay. Later, he'd even talked of going to fight in the Spanish Civil War. Only a recent promotion had prevented him from doing so. On second thoughts, he felt that he could do more to promote social justice working within the system.

Throughout lunch, Collis had been pleased to find his companion's militant idealism undiminished. Thus encouraged, the MP now made his first move, as the two men strolled beside the water.

'Sad, isn't it?' he ventured. 'All those years of struggle, all the writing and debating, all those cold hours on the picket lines, all the bruises, Jimmy Bent getting his arm broken by a policeman's truncheon … all that, and nothing's changed. The Establishment still rules, the bosses get fatter, the workers get thinner. Nothing's really changed, has it?'

Hunter was surprised. 'Yes it has. The Trade Unions are stronger now, there's unemployment benefit, safety regulations, welfare provisions …'

'All marginal,' said Collis. 'Nothing like the real Socialist equality we dreamed of. I still do.'

'So do I,' said Hunter. 'And that's just round the corner, surely. As soon as the war's over, Churchill has to call an election. And then we'll see a huge Labour majority, I'm certain of it.'

'Oh yes, of course there'll be a Labour government. Under Clement Attlee. But how much do you think that will alter things? Attlee's another toff. Bevin and Morrison have been sucked into the Establishment. There'll be a few changes, of course. But small, and cosmetic. Nothing like radical enough.'

'But they've promised extensive nationalization! The mines, the railways, steel, fuel, big chunks of industry! That's what we've always wanted!'

'Nationalization, yes. But have you heard the latest madness? They're going to pay compensation to shareholders! They haven't the guts just to take everything over, and to hell with the capitalists! The nationalized industries will start with huge debts hanging round their necks! It'll be milk-and-water socialism, not the real thing!'

'Well, you're a Labour MP, Gerald. You can demand more ruthless policies.'

'Don't think I haven't tried. But it's no use. A lot of the leadership's gone soft. Working with the Tories in the coalition has doused the fire in their bellies. They're even prepared to keep the monarchy!'

Hunter was downcast. 'My God! You really think so?'

'I know so. I've seen it all in close-up at meetings of the party executive. Our official leaders are Churchill's lap-dogs. They'll get power and they'll waste it. Five years on, the Tories will be back!'

'Bloody hell! What's to be done?'

It was the cue Collis had been waiting for. 'Direct action, Martin. Direct action! There are a lot of us in the party who do still have fire in our bellies! We're prepared to seize power and use it! Transform society! Create the democratic Britain you and I always yearned for!'

'Direct action?'

'It's the only way. Take control of the state's assets, and use them for the benefit of the people. Like Stalin did. And this is the year! There'll never be a better opportunity! Are you interested?'

'Obviously. I have to be.'

'Good. Because you can help. You'd have a role to play, Martin. Do you really want a genuinely socialist Britain?'

'Of course I do.'

'Even if it means breaking the law?'

'We broke the law often enough in the old days.'

It was the endorsement that Collis needed. As the two men completed their walk round the lake, he told Hunter of an audacious scheme. Carefully omitting names, dates and vital details, he outlined the plans he and his friends had made to change the face of Britain. Hunter listened in amazement and, Collis felt, with growing enthusiasm. Before they parted, he swore Hunter to secrecy, and promised to be in touch in the next few days. Then Hunter would hear the details and be told of his role in the operation.

Throughout the afternoon, Hunter's colleagues at the Ministry found him preoccupied. And so did his wife at home that night. He was wrestling with conflicting emotions, his conscience pulled in different directions. He'd long ago rebelled against the stern traditionalist values instilled by his father, a non-conformist preacher. But those values had never quite left him.

At ten o'clock he made the phone call that sealed his death warrant.

Jane Hart had found the reunion with her mother less embarrassing than she'd feared. She'd anticipated close questioning about recent events. And, while she knew her night with Adam must soon be public knowledge, she didn't want to be the one to disclose it to her mum. Also, she mustn't reveal where she was staying in London, or why.

On the train to Tilfleet, she'd concocted an elaborate story. The next production at the Windmill was to be much more spectacular, and she was to be heavily featured. So she was called to rehearsal every day at nine. Jane planned to talk long and loud about this theatrical excitement, hoping to swamp any awkward questions from her mother. But she needn't have worried. Mrs Hart was all set to do some swamping on her own account. After clasping her daughter to her bosom for ten seconds, she launched into a tumultuous recital of all that had happened at the Cavendish since they last met.

Clearly she'd enjoyed being besieged by reporters from the national press. And as for the local paper, that would actually carry a full-page interview including her picture, specially taken by their photographer, a nice man but rather arty. On the downside, she'd now lost the use of two rooms, Jefferson's and Adam's: out of bounds while the police searched for clues. And then beds and furniture would have to be replaced before the rooms came back into service.

Reactions in the house had varied. Jack Hardstaff had been a tower of strength, helping her with insurance forms and giving general support. Nice old Mr Donner had offered legal advice. But other residents had been less helpful. Some had complained that she'd been taking in the wrong sort of guest: dubious characters who allowed themselves to be murdered in their rooms. Mr Butler had actually given a week's notice.

The police had shown her pictures of the two men who died at Southend and she'd recognized one of them as the stranger who'd called recently, asking about accommodation. It was all very mysterious. They'd also quizzed her at length about Adam Webber, probing for anything Mrs Hart knew about his background. On this subject she had few facts. But that hadn't stopped her giving a generous flow of opinions and speculations. These she now retailed to her daughter.

Thus it was a long time before the question of Jane's London activities came up. But eventually it was bound to. Mrs Hart expressed surprise that her daughter was going back to London that evening. This was Jane's cue to tell her about the nine o'clock rehearsals, and embark on a lengthy and exuberant account of the new show, and her major part in it. She kept this going until Sergeant Monk came in and said that Inspector Jessett would like to see Miss Hart now. Jane then gratefully excused herself and followed the sergeant out.

The inspector had commandeered the lounge for his interviews. Emily Hart had offered the use of her office, but the inspector had foreseen the likelihood of her hovering in the vicinity. So he'd opted for the larger room, which was now closed to residents, except those summoned for questioning.

Jane found herself seated at a table opposite Inspector Jessett, while Sergeant Monk sat close by with his pencil and notepad.

Jessett began with a few pleasant enquiries about her welfare, and about life at the Windmill. He'd been there once, he said, to see the comedian John Tilley, a favourite of his on the radio. It was a permanent source of amusement to Jane and her friends that men always claimed they went to the Windmill to see the comics: it appeared that the presence of beautiful girls with very few clothes on had nothing to do with it.

Keen to keep on the right side of the police, Jane went along with this pretence, and told Jessett that the Windmill currently had a new comedian, Vic Dudley, who seemed likely to achieve the same success as Tilley and other past luminaries. She also mentioned the possibility of complimentary tickets. Would Jessett and Monk be interested?

Avoiding over-eagerness, the officers indicated that they might well be. 'Very funny, that Dudley,' said the inspector. 'I always enjoy him on the wireless.'

Jane said she'd see what she could do, and gave them a charming smile. Inwardly, she was trying to decide at what point, and in what manner, she should make the big statement that had to be made. She decided it would save time and reduce awkwardness if she volunteered it at the first opportunity. This came quickly. The preliminaries over, the inspector said, 'Now then, Miss Hart, I want you to tell us all you know about Maurice Cooper's death.'

This was the moment, and Jane spoke in a firm clear voice. 'The most important thing I can tell you, Inspector, is that Adam Webber didn't kill him. I know that for a fact.'

The inspector leaned forward. 'Really? How can you be so sure?'

'Because Adam was with me in my room all that night.'

The inspector was silent for a moment. Sergeant Monk looked up from his notes and studied Jane with new interest.

'I see,' said Jessett finally. 'That's certainly something we needed to know.'

'I'm hoping it's something my mother doesn't need to know. She's rather old-fashioned.'

Jessett was still assessing this new revelation. 'Yes, yes, I can see that. Of course, when evidence is given in court, it's hard to see how it can be kept quiet. But we shan't be rushing to tell Mrs Hart, unless it becomes necessary.'

'Thank you. I really will try to get those complimentary tickets.'

The inspector allowed himself a small smile. 'We shall wait patiently, Miss Hart. Mind you, I'm not sure that a Windmill show will be good for my sergeant's blood pressure.'

The sergeant looked pained. His moment of levity over,

Jessett stared hard at Jane as he asked, 'And when was the last time you saw Mr Webber?'

'When he left me the following morning, to go to work.'

Jessett maintained his stare. 'You haven't seen him since?'

'No.'

The inspector sighed. 'Well, I think you'd better give us an account of all the events of that night, from the time Mr Webber came home.'

With her secret now revealed, Jane was happy to tell the story in detail. She explained how they'd gone to sort out Jefferson's things. Then she told them about the confrontation with Cooper, and how they'd then gone on to finish the job.

'What happened then, Miss Hart?'

'We went downstairs and had hot drinks. Mum's managed to get hold of a jar of Horlicks.'

Mugs of Horlicks struck Sergeant Monk as an odd prelude to a night of passion. But it occasioned no surprise to Inspector Jessett: he'd been married for twenty years. He prompted her gently. 'And then you both went to your room?'

'I've had a lot of stress in the last few weeks,' said Jane. 'And I was still grieving for Mark, Mark Jefferson. Adam was comforting me. He's very kind and gentle, you know.'

'The policeman who went to arrest him on the pier might not agree with you.'

'Well, Adam was terrified, wasn't he? He thought they were out to kill him.'

'Did he? How do you know that, Miss Hart? Have you spoken to him since? A phone call, perhaps?'

Jane had realized her mistake as soon as the words were uttered, and she'd had a moment to recover. 'No, no, of course not. He's disappeared, hasn't he. But the story was in all the papers. Some people were chasing him. Obviously, he couldn't think straight.'

The inspector allowed a heavy pause to elapse. Then he said, 'You do realize, don't you, that withholding evidence from the police is a criminal offence?'

Jane was back in control of herself. 'Yes, of course, Inspector. I'll do all I can to help.'

'Good. I think that would be best. Let's go back to the hot drinks downstairs. You're saying you and Mr Webber were together from then until he left in the morning?'

'Yes.'

'So what time did he leave your room?'

'Around six. He had to be at work early.'

'But he must have gone to his own room to collect the things he needed.'

This was a tricky one, for which Jane had failed to prepare herself. There was a brief pause while she considered her options. Then she decided that from now on she would tell the truth wherever possible.

'Yes, he did,' she said.

'And did he find his room already wrecked?'

The die was cast now. 'Yes,' she said.

'That's extraordinary. He finds his room smashed up, but he doesn't report it to anyone. He just goes off to work, as if nothing had happened.'

'He realized that, if people knew the damage was done by then, they'd know he hadn't slept in his own room. He wanted to protect my reputation.'

'Hm. Well, that makes a sort of sense, I suppose.'

'He definitely didn't wreck his own room.'

The inspector ventured another wry smile. 'I may not be Sherlock Holmes, Miss Hart, but I'd already reached that conclusion.'

Then came the next crisis point. The inspector looked steadily into Jane's eyes. 'And you've had absolutely no contact with Mr Webber since six o'clock yesterday morning?'

Jane's nerve held. 'No. I went up to London mid-morning, to do my show at the theatre, and I stayed in town overnight.'

'Why was that?'

'I've just started being called for 9 a.m. rehearsals.'

'Really? They make you work hard at the Windmill.'

'Well, yes. Especially when we're preparing a new show.'

'So you'll be staying in town tonight.'

'That's right. I have to.'

'Please give Sergeant Monk your London address and phone number, in case we need to contact you.'

Fortunately, Jane had anticipated this one.

'I don't know where I'll be staying until I get back to town. I have to go backstage at the end of the show and see who can put me up. Best to contact me at the theatre. I'll give your sergeant the Windmill backstage number.'

Sergeant Monk's eyes lit up, and Inspector Jessett seemed satisfied. There were a few more questions about Adam's recent behaviour, and then the ordeal was over, apart from a final injunction.

'Miss Hart, if at any time you became aware of Adam Webber's whereabouts, you would let us know, wouldn't you?'

'Yes, of course, Inspector.'

'Good. Remember he's a wanted suspect, and anyone who helps him evade arrest will be charged with obstructing the police.'

'Yes. I understand.'

'Thank you, that's all for now. Don't forget that number for my sergeant.'

Jane supplied the number and left the room, trying not to look too relieved. Hating herself for her action, she avoided her mother, to escape further questioning, and sought out George Fowler. She found him alone in the scullery, drinking tea.

Now it was Jane's turn to be interrogator. She weathered an initial burst of opinions from Fowler, who was still getting huge entertainment from the Tilfleet drama. He had many theories about Cooper's death and associated events. These ranged from sexual jealousy, via black market rivalry, to wild plots involving German agents and collaborators. Possibly even a German U-boat, lurking in the Thames.

Jane heard him out patiently, and then began putting her questions.

'George, I believe the simple solution is usually the right one.'

'Yeah,' said George. 'I was wondering if Cooper and Jefferson done a robbery, and then fell out over the loot.'

'I suppose it's possible,' Jane conceded. 'But I think your black market idea's more likely. Cooper was in on that, wasn't he? He was always offering me nylons, and he seemed to have Scotch whisky for sale. D'you know anything about the local rackets, George?'

Fowler tapped the side of his nose with a grubby finger. 'Yeah, I know a lot, miss. But I'm risking my life if I talk about it.'

'Anything you say would be safe with me, George. I'd never let on I heard it from you. And there's a couple of quid in it, if you tell me anything useful.'

In George Fowler's mind, prudence grappled with an innate enthusiasm for cash, plus a relish for showing off his knowledge. It was an unequal struggle.

'All right, I'll trust you. Look, I've never been in on it myself. I don't touch nothing dodgy. But there's this pub out on the Fleet Road, right? Called The Bull. The word is, you can get a lot of things there you can't get at Woolworth's.'

'The Bull.'

'Yeah. The guv'nor's a bloke called Harry Paynter. His brother Reggie's an ex-boxer. They're both in with a gang who'll do anything for money, and quite a lot for small change. Right pack of villains they are. They got an enforcer called Sid Garrett; very handy with a razor.'

'My God! And you think Cooper was involved with that lot!'

'He'd never have been part of the gang. They're all hard men. Cooper was a jelly. But I reckon he did business with them. He was often out at The Bull.'

'How often?'

'Maybe two or three times a week. And, like you said, he could always get things. Booze and nylons and petrol and stuff. If you could pay over the odds for it. Which I couldn't, of course.'

'Do the police know about The Bull?'

'I reckon they must do. But they've never managed to pin anything on the Paynters – they're smart. Also the word is, one of the bobbies at the local nick is a mate of Sid Garrett. Seems they were at school together. Anyway, I reckon if the Bull mob don't trouble the coppers, the coppers won't trouble them.'

'That's not right, is it?'

'I dunno. To my mind, the law's got better things to do than go chasing black marketeers. I mean, they got to be watching out for Nazi spies, ain't they? And saboteurs. Don't rock the boat, miss. We got enough troubles here already.'

'Whatever happens, I won't involve you, George. And thanks for the information.' Jane rose, handed George two pound notes, and left the scullery. George poured himself a fourth cup of tea, and put in three lumps of sugar. Mrs Hart didn't take sugar, so George got her ration. Jane said a hasty farewell to her mother, explaining that she had to catch the six o'clock train. Then she hurried off to the station, thinking about the hard men who'd do anything for money.

Westley began the meeting with disagreeable news. 'I'm afraid we made the wrong decision about Hunter, Gerald. He's not on our side.'

Gerald Collis froze. Until that moment, he'd been convinced his old friend was ready to join them. There was a pause before he said, 'Really? I can't believe it.'

'You'll have to believe it. Last night Hunter rang me at home. He said he'd picked up a rumour of an attempt to overthrow the government.'

The meeting was aghast, and Ernest Cox was very angry indeed. 'Treacherous bastard!' he thundered. 'I said we shouldn't trust him!'

'This is disastrous!' said Jupp. 'How much does he know?'

Westley sought to calm his colleagues. 'It's not disastrous. Clearly he knows very little. I take it you didn't give him any details, Gerald?'

'Of course not.' Collis tried to sound reassuring. 'I just hinted at the general idea. But I'd have sworn he was going to come in with us. I'm shocked.'

Jupp looked anxiously at Westley. 'What exactly did he say on the phone?'

'He said he'd picked up a whisper at the Ministry that a left-wing group were planning to seize power, and that they have a secret source of men and weapons. Obviously, he was anxious to keep your name out of it, Gerald. He just said the government should check on extremists in the Labour Party.'

'That's bad enough,' said Cox. 'He must be silenced before he says any more.'

Collis protested. 'Just a minute! Martin's a good man, he won't say more. If he were going to, he'd have told Bob straight off.'

'We can't bank on that,' said Bell.

'Look, I'll go back to him, tell him it's off. There's been a change of plan.'

Jupp was not impressed. 'But then he might guess that Bob had told us about his phone call. In which case he'd know Bob was in on this.'

'There's no more to be said,' Cox insisted. 'The man has to be eliminated.'

'That's not necessary,' said Collis. 'He just has to be kept out of the way for a while. A quick posting back to Australia. Bob, you could arrange that.'

Westley was making notes on the pad in front of him, but remained silent.

Jupp stared at Westley. 'What did you tell him when he rang?'

'I thanked him for the tip-off, and said I'd get Intelligence on to it. I told him to keep everything to himself for now, to avoid alerting the opposition.'

'Good,' said Cox. 'Well done. Now get rid of him. And quick!'

'For God's sake!' cried Collis. 'We're not a bunch of assassins!'

'No, we're not,' said Cox. 'We keep the killing to a minimum.

But we all know we can't achieve our objective without some bloodshed. We can't jeopardize the whole operation because one man hasn't the courage of his convictions!'

'Right, gentlemen,' said Westley, with suitable firmness. 'I think that's enough discussion on this issue. I will arrange for appropriate action. But take note that we'll have to stick with Neville Straker doing that particular job, as originally planned. Bill, you know the man. Tell him to cut down the drink.'

Bill Ford nodded. 'Yes, I'll do that. And I have a point I'd like to raise.'

'Go ahead,' said Westley.

'I'm told there's been a breach of security in Tilfleet.'

Westley frowned. 'That information hasn't been officially released yet. How do you come to know about it?'

'I have contacts in the Tilfleet area. It borders on my constituency.'

Westley was stern. 'Our cells are not supposed to speak to each other laterally. Communication has to be done through the chain of command.'

'That's as may be,' Ford persisted. 'But you can't stop people talking. And I'm reliably informed that confidential papers are missing.'

There were murmurs of alarm around the table.

'I'm also told,' continued Ford, 'that the bizarre events on Southend Pier the other day have something to do with it. I think we should know the facts.'

Several voices were raised in agreement. Westley sighed. 'Obviously I'd have told you about this matter in due course. But I had intended to wait a day or two, till things became clearer.'

'I think you should put us fully in the picture,' said Jupp.

'Very well,' said Westley. 'I'll tell you all that's known at present. There was a break-in at our Tilfleet unit the other night – almost certainly a petty thief. A few items were stolen, including cash. More seriously, a notebook disappeared, containing some confidential information. The culprit was caught and eliminated, in case he'd stumbled on anything compromising.'

'And the notebook?' asked Ford.

'It's not yet been recovered, but it will be. Our people know who's got it.'

'Who?' said Cox.

'The thief had somehow passed it on to an accomplice, who'll have no idea of its importance. The contents are encoded, of course.'

'And what about the men who died on the pier?' asked Ford. 'I hear they were East End gangsters, working for us. Were they involved in the search?'

'I believe so. But I'm assured they can't be linked to our organization.'

Charles Bell let out a deep breath, and expressed his concerns with gravity. 'It saddens me,' he said, 'that we employ professional criminals. Surely our work should be done by genuine supporters. People who believe in our cause.'

'On the day, it will be,' said Westley. 'In the meantime, there are certain jobs which are best carried out by experts.'

'Not expert enough, it seems,' said Cox.

'On this occasion, apparently not,' Westley agreed. 'However, this is the first mishap in a year of preparation. And it will be rectified.'

'Let's get this straight,' said Cox. 'Somewhere in the Tilfleet area there's a thief in possession of a notebook with some details of our operation, which we hope he won't understand.'

'Which he certainly won't understand,' said Westley.

'But there's always the chance that it could fall into the hands of someone who might understand. The police, for instance.'

'A remote possibility. But that's why the theft was not reported. And that's why our people are vigorously seeking the man Webber.'

'Webber?' said Jupp. 'The man whose picture's in all our papers?'

'That's right. The police want him for the Tilfleet murder. Our people have to catch him before the police do. And I'm sure they will.' And with that Westley closed the subject. 'Now, I'd like to hear your local area reports.'

When Jane got back to the flat, she found Adam somewhat morose. Sitting indoors doing nothing all day was something he wasn't used to. The afternoon had been pleasant enough, listening to Maggie's theatrical stories, which were highly scandalous and very amusing. But then Maggie had to go out, and the evening had been tedious. He'd read the newspaper from start to finish, without taking in much, except the Tilfleet story. He'd tried listening to the radio, but his mind had been too troubled to concentrate. He was looking serious when Jane joined him in the lounge, bringing with her a carrier bag. From it she took two bottles of brown ale.

'First aid!' she announced brightly.

Adam sighed, but managed a smile. 'Jane, you're a genius. Thanks.'

'How was the day?'

'OK. Maggie was fun this afternoon. She's got some good stories.'

'Right. And some of them are almost true. Where is she now?'

'She went out to meet someone called Phil. They were going to the pictures.'

'Oh yes, she's seeing one of the boys from the 'Mill. Fine waste of time that'll be. Still, it shouldn't upset her gentleman friend.' Jane removed the caps with a bottle opener and poured the beer, tilting the glasses to minimize froth. 'Did she give you some lunch?'

'Yes. Baked beans on toast and a tin of rice pudding.'

'She likes you. That's two tins off her points ration.'

'The trouble is, I think she knows who I am.'

'I'm sure she does. I'll bet she twigged the minute I brought you here. All that stuff on the news about Tilfleet. And she knows I come from there. When your picture turned up in the papers, that'll have clinched it.'

'And she still doesn't mind my being here?'

'Of course not. I'm her friend. You're my friend. So you're her friend. That's the way it works in the East End.'

'Has she said anything to you about me?'

'Only that if you've got a brother, she'd like to meet him. Officially, you're on leave from the army, by the way. Don't worry, Adam, you're safe with Maggie. She's all right.'

'Thank God for that.' Adam was silent for a moment. Then he took a long swig of brown ale, and voiced the words that had been on his mind for the last two hours. 'Listen, Jane, I don't think this is fair on you.'

'Of course it is,' said Jane. 'You can buy the next round.'

'I don't mean the beer, I mean this set-up. I'm dragging you into a mess you don't deserve. I've been thinking.'

'Always a mistake,' said Jane cheerfully. 'Have some more of this.' She topped up Adam's glass.

'Seriously,' said Adam. 'If you're caught helping me you could go to jail. And what would that do to your career?'

'Nothing,' said Jane. 'One good thing about the stage: going to jail doesn't finish you. Ivor Novello's still working, isn't he?' Novello, a prominent actor, writer and composer, had been jailed for contravening petrol rationing. Jane took Adam's hand. 'Listen, fathead. You came to me for help, remember? So help is what you're going to get.'

'I still reckon I should try and get to Canada. Link up with my parents.'

'Don't be daft. That's the first place the authorities will be looking for you. They're probably on to the Canadian police already, chasing your mum and dad.'

'They won't be looking in Canada, will they? They'll be trying to trace Adam Webber's parents, and they'll find they were killed in the Blitz.'

The reminder took Jane by surprise. She sipped her beer and nodded. 'Oh yes, that's true, I suppose.'

'My parents are Mr and Mrs Carr. We may not be close, but they wouldn't turn me away. If I join them, I can go back to being Adam Carr. I could start a new life over there. When I got things going, I'd send for you.'

'Well, I'm afraid I wouldn't come. Like I said, I'm not spending my life on the run. Anyway, Canada's in the war too, right? You'd be called up for the Canadian army. No, Adam, it wouldn't work.'

'But what's the point of staying here? I can't spend the rest of my life hiding in Maggie's flat.'

'You know my solution. Give yourself up in an orderly fashion. Let the police sort it all out.'

'No, sorry. I'm not doing that.'

'Then the other option is to sort it out ourselves. Find out what's going on. I asked you to rack your brains, didn't I? Did you get any ideas?'

'Well ... there was one thought. When those sods were roughing me up on the pier, they got excited about a booklet in my pocket. It was just pier safety regulations, but they thought it was something they were looking for. It occurred to me it might tie up with that notebook we found in Mark's room.'

'I remember. It was in some kind of code, wasn't it? You were going to show it to someone.'

'I gave it to my friend Leo, on the pier. I hoped he might decode it. If he could, we might learn something. The trouble is, I couldn't turn up there now without getting nicked. And I don't know his phone number, or even if he's got one.'

'Perhaps I could go there.'

'You couldn't get on the pier without a permit.'

'All right, that's something we'll have to work on. But I still think there's a black market connection. George Fowler confirmed that Cooper was up to his neck in the local racket. And it operates from a pub called The Bull.'

'Maybe I should go there and have a look round.'

'You can't do. Your picture's on every front page; they'd be on to you at once. No, I'm going to ring the police inspector and tip him off. If they look into that lot, they might unearth something. And it'll show I'm co-operating.'

'Yes, that's worth a try.'

'George said the police don't bother too much with the goings-on at The Bull. But if they think they're involved in murder, they might feel differently. I'll lay it on thick about Cooper's black market dealings. George even gave me some names I can throw in.'

'My God, Jane, you're certainly a fighter!'

'We've both got to be. There's no point in giving up. And talking of not giving up, why have you got all that stubble? I brought you a razor.'

'It's intentional. Eventually, I'm going to have to go out, aren't I? And a spot of beard and moustache might make me less like my picture in the papers.'

'Good idea. I'd thought about that. I found some old glasses that belonged to my dad. They're not strong, he had quite good eyesight. Anyway, I can see through them all right. You could wear those in an emergency – that might help.'

'Thanks, I'll give them a go.' Adam smiled ruefully. 'Glasses, moustache and beard! A Child's Guide to Disguising Yourself!'

'Don't knock it,' said Jane. 'It could work, especially at night. Besides, it won't just be a disguise, it'll be an improvement. Now we're going to need to eat. I've brought some tins from Mum's store cupboard.'

'Well done, I'm starving. What have we got?'

'Good stuff. Baked beans, followed by rice pudding.'

London was enjoying another afternoon of autumn sunshine and, in St James's Park, strollers were making the most of it. The flamingos were a little more animated today, sauntering around and showing off. Moorhens were hurrying about, pecking at insects, and ducks were basking in the warmth.

On the flat roof of one of the tall Regency buildings facing the park, a trap door was raised, and a man in workman's overalls emerged. He was carrying a tall canvas bag, in which stood several lengthy implements. There were two or three long-handled brushes, some metal rods, and other items less easily identifiable. Clearly, the man was about to do something useful to some of the chimney pots which abound on that old London roof. Indeed, he began by selecting a thick iron rod and inserting it into one of the chimneys, while peering earnestly down the hole. After half a minute he shook his head thoughtfully, withdrew the rod, and returned it to the canvas bag. Then he stood upright and surveyed the pleasant vista around him: the deserted roofs bathed in sunshine, and the park below gently alive with leisure activities.

Up there he was totally alone, and he wasn't overlooked by any windows. Satisfied, the man laid the canvas bag flat and knelt down beside it, beneath the level of the parapet. He took from the bag another lengthy object, this time a rifle: a rather sophisticated one with silencer and telescopic lens. He also produced a pair of binoculars and, from his pocket, a photograph of a man. Then he settled into a dark space between two chimney stacks and began to scan the park.

On the path by the bridge, Martin Hunter was taking his usual post-prandial walk. To park regulars, who were used to seeing him, it seemed like his customary casual afternoon stroll. But, in fact, Hunter was not in the relaxed mood that these perambulations usually induced. His agonized decision of a few nights ago still obsessed him.

Had he betrayed his friends and left them open to dire consequences or had his telephone warning been discreet enough to avert a national struggle without ruining the plotters' lives? On the other hand, had he said enough? Had his mild words been sufficient to produce the necessary action? Deep in thought, he nearly collided with a small girl on a red tricycle. Indeed, he would have done, had the mother not pulled the child back.

Hunter doffed his bowler hat and apologized, before walking on. He took just a few more paces, the last of his life. And then, suddenly, all his heart searching was ended. A bullet hit him just above the left ear, leaving a neat hole, from which blood had started to trickle even before he hit the ground.

5

'TWENTY-SEVEN ... PENN STREET,' Sergeant Monk repeated, as he wrote down the words. 'Right, I've got all that. Thanks. I'll tell the inspector.'

He replaced the receiver.

'Good news, sir. Southend police have identified the jokers who got themselves killed on the pier.'

'About time,' said Jessett, carefully taking another biscuit. He was a meticulous man, one of the few individuals who could extract a digestive biscuit from the packet without damaging either. 'Names mean anything?'

'Frank Cregan and David Stanley Clark, both with addresses in Stepney.'

'Cregan rings a bell,' said Jessett thoughtfully. He stirred his tea and gently dipped the biscuit. 'See if anything's known.'

'Southend have done that. They got the prints off the national records. Both men had form. Each done once for affray, Cregan twice for GBH.'

'I remember now. Cregan was a strong-arm man for the Plaistow mob, wasn't he? Moved into our manor last year. Friend of Reggie Paynter.'

'That's right, sir. And that reminds me.' Monk pulled a pad from his pocket. 'I had a chat with Sniffer Dean the other night. Cost us a tenner, but he's ready to give us enough evidence to nail Reggie Paynter for that post office job.'

The phone rang, and he picked up the receiver. 'Inspector Jessett's office ... Who? ... Oh, Miss Hart ... hang on, I'll see if he's free.' He put his hand over the mouthpiece. 'Jane Hart, sir. Will you take it?'

'Yes,' said Jessett. 'Hold on a minute.'

The bottom of his biscuit had fallen into the tea, and the inspector was trying to retrieve it with his teaspoon. Now he gave up, and knocked the whole lot back with a couple of gulps. 'OK, put her through.'

Jane came on the line, sounding bright and eager. 'Hello, Inspector, it's Jane Hart. You remember? From the Cavendish?'

The inspector responded affably. 'Yes, Miss Hart, of course. How are you?'

'Life's a bit hectic, with all the rehearsals, but I've been trying to think about Maurice Cooper, as you asked. You said to let you know if I had any ideas.'

'Yes, please. Has anything occurred to you?'

'Well, I wondered if you knew that Cooper was up to his neck in the local black market?'

'It doesn't surprise me, Miss Hart. But he never actually turned up in any of our enquiries. Are you sure of this?'

'Absolutely. He was always promising me nylons, if I was nice to him. Which I wasn't, of course. And he hinted to various residents that he could get things like whisky and petrol, if they could pay silly prices.'

'That's useful to know, Miss Hart. Anything else?'

'Mark Jefferson was interested in Cooper. He told me Cooper used to hang around a pub called The Bull. He was involved with an ex-boxer called Pointer or Paynter or something.'

'Reggie Paynter?'

'Yes, I think that was the name. They sound like a pretty tough bunch. It struck me that if Cooper fell out with them, they could have done him in.'

'Possibly. We know a bit about Reggie Paynter. What are Adam Webber's thoughts on the subject?'

Jane avoided the trap. 'I don't know. I never talked about it with him. I got that last stuff from Mark.'

'You've still heard nothing from Mr Webber?'

'I'm afraid not. Have you had any news, Inspector?'

'We've identified the victims on Southend Pier. A couple of small-time criminals. We'd like to know how they were involved with Mr Webber.'

'Sorry, I've no idea.' Jane changed the subject. 'Oh, I've given the Windmill box office your name and your sergeant's. It's Sergeant Monk, isn't it?'

'That's right.'

'You'll come in free any time you'd like to turn up.'

'You're very kind,' said Jessett. 'Could I now have your London address?'

Jane was ready. 'Sorry, but it changes all the time, according to which of the girls can put me up on her sofa. I shan't know till after the show tonight.'

Jessett sighed. 'I see. Well, please keep in touch.'

'I certainly will. Good luck with your enquiries, Inspector.'

The line clicked off at the other end.

Jessett let out a deep breath and peered at his empty mug. 'I could manage more tea.'

'Right you are, sir,' said Monk, transferring Jessett's mug to the table, on which stood the tray with teapot, electric kettle and tin of powdered milk. 'Anything helpful from the girl?'

'She wanted to tell me that Cooper was in with the black market crowd at The Bull. She even mentioned Reggie Paynter.'

'There's a coincidence.'

'Yes. I think we'll pull Reggie in, now we've got evidence. Apart from the post office job, I reckon he can tell us something about Cooper and Cregan. Have Sniffer sign a written statement. I'll get an arrest warrant.'

'Very good, sir.' Monk poured more tea for both of them. 'You're right. Cregan and Paynter were certainly mates. Cregan was Paynter's second in his boxing days. Maybe Paynter can tell us something about the scrap on the pier.'

'It's a bonus if he can. But I'm more concerned with who killed Cooper. That's the blot on our patch.'

'Right, sir.' Monk handed the inspector his tea.

'Ta,' said Jessett, once again wrestling with the biscuit packet. The closer he got to the bottom, the more difficult it was.

'Now I'll tell you the really helpful thing about that phone call.'

'Yes, sir?'

'It tells us that Webber and that girl are thick as thieves. She's desperate to lead us away from him by babbling on about Cooper and the villains at The Bull. Either she's with him, or she knows where he is. If we play our cards right, she'll lead us to him.' Jessett succeeded in extricating another biscuit. 'It may be time for our visit to the Windmill.'

'Yes, sir,' said Monk cheerfully. 'The sooner the better.'

'And the biscuits are running low. Ask Sergeant Fairweather to rustle up some more, will you?'

'Sergeant Fairweather?'

'Yes, you remember. He gets them off-ration from a girl at the grocer's.'

Alfred Jupp alighted from the taxi and handed the driver half a crown.

The sixpence tip was over-generous, but he was in an expansive mood. Tonight he was putting the impending coup out of his mind: tonight was a special anniversary.

It wasn't a wedding anniversary. Next March he'd mark his twenty-six years of marriage to Muriel with half a dozen red roses and, perhaps, a quiet supper for two at the House of Commons. Tonight was more exciting.

It was exactly a year since he'd met his mistress. And, despite a stolid appearance, Jupp was a romantic. As far as he was aware, his girl hadn't noticed the anniversary approaching, and he was going to surprise her. He knew her work schedule: she was free this evening. He intended to take her to Silvio's, the club where he'd first encountered her. Then she was in the chorus line. Tonight she'd be sitting at the best table.

He pushed open the street door, crossed the foyer and went up the stairs. He was confident she'd be at home – if not now, then soon. Tonight was the night she washed her hair, and listened to *Jazz Club* on the radio.

He reached the first floor, pushed his key into the door on the right, and turned it with his right hand. In his left hand he held a bunch of flowers.

The hall light was on: so she was in. And there were voices in the sitting room. Jupp closed the front door, opened the sitting room door and went in.

His girlfriend had company. She was sitting in an armchair, enjoying a lively conversation with another girl and a man, both of whom were relaxed on the sofa. The man's face looked vaguely familiar.

Maggie Rayner looked up, startled. Then she leaped to her feet and came towards him with outstretched arms.

'Alfie! What a lovely surprise! I wasn't expecting you!'

Jupp gave her the flowers and kissed her on the cheek. 'It's intended to be a surprise, my dear. For a special day. Exactly a year since we met. At Silvio's, remember?'

Maggie was starting to collect her wits. 'Of course! Silvio's! How could I forget? But I thought you were away, working somewhere.'

'I was. But I told them I had to be in London for the night. I felt we were due for a celebration.'

'A celebration! Alfie, that's wonderful!'

Jupp was looking at the couple on the sofa, trying hard not to stare at the man, and wondering where he'd seen that face before. 'I hope I'm not interrupting anything.'

Maggie laughed. 'No, we're just having a drink and a chat. This is my friend Jane, who's in my show at the Windmill. And John's her boyfriend. He's home on leave from the army.'

'How do you do?' said Jupp. 'You're in the army, young man?'

Adam rose and shook his hand. 'Yes. This is my last day in civvies for a while.'

'Well, well, pleased to meet you. And you ... Jane, is it? You're in Maggie's show.'

'That's right,' said Jane. She gave a tense little laugh. 'We're the stars! Only we're both off today.'

Maggie's words tumbled out. 'John came up from his parents' home yesterday, and he has to catch a train up north late tonight. So he and Jane stayed here last night.' This she announced forcefully, aware that there were signs of male habitation that needed to be explained. 'You always said I could put up friends when you're not here.'

'Of course,' said Jupp. 'Always glad to help your chums, especially when they're doing their bit for the war effort. Please sit down, all of you, and have another drink.'

'Thank you,' said Jane. 'But now you're here, I think we ought to go. I'm sure you and Maggie have a lot to talk about.'

'Maggie and I are going out,' said Jupp. He turned to Maggie. 'How does Silvio's suit you?'

Maggie gushed. 'Oh Alfie, that would be smashing!'

'So you two stay here till it's time for John's train,' said Jupp. 'I'm sure there's a bottle of wine for you in the cabinet. And if Maggie's left any food in the fridge, you're welcome to it.'

'That's very kind of you,' said Jane. 'What do you think, John?'

'Fine with me. It's very comfy here. Thank you, sir.'

So they all sat down for a brief spell of nervous conversation.

And then Jupp got to his feet. 'Maggie, I have to leave you for ten minutes. I need some pills from the chemist. You start getting ready. John and Jane, relax and make yourselves at home.'

Maggie smiled. 'Oh, they'll do that all right. But I hope you won't expect me to be ready in ten minutes!'

'No, no, just get started. But we'll be on our way as soon as we can, eh? Leave these two together. They may not be meeting again for a while. I'm afraid this wretched war's going on for some time yet.'

And with that, Jupp made his exit, pausing at the door to add, 'Don't forget, you two. You can stay here for as long as you like.'

He closed the sitting room door behind him.

As soon as they heard the front door shut, Maggie jumped up. 'Right, you two! Get out of here fast!'

Jane was not surprised. 'You think he recognized Adam?'

'I'm damn sure he did! First he was staring at him, and I could see his mind working. Then something clicked and he stopped looking and started thinking what to do. Don't forget, Adam's picture's been in the papers all week.'

'So what's he up to?'

'He's gone to call the police, hasn't he?' said Maggie. 'He'll reckon it's his duty. He might even think I'm in danger. All he knows is there's a man here who's wanted for murder!'

'How far's the police station?'

'He won't bother with that, he'll ring them. He couldn't use the phone here, with you listening. He's on his way to the call box in Carlton Avenue. That's five minutes away. You can bet the coppers will be here ten minutes after that. So you've got just under a quarter of an hour to disappear!' She noticed Jane hesitating. 'Don't hang about! Go now!'

Jane sighed. 'You're right, of course. I'm trying to think where to head for.'

'Try some of the other girls. Or Vic Dudley. He's a good sport. And he's cross with the police, since they tried to nail him for fiddling petrol.'

'Vic Dudley, yes! He's got a big flat, hasn't he?'

'Yes, he has. And that reminds me, he owes me a favour.' Maggie winked. 'Tell him I'm asking.'

Adam and Jane delayed no longer. Jane had brought a suitcase the previous day, with items from the Cavendish. They threw all their things into the case, and five minutes later they were gone.

When Jupp reached the phone box, there was a man already in there, making a call. Jupp fretted as he waited outside, wondering if it would be quicker to look for another one. He decided against it. When he found one, that too might be occupied. Or it might have been vandalized. At least he knew this one was working.

Eventually, he opened the door and said, 'Excuse me, but could you be quick, please? I have to make an urgent call. A matter of national importance.'

The man moved the receiver away from his face long enough to say 'Bugger off!', and then he resumed his conversation.

He was a big man. Jupp withdrew.

Five minutes later the man came out, scowled at Jupp, and went on his way. Jupp entered the call box and dialled a number. Then he waited impatiently, drumming his fingers on the ledge.

When the phone was picked up at the other end, he spoke with speed and authority. 'Listen carefully, this is vitally important. Alfred Jupp here, and I've got the man Webber for you … yes, he's in my flat at 9 Rochester Court, Trent Road, Maida Vale. Now I have a friend there, and I don't want her involved, so give me time to get her out. Have your people there in forty minutes. Tell them to say they're police. They'll find a man there with a girl. Have them leave the girl and take the man. He's slightly disguised, but he's definitely Webber.'

Jupp repeated the address, got an acknowledgment from the other end, and hung up. Then he left the box, and started walking briskly back to the flat.

In fact, he was too brisk. As he stepped off the pavement, there was a screech of brakes and a car, whose dimmed headlights he hadn't seen, skidded to a halt. It had almost stopped before it knocked him over. It took only a moment for Jupp to collect himself and get to his feet. But already the driver, a middle-aged man in a dark overcoat and a bad temper, had got out of the car. He confronted Jupp angrily.

'Why don't you bloody well look where you're going!'

Jupp's first reaction was governed by the politician's compulsion never to admit he's in the wrong. 'I could say the same to you!' he snapped. 'You could see I was going to cross!'

'Rubbish!' said the driver. 'You just stepped out without any warning!'

By now, Jupp's urge to argue had been overtaken by his need for haste. He brushed some mud off his trousers and said, 'Never mind. No harm done. Let's forget about it.'

Alas, passers-by had heard the brakes, and seen Jupp fall, and several of them stopped to enjoy the drama. Now a sturdy, belligerent man spoke up.

'Don't you let him bully you, mate!' he advised. And he turned to the driver. 'You were going too fast. You're not supposed to go that fast in the blackout.'

A small crowd had now gathered, and a woman's voice concurred. 'That's right! He come round the corner too quick!'

'You stay out of this!' bellowed the driver.

Jupp now needed to get away. 'It's all right,' he said. 'Forget it. I'm not making a complaint.' And he started to move off.

'Well, I am!' said the driver, barring his way. 'Look! The visor on my headlamp. You've knocked it sideways!'

'I never touched it,' said Jupp. 'Kindly get out of my way.'

'He's trying to con you!' said the belligerent man, who'd hated drivers since childhood. Their neighbours had owned a car, and never offered him a ride. 'Don't let him get away with it!'

'Why don't you mind your own business?' said the driver.

And then the policeman arrived. It had been a quiet evening on his beat, and his report book was almost empty. This was his chance to start filling it.

By now, both Jupp and the driver wanted to move on, but the belligerent man and another witness were keen to tell their stories, and the constable was eager to record them. And first there were essential formalities to be completed.

The policeman took a pencil from his pocket and licked the point. 'Now then,' he said, 'I'd better take some names and addresses.'

As Jupp finally mounted the stairs to flat nine, he knew that time was short. Perhaps he wouldn't be able to get Maggie out before the men came. He was glad he'd said they should pose

as police. If the force traced a wanted man to his address and
came to arrest him, there was no reason for Maggie to suppose
Jupp was involved. He'd affect surprise that Maggie had let her
friend bring such a man into his flat. He wondered if Webber
would put up a fight.

As he turned the key and opened the door, he had all his reactions prepared: except for the one he was going to need in five
minutes. He closed the door behind him.

Maggie emerged from the bedroom, her dressing and make-
up still incomplete.

'You've been a while,' she observed. 'Have they moved the
chemist's?'

'There was a long queue,' said Jupp. Of course, he could have
told her about the car accident, but decided that would take too
long. 'And there was a new pharmacist. He took an age making
up the pills.'

The place seemed quiet. Jupp peered through the open sitting
room door. 'Where are your friends?' he asked.

'They decided to go after all,' said Maggie casually.

Jupp went pale. 'Go? Go where?'

'John remembered he had to phone a friend. They're going to
meet him for a meal before John catches his train.'

Jupp raged inwardly, but tried to appear calm. This wasn't
supposed to be important to him. He didn't quite succeed with
the calmness.

'Where are they eating? What station is he going to?' His
voice had gone up an octave.

'I think they were meeting at Joe Lyons. And it's probably
Euston. I'm not sure. Does it matter?'

'No, no, of course not. Pour us both a drink. I have to make a
phone call.' At that moment the phone rang on the hall table.
Maggie picked up the receiver.

'Hello?' Her voice became enthusiastic. 'Oh, Kathie, hello!
How are you? Great! Well, the new show starts in ten days, so
we're working hard ... oh yes, I'll have some time free. Not the
next few days maybe, I have a friend here ... Next week, yes,

you bet ... Good. Listen, how's Les? ... What? Really? ... Well! I never thought he was that sort....'

Jupp listened with mounting frustration. What capricious god had delivered Webber into his hands, and then put all this trivia in the way? After two minutes he could wait no longer.

'Sorry, Maggie. That call of mine, it's urgent! Can I use the phone?'

'Hang on,' said Maggie to the phone. And then to Jupp: 'I'll only be a minute. I haven't spoken to Kathie for ages.'

'Tell her you'll ring her back,' snapped Jupp. 'This is important!'

'All right. Kathie, my friend wants the phone in a hurry, I'll have to ring you back. Where are you? ... Oh, you're back at the Casanova! I thought you said you'd never work there again ... Oh well, I suppose that's different. I mean, as long as they treat you right. I always say, at least the Casanova does a lovely show.... Is that red-haired boy still there?'

Jupp snatched the receiver. 'Sorry, Kathie, I need this phone urgently! Maggie will ring you back.'

He pressed the phone rest to clear the line, and began to dial.

Maggie frowned. 'That wasn't very nice, Alfie! What's come over you?'

'Sorry, it couldn't be helped. I'll explain later.... Blast! It's engaged!'

'Serves you right,' said his lover.

And then the doorbell rang.

'I'll get it,' said Maggie.

'Just a minute,' said Jupp, his brain racing.

But Maggie had already opened the door, and two burly men were barging in. 'Police!' said the first man. 'I'm Inspector Collins and this is Sergeant Digby.'

Maggie wasn't surprised: this was what she'd been expecting, and she was ready. 'I'm glad you're here,' she said brightly. 'Is it about that Peeping Tom I reported last week?'

'No, miss, we don't know anything about that. We're here to

arrest this man. Adam Webber, I must ask you to come with us to the police station.'

The MP was astounded: he hadn't foreseen this one. 'Don't be a fool, man! I'm not Webber!'

And, indeed, he didn't look much like Adam's picture in the papers. But the visitors were men whose perusal of the newspapers was normally confined to the strip cartoons. They rarely reached the news pages. They'd been told to grab the man at 9 Rochester Court, and that's what they were going to do.

'We'll sort that out at the station, shall we?' The first man gripped Jupp's arm.

Jupp was in a quandary. How much could he say in front of Maggie, without revealing things she mustn't know? He decided to keep it simple. 'I don't believe you're the police,' he said. 'Prove your identity.'

'Right, son, you asked for it!' The second man reached inside his jacket and brought out a truncheon.

'No!' screamed Jupp. 'There's no need for that!'

Maggie was aghast. 'Let him go!' she cried. 'He's not the man you want!'

The second man picked her up, threw her into the bedroom, and shut the door. Then, as Jupp protested, he hit him with the truncheon and grabbed his other arm.

'Go easy with that!' said the first man. 'He's got questions to answer.'

Then the two men supported their semi-conscious captive out through the door and down the stairs.

'The spokesman added that the German counter-attack had been repulsed, and Allied Forces were again advancing on all fronts.'

Having rounded up the day's war news, the BBC announcer's voice changed gear slightly as, after a short pause, he moved on to domestic items.

'It's been confirmed that the man who died in London's St

James's Park yesterday was killed by a single bullet fired at long range. It's now thought that the shot may have come from an upper window or roof of an adjoining building. Police ask anyone who noticed anything unusual in the area to contact them on Whitehall 1212. That number again, Whitehall 1212.

'The victim has been identified as a senior civil servant, Martin John Hunter, who worked in Whitehall. Mr Hunter, who was forty-two, had a long and distinguished career in public service—'

'Turn it off, George,' said Emily Hart. 'I don't really get on with that chap Pickles.'

Traditionally, the BBC News had always been read by gentlemen with English public school accents. But, as a sign of national solidarity in wartime, the BBC was now employing a few announcers with regional accents. The most notable of these was the North Country actor Wilfred Pickles, who delivered his lines in broad Yorkshire tones.

It was known that BBC announcers wore dinner jackets when broadcasting in the evening, even though they weren't seen by the listeners. In contrast, Pickles sounded as if he were wearing tweeds and cloth cap. Mrs Hart did not approve.

'I think he's all right,' said George. 'Makes a nice change from all those posh voices.'

'Posh voices are what you want on the news,' Mrs Hart declared. 'They make you feel safer. Specially when the news is bad.'

'But it's not so bad these days, is it? Except for that poor devil in the park.'

'Well, just remember Dunkirk and the Blitz. I was less worried if Alvar Lidell or Bruce Belfrage was on. No matter how bad the war was going, you felt it would turn out all right in the end, cos the right people were in charge.'

'Well, now things are better, we can have a bit more variety, can't we?'

'That's not fair,' said Mrs Hart. 'I think the people who had to read all the bad news should be allowed to carry on and do the good news. And that murder wouldn't have sounded so bad if it had been Alvar Lidell telling us.'

Letting his employer have the final word, as always, George switched off the radio. Then he began to voice his thoughts on the murder in the park.

'I reckon the Germans got that bloke,' he observed. 'Senior civil servant. He was probably one of Mr Churchill's top men.'

'I wouldn't put it past them,' Mrs Hart agreed. At the end of the day, she was relaxing with hot cocoa, and a copy of *Picture Post*.

'They got agents everywhere, them Nazis,' said George. 'That's what I said to Millie yesterday. She was telling Mr Hardstaff about her boyfriend being in France with the army. In the lounge, in front of other people! I said, "Careless talk costs lives, my girl!" Them Nazis got agents everywhere.'

'Not among our guests, I hope.'

'You never know, do you? That Mr Donner, his name could be German, couldn't it? Them Jerries are always shouting "Donner and Blitzen"!'

Mrs Hart looked up from her magazine. 'Have you repaired that shelf in Miss Jane's room yet?' she enquired. The end upright had come off, and the vertical books were kept upright only by a pile of horizontal volumes at the end. It was very untidy.

'Not yet,' said George. 'I was all day fixing the boiler, wasn't I?'

'Ah yes, of course.' Mrs Hart was conciliatory: boilers were more important than shelves. 'Have another one?' She pushed towards him the precious tin of chocolate biscuits her cousin had sent from Australia. George took one, and Mrs Hart replaced the lid firmly.

'Course, it didn't have to be a high building,' George resumed. 'That bloke could have been shot from one of them big cranes you see these days. Or the Germans could have used a balloon.'

'If there'd been a balloon, the police would have noticed,' Mrs Hart objected.

'The police don't always notice everything,' said George darkly. 'But I do. I spotted an envelope in Adam Webber's drawer that was addressed to 'Adam Carr'. D'you think I should tell the inspector?'

Maggie was breathless as she came into the dressing room and shut the door behind her. 'I got your message,' she puffed. 'Sorry I couldn't take the call, I was in the bath.'

'That's OK,' said Jane, who was sitting alone in front of the mirror, working on her eyebrows. 'I couldn't say much to your gentleman on the phone. But I thought if we both got here early, we could have a chat before the others get in.'

'Good idea,' said Maggie. 'So here I am.' She sat down and lit a cigarette. 'And the first question is, did you two find somewhere to stay last night?'

'Yes, we took your advice. We're at Vic's.'

'Good old Vic, I knew he wouldn't let you down. Does he know it's Adam Webber with you?'

'I don't know. Like you, he didn't ask. I just said we had nowhere to stay, and that was it. When did you guess who my friend was, by the way?'

'About five minutes after we met.'

'I thought so. Well, thanks for not letting it put you off.'

'Honey, I don't know what this business is all about,' said Maggie. 'But I do know a good man when I see one. Adam wouldn't kill anyone. Well, not unless they had it coming. Is Vic in yet?'

'Yes, we came in together. He was meeting a writer in his dressing room. Listen, I want to know what happened last night, after we got out.'

'It was weird. Alfie was ages coming back and then he was a bag of nerves.'

'Had he tipped off the police?'

'He must have done, but he didn't say. He was talking about

the chemist. Then, when he found you and Adam were gone, he went crackers. But he still didn't say he knew who Adam was.'

'Perhaps he didn't. Perhaps he really went to the chemist.'

'No, of course he knew. Just listen to the rest of it. He was all agitato, wanting to make a phone call, only it was engaged. And then you'll never guess what happened!'

'Did the police come?'

'Yes, they did! And they arrested Alfie!'

'They arrested your gentleman?'

'That's right! Cos he was the only bloke in the flat, wasn't he? So they thought he must be the one they'd been sent to nick!'

'I suppose it was quite funny really.'

'Alfie didn't think so. Very tough they were, too. One of them grabbed me and threw me in the bedroom.'

'That could have been fun.'

'Well, it wasn't. He hurt my arm and then he shut the door on me, and I heard them roughing up poor Alfie. When I came out, they'd taken him away.'

'I'm afraid Adam hit a policeman on Southend Pier. They were probably getting their own back.'

'Alfie thought they weren't real police when they burst in. But when he came back he said they were.'

'How long did they keep him?'

'He was gone about an hour, then he turned up with a bruise on the side of his head. He said they'd apologized for the mistake. But he was still thinking of making a complaint. You know, about police brutality.'

'Did he admit he'd tipped them off?'

'Yes, when he finally got back. It seems at first he just *thought* it was Adam but he felt he should call the police just in case.'

'Thank God you guessed what he was up to!'

'Funny, he didn't let on when he first got back; he was fussing about waiting at the chemist's. He says he still wasn't sure, and didn't want egg on his face.'

'So he got a bang on the head instead.'

'Anyway, when he got back from the rozzers, he said it definitely *was* Adam Webber – they'd shown him more pictures. He told me I'd been hiding a criminal in his flat.'

'Was he very angry?'

'He was at first. But I convinced him I really thought he was just your soldier boyfriend.'

'So you got your night out after all?'

'Eventually. Of course, he pretended he was still cross, so he had an excuse to give me a good spanking. He always feels better after that. And then, after a bit, we went to Silvio's.'

'A bit of what?'

'Well, you know how one thing leads to the other. It was nearly 10.30 when we got to the club. But we had a great time – he spent nearly twenty quid!'

Having finished her story, Maggie stubbed out her cigarette and looked intently at Jane. 'Listen, honey, tell me to mind my own business if you like, but I have to ask. What are you planning to do now?'

'Vic says we can stay with him for a week or two.'

'Good. I expect he's glad of the company – he's between girl-friends. But I meant what are you going to do about Adam? He can't hide for ever.'

Jane sighed. 'I don't know, Maggie, I really don't. I want him to give himself up and let the police sort things out. But he won't.'

'Why not? Like I said, I'm sure he's not a murderer.'

'I know for a fact he's not a murderer. But … well … there are some other things that could get him into trouble. Nothing wicked, I promise you.' There was a brief knock at the door, and Vic Dudley came straight in.

'Do you mind?' exclaimed Maggie. 'We might have had no clothes on!'

'That's what I thought,' said Vic. 'But it's not my lucky week. I should have known. Yesterday I bought a suit with two pairs of trousers and burned a hole in the jacket. Listen, I want to try out some new gags on you.'

'I hope they're better than that one,' said Maggie.

'They're all winners,' said Vic. 'Get these.' He cleared his throat. 'Fellow stopped me in the street today. He said, "I've seen you on the wireless. Why aren't you in the army?" I said, "With a war on? You think I'm crazy?"

'Actually, the fact is, I failed my medical. Not enough blood in my alcohol stream. And they didn't like the look of my alimentary canal. I think it had a barge on it. Anyway, it's true, they wouldn't take me.

'Even today I need check-ups. Last week I had these tests. When I went back for the results, the doctor said, "There's good news and bad news." I said, "Better tell me the bad news first." He said, "You've only got a month to live." What a shock! I tried to be brave, I said, "Well, what's the good news?" He said, "I made it with that new receptionist last night."

'He could see I was upset. He said, "Don't worry, that was a joke."

'I said, "Could you come to the Windmill and explain to the audience?"'

'You may need him to do that,' said Maggie. She lit another cigarette.

The short man had missed last night's shambles. He'd been in Bristol, arranging a fatal accident. Now he was back, and holding an inquest.

'Bloody fools!' he said. 'You managed to mistake a middle-aged pen-pusher for a young bruiser! The brute who saw off Cregan and Clark and knocked out a policeman! Crass stupidity! It's incredible!'

Reggie Paynter's fists tightened. He didn't like being talked to like this. One day he was going to hit the short man extremely hard. Several times. But not yet. These people paid good money. And he knew they had some ruthless men behind them. He clenched his fists, and let Sid Garrett do the talking.

'No one give us a picture of the bastard, did they?' Garrett protested. 'Your number two just said there was a bloke called

Webber in Maida Vale giving you trouble. We was to go to his flat, make out we was coppers, and bring him here. That's what we did.'

'But you must have known what Webber looks like! You haven't been living up a mountain, have you? You've seen his picture in the papers!'

'I don't bother with papers,' said Garrett. 'Anyway, there was no other geezer around. We brought back the only bloke who was there.'

The short man sighed. Then he opened a drawer and picked up a bunch of newspaper cuttings. He gave one to each of them, and they peered at the grainy photographs.

'That's Adam Webber. It's vital we take him before the police do.'

'The coppers are after him too?'

'Good God, you have been living up a mountain! It's not just been in the papers, man, it's been all over the radio! Every day! The police want Webber for murder. We want him because he has a notebook that could make trouble for us. Our people are now offering five hundred pounds to anyone who can get him into our hands.'

Garrett whistled. 'A monkey! Strewth! Just tell us where he is now and we'll bring him in double-quick!'

The short man's voice rose. 'We don't know where he is now! We had this chance last night, and you blew it! He's hiding somewhere else now!'

'So how do we find him?'

'Through his girl. We now know for sure he's with the young woman from the Cavendish. They were together at Mr Ju—' He corrected himself. 'At the Maida Vale flat. And they left together. Find the girl and we'll find Webber.'

'OK, how do we find the girl then?'

'She's a dancer at the Windmill Theatre. You see the show there and, at the end, you watch for her at the stage door and follow her home.'

'How do we know which is her?'

'Her name's Jane Hart. You buy a programme, then you'll know what she looks like when she comes on. You can read, I take it?'

6

VIC DUDLEY'S RENTED flat in Notting Hill was functional rather than luxurious but at least it did have two bedrooms, as well as a sitting room and kitchen. Vic's first two years in show business had been a struggle. But now Windmill wages and radio fees had brought a measure of prosperity. There was a radiogram, with a stack of dance-band records. Vic had bought a rather stylish electric heater to augment the gas fire. And there was a fridge, to keep the beer bottles cold.

Adam had stayed warm and comfortable all day but boredom had been a problem. It was a working day for Jane. And comedians at the Windmill worked every day. So Vic and Jane had gone off together to the theatre after the three of them shared a late brunch.

Vic had offered his large collection of men's magazines to keep Adam amused and for a while it did. He'd chuckled at the jokes and light-hearted articles in *Lilliput*, *Men Only* and *London Opinion*, admired their occasional, rather demure, black-and-white pictures of naked ladies, and failed to finish several crossword puzzles. By late afternoon Adam was feeling the need for more positive activity. He studied himself in the mirror. His facial hair had grown quickly, and could almost be regarded as moustache and sideburns, with the beginnings of a beard around his chin. Every day he'd practised wearing the glasses and found they did little to impair his vision. He was starting to feel he could venture into the outside world without being instantly recognized.

He sat down with pencil and paper and began to list all the things that needed thinking about: Cooper, The Bull, black market activities, and the thugs' interest in a blue notebook, which must surely be the one he'd taken from Jefferson's room.

Then he saw that it was six o'clock: time for the news. He wondered if he'd hear an explanation of last night's alarms. There'd been two big blasts in London for the first time in many months and this morning had brought much speculation. Were the Germans about to launch a new bombing campaign? A last-ditch attempt to turn the tide?

Adam switched on the radio and found that the news had already started. It was not good news, but the announcer's voice was calm and reassuring.

'It's now been confirmed that the two explosions in the Greater London area last night were the result of enemy action. Two high-explosive rockets had been fired from enemy territory across the English Channel.

'The explosion in Chiswick demolished two houses, causing twelve casualties, five of them fatal. The second rocket landed on farmland near Edgware, destroying some barns and outhouses, and injuring two farm workers. Their injuries are not thought to be serious. These rockets appear to be of a new type, and have been designated V2s, as successors to the V1 flying bombs, which the Germans have now abandoned.

'The War Office says that the V2s will be defeated in the same way. Additional fighter squadrons are already being deployed over southern England, to destroy the slow-moving rockets before they cross the coastline. There are no plans for evacuation, and the government is stressing that danger to the public is far less than that faced during the Blitz.'

Adam reflected on this new threat. Perhaps Canada wasn't such a bad idea after all. The newsreader moved on.

'Police are investigating the death of a city councillor in Bristol today. James Baxter, aged forty-five, who died of gunshot wounds, was a captain in the Home Guard. He died when a pistol was fired during a military exercise. It's believed that Captain Baxter may have accidentally discharged the gun himself.

'And now the weather....'

Adam switched the radio off, so that he could stop and think. Something in that last item had started his brain working. He remembered that Mark Jefferson had been in the Home Guard. And he'd also met an accidental death. That was something else to think about.

The new twist in the war against Hitler was the first topic when Westley and his friends began their meeting.

'What's the truth about these V2 things?' Charles Bell demanded. 'The press seem to be playing down the whole issue.'

'That's government policy,' Westley replied. 'In fact, the Cabinet are extremely worried. In private, Churchill is saying this is the biggest danger Britain's faced since we saw off the threat of invasion.'

'Hell!' said Hugh Denby. 'Just when we thought the bastards were finished!'

'They are finished,' said Westley. 'Nothing can stop the Allied advance in Europe. But Hitler wants to kill as many people as he can before we hang him.'

'What's known about the actual rockets?' Jupp enquired.

'Just the basic facts. They carry high-explosive warheads, which go off on impact. They can't be aimed with any accuracy. They're fired from occupied Holland, pointed in the general direction of London. They can land anywhere within a fifty-mile radius and, needless to say, they can cause a lot of damage.'

'What defence is there?'

'None,' was Westley's blunt answer.

'The War Office says that our fighters will destroy the rockets in mid-air,' said Bell.

'Window dressing, I'm afraid,' said Westley. 'The damn

things go too fast. If our aircraft can hit one in twenty, they'll be doing well.'

'So what will the government do?'

'The rockets will only be stopped when our army reaches the launching sites. That may take some weeks.'

'Has anyone thought of bombing these launch sites?' asked Cox.

'They'll be trying,' said Westley. 'But our agents say they're deep underground and heavily camouflaged.'

'Could we drop paratroops to take the area in advance of the main force?'

'That's been suggested. But there's opposition. The army don't want another Arnhem.'

'So, for now, any of us can be blown up at any time?'

'That's about the size of it,' Westley conceded. 'The government's only option is to belittle the danger and prevent panic, while we wait for our troops to do the job.'

Denby voiced the question that was in everyone's mind. 'Is this going to affect our plans?'

'Basically no. As I said, V2 impact is indiscriminate and unpredictable, affecting friend and foe alike. What we can't foresee, we can't take into account. So we carry on, exactly as planned.'

There were murmurs of approval around the table.

'Of course, there could be complications,' Westley continued, 'if the Cabinet decided to evacuate certain public figures to the provinces.'

'Is that a possibility?'

'It has been discussed. They might move Churchill and his headquarters staff out into the country, probably somewhere up north, beyond the V2 range. Also, the King and Queen, plus some ministers considered vital to the war effort.' Westley allowed himself a rare smile. 'I believe I may be one of them.'

'So you would be fully in the picture?'

'Exactly. In that event, the job of making arrests would be handled by our local units, instead of our metropolitan strike force.'

'And they'd have sufficient warning?'

'Certainly. But I don't think the situation will arise. Even if the decision were taken, I don't believe the moves could be arranged before our day of action.'

'It seems to me,' said Bell, 'that this V2 scare could work in our favour. The police and the army will have their hands full dealing with these V2s. Plus the public alarm they're going to cause.'

Westley smiled again, using up his ration for the week. 'Exactly. Furthermore, in due course the army will overrun these sites and put a stop to the rockets. If that happens after our takeover, we'll get the credit. Now let's move on.' Ernest Cox had raised a hand. 'Ernie, you wanted to say something?'

'Yes,' said Cox. 'I want to congratulate you and our active-service unit on the efficient way the traitor Martin Hunter has been silenced.'

Westley looked stern. 'Ah. Please be careful, everyone. Don't assume Hunter's death had anything to do with our organization. The police are checking on enemies he may have made at the time of the Spanish Civil War.'

Gerald Collis now spoke quietly. 'I for one deeply regret Martin's death. I still believe that there were other ways of dealing with the problem.'

'Your views are noted,' said Westley.

There was an awkward silence. Then Bill Ford spoke up.

'What's the latest on the Tilfleet cock-up? Have they recovered that notebook yet? And what about the thief? Have they caught him?'

'Not yet, I'm afraid. There was a reported sighting of the man Webber in London on Tuesday. Our men moved quickly but by the time they got there the man had gone. Of course, it may not have been Webber anyway. I have no more details.'

Jupp's eyes remained firmly fixed on the papers in front of him. The pound notes he'd handed out had been money well spent.

'Our people are continuing the search,' said Westley. 'We're now offering a reward of five hundred pounds to the London underworld for anyone who can deliver Webber alive.'

'Oh dear,' sighed Bell. 'More gangsters.'

Westley produced words that had served him well in the past. 'You can be sure that we're leaving no stone unturned.'

Onstage, Vic Dudley was in full flow. He'd been promoted to the penultimate spot in the show, and he was making the most of it. 'Got a question for you. Little question. Do infants get as much fun from infancy as adults do from adultery? There's a lot of it goes on, you know. Friend of mine came back from the Far East, he'd been away a year. First night home he was in bed with his wife; they'd left a light on downstairs. Air-raid warden banged on the door. My mate woke up in a panic, he said, "My God, is that your husband?" His wife said, "No, don't worry, my husband's in the Far East."

'Course, we shouldn't do it. All these good people tell us we shouldn't. There's a big notice outside our local church. "If you're tired of sin, come in." Underneath, someone's written "If you're not, ring Bayswater 2429".'

Vic was getting a few laughs, but not from Paynter or Garrett. They'd heard all this twice before. Entertainment at the Windmill was non-stop, the same programme being played five times a day, with a ten-minute interval between shows. No one had to leave. You could come in when you wanted, and leave when you chose. The audience consisted almost entirely of men, all eager to get to the front rows for a closer look at the girls.

So, when front seats were vacated by customers who had to get back to the office or go home, men from further back rushed forward to grab the empty places. Climbing over the back of the seats was forbidden, and punished by expulsion. So experienced Windmill-goers always sat at the end of a row when they first arrived, ready for the spring forward, until they finally reached Row A.

Paynter and Garrett had come into the theatre at four, and had made it to the front row at 8.30, in time for the start of the last show. As they'd made their final charge, they'd faced competition from another man, slightly closer, approaching the vacant seats from the opposite direction. But this was a small man in a suit, with fountain pen and propelling pencil protruding from his breast pocket. Paynter had glared at him and he'd melted away. Thus they'd been watching the final run from the best possible vantage point. Seeing the girls repeat their routines had brought nothing but pleasure. Hearing Vic Dudley's jokes for the third time was a small price to pay.

With the help of the programme, they'd identified Jane Hart as the fan-dancer in the South Seas number, and they'd studied her diligently, to ensure they'd recognize her later. They'd also spotted Maggie early on, standing on a pedestal at the back, pretending to be a classical statue. Garrett had made the connection.

'Blimey, that's the bint at the flat – the one I shoved in the bedroom!'

'You're right,' Paynter had observed. 'You missed a chance there, Sid.'

'Yeah, well, she didn't look so good with her hair in curlers and that white stuff on her boat.'

Now Vic Dudley was coming to the end of his act, and the two men were looking forward to the finale. They'd done their reconnaissance and located the stage door before they came in.

'There's been a bit of trouble backstage,' Vic Dudley was saying. 'They found a little hole punched in the wall between my room and the girls' dressing room. That's right, a little hole in the wall. The manager was furious, he said, "This is disgraceful! We can't have that sort of thing here!" I said, "Don't make a fuss, it doesn't bother me. If it gives them pleasure, let them peep."

'Anyway, there it is. There's a hole in the dressing-room wall, and I'd better go and look into it. So I'll leave you with this thought. A happy life depends on working well and sleeping well. So watch out who you work with and who you see as a friend. Good night.'

Vic took his bow to a sprinkling of applause, the pianist went into his play-off music, and the red plush curtains swished together.

Paynter and Garrett settled down to enjoy the seaside spectacular for the third time. They could relax. There'd be plenty of time at the end to get to the stage door before the performers began to leave.

Bert Bailey had left his den behind the counter and was standing at the open stage door, taking the air. A portly, fifty-ish, balding man, short of exercise, he found even the Soho air refreshing after a long spell inhaling the stale smells of greasepaint, sweat and cigarette smoke. He surveyed the scene outside in Archer Street. It was a mild night, bright with moonlight, and the tart on the corner was looking relaxed and cheerful. People, on their way to pubs and clubs, were content to stroll at a leisurely pace.

The tart exchanged friendly words with all the male passersby who weren't accompanied by women and was not offended when they continued on their way. From the next street came the sound of a team of buskers, one with a concertina, the other playing the spoons. And then, of course, there were the loiterers.

'Cheerio, Bert. See you tomorrow.'

The first of the company to leave was the pianist, Ronnie Bridges. It didn't take him long to change from dinner jacket to casual clothes, and he was keen to get back to his home in Essex.

'Good night, Ronnie,' said Bert. It was all first names at the Windmill: except, of course, for the manager, Vivian Van Damm. He was always 'Mr Van Damm' to his face, and 'VD' behind his back.

Bert resumed his survey. He was used to men lingering near the stage door. Many of them he knew: regular boyfriends of Windmill girls. Others were fans or admirers, anxious to greet a favourite as she came out and perhaps strike up an acquaintance.

The girls were adept at brushing off unwanted approaches politely but firmly. If he saw a girl being harassed, Bert was always ready to step out and intervene. It seldom happened. But he liked to keep a watchful eye.

Tonight he was a little concerned about two large men standing together in a doorway across the street. They seemed anxious to stay back in the shadows. But the reflected moonlight allowed Bert to see two craggy faces, watching the stage door intently. He sensed something different about this pair: something, perhaps, a little sinister. One was smoking a cheap, small cigar, and the aroma was filtering across the street in the still air. Bert felt these two could be trouble.

Monk wished Inspector Jessett wouldn't smoke those damned little cigars. To him, they smelt like a garden bonfire, on which someone had carelessly left a Wellington boot. But it was something he'd had to learn to live with.

Jessett glanced at the luminous dial on his watch and found it was 10.40. 'Why does it take them so long to put on a few clothes?' he grumbled.

Monk grinned. 'Well, most of them have to start from scratch.' And then, savouring a happy memory, he added, 'I reckon that Hart girl's quite a looker.'

'Yes. I noticed you studying her features very carefully.'

'In the line of duty, sir. We need to spot her quickly when she comes out, don't we? She won't hang about. And she might be with a bunch of people.'

'We'll spot her all right. And then we'll have to be quick. You parked your car in Rupert Street?'

'That's right, sir. As instructed.'

'Good. And my car's in Great Windmill Street. So, if she turns left when she comes out and gets in a car, we follow her in mine. If she goes the other way, we use yours.'

'She doesn't look the sort who'd be running a car. Specially in wartime.'

'You never know. These theatricals often have rich friends.'

'I bet she goes home on the tube.'

'Tube or bus, there's no problem. We follow her wherever. We could leave the cars where they are till the morning.'

Jessett's cigar was burned almost down to his lips. He dropped the stub and ground it under his right boot. 'I wish they'd get a bloody move on.'

Monk could see that his boss was getting irritated. He switched the subject. 'That was a long spell with the superintendent this afternoon, sir. Was he giving you a hard time?'

'He tried to. It seems we're under pressure from the Tilfleet Chamber of Commerce. They want a result on that post office blag. The local shopkeepers are worried.'

'You told him we'd fingered Reggie Paynter?'

'Yes. That pleased him. The super's been wanting Paynter locked up ever since he turned up on our patch. I told him I've got the warrant, and we can do him for robbery and GBH.'

'Ah. That'll put him away for eight to ten years.'

'Right. Now the only problem is finding him. Ever since he left his wife, there's no address.'

'We can pick him up at The Bull, can't we?'

'I doubt it. Once news of the warrant gets round, he'll be making himself scarce, and you can bet it's got round already. Ah, they've started coming out.'

Several of the male dancers had emerged from the stage door, and were being warmly greeted by some of the waiting young men.

'The boys,' Monk observed. 'Always the quickest.'

'That's true,' said Jessett. 'They don't put on quite so much make-up.'

'We could nick a few of them, if we followed them down to Leicester Square.'

'Not tonight, Josephine,' said Jessett. 'Tonight we follow the lady.' And then he checked himself. 'At least, I think we do.' His gaze had fallen on two men waiting on the other side of the road, close to the Windmill stage door. He'd been vaguely aware of them standing around almost as long as he and Monk had: now he'd noticed something. He lowered his voice. 'What d'you make of those two jokers over there? Anything familiar about the tall one?'

'Not really,' said Monk. 'I can't see his face.'

And then, for a moment, he could. The tall man had struck a match to light his cigarette, and his face was briefly illuminated.

'Yes, I can!' said Monk, with quiet excitement. 'That's Reggie Paynter!'

'Talk of the devil!' said Jessett, equally quietly. 'It's Reggie Paynter all right. He must fancy one of the Windmill birds.'

'So what do we do?' asked Monk. 'Do we still wait for the Hart girl?'

'No,' said Jessett. 'She's always here, we can come back another night. We can't miss this chance of nabbing Paynter.'

Monk had a suggestion. 'What if you nick him while I wait for the girl?'

'No, thank you, Arthur,' said Jessett. 'There's two of them. And it's a pound to a penny his oppo's another villain. It needs both of us. Have you got cuffs?'

Monk checked the handcuffs in his overcoat pocket. 'Yes, sir.'

'OK,' said Jessett. 'Here we go. Don't bother with the other bloke. Get the cuffs on Paynter, double-quick.'

The two policemen strolled casually across the street. As they neared their prey, Monk detached himself, on a course that would take him round behind Paynter. Jessett approached from the front, with a friendly smile on his face.

'Evening, Reggie,' said the inspector. 'We'd like a word if you don't—' He didn't finish the sentence. Reggie Paynter still had the fast reflexes of a boxer, and he could spot a policeman a mile off.

Before Monk could grab his arm, Paynter punched Jessett hard in the stomach, doubling him up. Then, sensing danger behind him, he spun round and butted Monk hard in the face. 'It's the law!' he shouted to Garrett. And then he ran. As Jessett and Monk staggered back, Garrett also took to his heels. With the hunted man's instinct to halve the pursuit, he fled in the opposite direction. Paynter was running west towards Great Windmill Street. Garrett ran east into Rupert Street.

Monk and Jessett were not confused: Paynter was their target. Recovering swiftly, they set off after him, scattering pedestrians as they charged along the narrow pavement. Monk produced a police whistle, and was blowing it with all the breath he could muster.

Piccadilly Circus was still shrouded in wartime gloom, with Eros boarded up for the duration. No one was sure why. The planking would offer no protection against bombs. The popular view was that the boards were there to protect the statue from revellers when Victory Night finally arrived. But that still seemed a long way off, as Paynter ran down Great Windmill Street and into the darkened Circus. The neon lights which once lit up the hub of the British Empire were still extinguished. There was some traffic but it moved cautiously.

Cursing the moonlight, Paynter sprinted on. His first instinct had been to dash into the tube station and get on a train. But then he realized that could be a trap. Waiting for a train that didn't come, he'd have nowhere to run when the police caught up with him. He decided to charge on, down Lower Regent Street, and lose himself in pitch-dark St James's Park.

Walking up Lower Regent Street, in the opposite direction, was Police Constable Henry Day, coming to the end of his evening patrol. He'd had two lights put out that were contravening the blackout, and he'd cautioned three courting couples in the park. Otherwise, it had been an uneventful spell of duty. But now, as he approached Charles the Second Street, he heard shrill blasts from a police whistle and saw a man hurtling towards him. He read the situation instantly, stood in the middle of the path, and raised one hand, in the way he did when stopping traffic.

Reggie Paynter saw this uniformed figure blocking his way, and knew what he had to do. Adding pugilistic skill to the momentum of his run, he swung a huge round-arm punch at the constable's head. This was a misjudgment. Constable Day was at that time a Southern Area Amateur Boxing Champion. He easily ducked the swinging fist, and then felled Paynter with one mighty blow. As Paynter hit the pavement, Jessett and Monk came puffing towards them, the latter gratefully taking the whistle from his lips.

Back in Archer Street, Vic Dudley and Jane Hart were about to pass through the stage-door. They'd heard the police whistle.

'What's up out there?' asked Vic.

'Bit of aggro,' said Bert. 'Couple of heavies been hanging round for half an hour. They got into a punch-up with some other blokes, then they all ran off.'

'Oh well, that's Soho for you,' said Vic. And with that, Vic Dudley and Jane Hart walked to Rupert Street and hailed a taxi.

Unlike Maggie, Vic Dudley liked to eat in the morning. Before going off to work, he always required a large brunch, and this he now shared with his guests. At heart, Vic was an egg-and-bacon man, but wartime rationing limited that to Sundays. Happily, baked beans were still plentiful and played a large part in Vic's diet. For brunch, they were always preceded by porridge. Vic was now eating a large bowl of what he called Tartan Tack. This meant that, before tipping milk and sugar onto his porridge, he'd stirred in a measure of whisky. 'A mark of respect for our Scottish friends,' he maintained.

He savoured his first spoonful, swallowed it, and said, 'I've been thinking about last night.'

Adam and Jane were eating cereals and drinking large quantities of tea.

'What about last night?' asked Adam.

'Bert said there were two heavies hanging round the stage door. I reckon they might have been coppers. Someone out there was blowing a police whistle, right?'

'Why would police be watching our stage door?' asked Jane.

'They could have been waiting for you.'

'Me?'

'Listen, they want to nick Adam here, right? They might have guessed he's likely to be with you. No use asking, you wouldn't let on. But they could have sussed that if they followed you home from the 'Mill, they might get lucky.'

'But no one did follow us, did they?' said Jane.

'Apparently not,' said Vic. 'Or they'd have been knocking on the door by now. But Bert said these geezers got in a punch-up. Maybe they were going to follow you and that stopped them.'

'In which case we've got a problem,' said Adam. 'If Vic's right, they'll follow you another night. What can we do about that?'

'I can't stop going to work, can I?'

'Don't worry, darling, Uncle Vic's got it all worked out. There's a fire door on the other side of the theatre, opens onto the mews, where VD parks his car.'

'I didn't know about that.'

'Not many people do, that's the idea. There's room for two cars by that door. I'll square VD to leave my car there and let us use that exit. No one will be watching there. I can have you out of the building and on your way home quicker than a rat up a drainpipe.'

Jane gave him a big smile. 'Vic, you're an angel. I've never been compared to a rat before, but it's a great idea. But will VD agree?'

'Yes. He wants me to sign a new contract.'

Adam drained his tea mug. 'I don't know about angels, Vic, but you're a hell of a good friend.'

'Can't help it, chum. My mum was bitten by a nun.' Vic poured more whisky on his porridge and offered some to Jane and Adam, who declined. 'Right, that's that problem settled. What plans have you two got?'

'I'm working today,' said Jane.

'You worked yesterday, you should be off today.'

'I agreed to swap with Annie Baker. She has to go to the dentist.'

'Oh well, that'll be more fun than listening to the Accordion Aces. So we'll go in together again, OK? And for the next few weeks I'll use the car.'

'Thanks. Have you got enough petrol?'

'Gallons. Alfie Allen sold me his coupons.' Vic finished his porridge and turned to Adam. 'Sorry, mate. You've got another day indoors on your own.'

'Until this evening,' said Adam. 'Then I'm going to a pub.'

'Hey! Is that wise? I thought you were lying low?'

'Can't lie low for ever, can I? Jane and I have talked it over. The best way to prove I didn't kill that bastard Cooper is to find out who did.'

'Come off it – you've seen too many Hollywood movies. You're not Alan Ladd. How are you going to start? You've got nothing to go on.'

'Yes, I have. Cooper was up to his neck in the Tilfleet black market, involved with some very rough characters. We reckon he may have got himself killed by crossing the local gangsters. Anyway, it's a starting point.'

'And if they're as rough as you say, it could be a finishing point. You'll have to be careful.'

'I'll be careful. Jane's discovered the Tilfleet villains hang around a pub called The Bull. That's where I'm going. I'll say I was a friend of Maurice Cooper, and I'm after some black market booze. See who reacts.'

'Just a minute. If you go to a pub, someone's likely to recognize you. Your picture's in all the papers.'

'Not any more, Vic, haven't you noticed? I've been pushed out by the Cleft Chin Murder.'

The police were currently searching for an American army deserter and his girlfriend, who'd robbed and killed a London cab driver. The victim had a cleft chin, which enabled the newspapers to pin a label on the case. Pictures of the cabbie and the American had largely replaced Adam's on the front pages.

'I'm getting to be old news,' said Adam. 'Also, I hope this face fungus is starting to hide my natural good looks. And I'll be travelling in the dark.'

'Do you approve of this, Jane?'

'Not much. But we have to do something. I just wish Adam would wait till tomorrow, so I could go with him.'

'Now that would be daft, wouldn't it?' Adam protested. 'The two of us would be far more likely to be spotted than me on my own.'

Vic had to agree. 'I'm afraid he's right, Janie. A man can sometimes be overlooked. But a girl like you is always going to be looked over.' A thought struck him. 'Listen, if someone comes up with some naughty liquor, what are you going to use for money?'

'This wonderful girl's been subbing me. I've got about ten quid.'

'Which won't go very far. Dodgy Scotch is costing more than five a bottle these days. Besides, you're going to need that cash to carry on living.'

Vic got up, opened a drawer, and took out a wad of notes in a rubber band. 'I did a gig at Benny's Club last week. Got paid in readies. Here's twenty.'

'Vic, you're amazing. That must have been a very generous nun.'

'It's only money,' said Vic. 'Money doesn't buy friends. But it does give you a better class of enemy. Take it.'

Adam took it. 'All right. Thanks. Just a loan, of course.'

'We'll see. If you come back with some Scotch, I'll take that instead. Just make sure you come back.'

7

AT THE JOINT Services Supply Depot in Leatherhead, Staff Sergeant Whittaker was puzzled. He put down the sheaf of papers, scratched his head, and looked across at the adjutant, sitting at the opposite desk.

'Excuse me, sir, have you seen these latest orders from HQ?'

Captain Hazell looked up from *The Times* crossword puzzle. 'You mean the Home Guard requisitions?'

'Yes, sir. It doesn't make sense. Why do these toy soldiers suddenly need all this extra ammunition? They're not doing any fighting.'

'They say they need it for their exercises. And it seems there's a big one coming up.'

'They don't use live ammo for exercises, do they?'

'Apparently, sometimes they do. That's how that poor devil in Bristol bought it. And, of course, they need live stuff on the firing ranges.'

'Beats me why they haven't been disbanded yet. Jerry's not going to invade now, is he?'

'Quite a lot of people share your view, Sergeant. But it seems somebody up there likes them. And I suppose they could still be useful if these damned V2s started causing civil unrest.'

'Well, I hope they wouldn't be using live ammo for crowd control!'

Hazell's brain delivered the word he'd been searching for, and he wrote it into his crossword puzzle. Then he sat back. 'Actually, Sergeant, I did query those orders when they came through. I had a word with the colonel, and he took it up with the top brass.'

'I'm glad to hear it, sir. Puts us in the clear.'

'The answer came back, yes, the stuff had to be despatched. And quick. It seems to have been decided at government level. So we'd better get on with it.'

'Very good, sir, I'll start things moving at once. "Theirs not to reason why", as Shakespeare put it.'

'Tennyson, Sergeant. Any chance of a coffee?'

Reggie Paynter was not inclined to be co-operative. He glared across the table and snarled, 'You're wasting your time. You got no evidence.'

Jessett stared back. 'Evidence of what?' he asked innocently.

The question threw Paynter. He hesitated before saying, 'The post office job. That's what you pulled me for, innit? You haven't got me here for fun.'

'That's true,' said Jessett. 'Nobody's laughing. But I'm glad you want to talk about the post office job. Get it off your chest, eh?'

'What's your game? It isn't on my chest. I didn't do it!'

'So it's funny you led off about it. I was going to talk about resisting arrest. Obstructing the police. Assaulting a constable.'

'I never touched him!'

'Only because you weren't good enough. You threw a pretty hefty punch. Just a bit too slow.'

'Sod off,' said Paynter. He folded his arms across his chest.

'Last night's caper's enough to lock you up for a bit,' said Jessett cheerfully. 'So let's move on to this post office raid you were so anxious to discuss. Fifteenth of February. Tilfleet High Street.'

'I didn't do it,' Paynter reiterated.

'We've got a statement from a witness who heard you admit the crime.'

'Rubbish! Why would I do that?'

'Because you can't resist bragging when you've had a few

jars. We've also got a bookie who says you suddenly had a great deal of cash.'

'A present from a friend.'

'You haven't got any friends, Reggie. And, if you had, they wouldn't be the sort to give away money. Best of all, you were picked out by both witnesses at the identity parade.'

'That was rigged. How could they know me, we was wearing ... the blokes who done that job was wearing masks.'

'How do you know?'

'I read it in the papers.'

'That'll be the day. Anyway, witnesses saw your eyes and hair, and those bloody great cauliflower ears. Face it, we've got you bang to rights.'

'My brief doesn't think so.'

'He's paid to bring hope to the desperate.'

'And he told me not to answer any more questions.'

'You don't have to, Reggie. I'm just trying to help you, that's all.'

'Help me? You're joking!'

'No, I'm not. Like I said, we've got you fair and square. Robbery with violence, GBH. With your record, that's eight years, maybe ten.'

Paynter pondered for a moment. 'So how are you going to help?'

'We can't stop you going down, Reggie. But I could get you a shorter sentence.'

'What? Fix the judge, you mean?'

'No, that's something we can't do. But there's something I can do. I can get them to reduce the charge from GBH to common assault, go easy on the gory details. I can say you've been co-operative. That way you might get off with a couple of years. If you smile nicely at the judge.'

Paynter thought it over. A six-year difference. That was a lot of living time. Eventually he spoke, with slightly less arrogance.

'So what do I have to do? I ain't going to grass on anyone.'

'I wouldn't expect it, Reggie. We'll get your mates in our own good time. What I want from you is information.'

'Information … grassing … same thing. I don't do it.'

'Not the same thing. I'm not asking you for names. You don't have to put anyone in the frame. I just want a rough idea of what's been going on.'

'Going on?'

'You were a friend of Frank Cregan, right?'

'Yeah. We used to train together.'

'And I bet you knew Dave Clark too. So you should be able to tell me what the hell they were doing, roughing up a bloke on Southend Pier.'

'Oh. That.'

'Yes. That. Spilling the beans on the pier shambles can't hurt Clark or Cregan now, can it? In fact, if you tell me about it, you'll be doing them a favour. We want to find out who topped them.'

'I don't know who topped them. If I did, I'd be after the bastards myself.'

'Just tell me what they were doing.'

Paynter pondered again. As the man said, telling what he knew couldn't do his mates any harm.

'So if I tell you that, you'll do what you said?'

'If you tell me the truth about the pier, I'll go easy on your previous. I'll want to know a few other things before I reduce the charge.'

'Like what?'

'Like why you and your pal were waiting outside the Windmill stage door.'

'That's easy. We seen the show, and we was waiting to see if we could chat up a couple of the girls. That's not illegal, is it?'

'Were you waiting to see Jane Hart?'

Paynter's reply was not quite quick enough, but eventually it came. 'Who?'

'Jane Hart. The girl from the boarding house where Maurice Cooper had his head bashed in.'

'I don't know their names. I took a fancy to a redhead, and my mate would have settled for anyone.'

'What do you know about the Cooper murder?'

'Only what I hear in the pub. That bloke on the pier done it, right?'

'He's the one we're looking for. And that brings us back to the pier, doesn't it? So what were Cregan and Clark up to?'

Paynter sighed. 'Yeah, well, I do know a bit about that, cos I was due to meet Frank that evening. We was going to the dogs.'

'And he cried off?'

'Yeah. Rang me in the afternoon, said he'd got a job. Him and Dave had to nab this bloke on the pier. They was to take him somewhere quiet and lean on him till he coughed up. About some notebook he'd nicked.'

'A notebook? Are you sure?'

'That's what Frank said.'

'And who'd given them this job?'

'I dunno.'

'I think you do, Reggie. The word is, someone round here is paying good money to the local villains to do naughty things. Who is it?'

'I told you, I dunno. None of it's come my way.'

'What about the ten fivers in your pocket when we nicked you?'

'I'd like them back.'

'You'll get them back, if they're legit. Where did they come from?'

'The dogs. I had a couple of wins. Listen, you said you'd go easy if I told you about Frank and Dave on the pier. I done that.'

'And I've said I'll knock a couple of blots off your record. Before I talk about reducing the charge, I'll want to know a lot more.'

'Well, I ain't saying nothing more.'

'Ah, but you will. All in good time. Just go away and think about it.' Jessett nodded to the constable. 'All right, Thompson, take him back to his cell. Have a good night's sleep, Reggie. We'll talk again tomorrow.'

'Sod you,' said Paynter. He got up and Thompson led him away.

Sergeant Monk came in.

'Any luck, sir?'

'We've made a start.' Jessett told Monk what he'd learned. Then he summed it up. 'Someone else is after Webber. You can bet they paid those two to go to the Windmill and follow the Hart girl.'

Monk grinned. 'Not a bad way to earn a few quid.'

'I'm glad you think so. We'll be back on stage-door duty tonight.'

'Right, sir. Do we get to see the show again?'

'Of course. So we know when it ends. Any news on Webber's history?'

'The Marine Research Centre recruited him from Imperial College, London, so I got on to them. It seems he studied marine biology there for three years and got a good science degree. Never known to be in trouble.'

'Background? Family?'

'They don't know much. His parents were killed in the Blitz. Webber shared digs with a fellow student called Adam Carr.'

There was a sharp intake of breath from Jessett. Monk looked at him enquiringly, but the inspector merely said, 'Go on.'

'Just before they were due to leave Imperial, their house got a direct hit from a V1. Webber was the only survivor – he'd gone out to buy fags. He went straight from college to the Marine Research place, and booked into the Cavendish, where they don't seem to know anything about his background.'

'I see. Well done, Arthur.'

'Fancy. No one wants to know about their guests.'

'Ah. Not quite true, Sergeant.'

'You don't agree, sir?'

'An hour ago I had a phone call from George Fowler. You know, the Cavendish handyman.'

'Oh yes. The chap who thinks he's Sexton Blake.'

'Well, he does try to be helpful. He rang to say he'd found an envelope in Webber's room. Not addressed to Adam Webber. Addressed to Adam Carr.'

Now the intake of breath came from Sergeant Monk. 'Webber's mate at college. That's interesting.'

'Isn't it? Get back to Imperial and see if they can tell you the exact date the bomb hit Webber's digs. Then contact Civil Defence and ask if they have a full casualty list for that incident.'

'Right, sir. What was in the envelope, by the way?'

'Nothing. It seems someone had chucked the contents and scribbled on the envelope. Some kind of list, Fowler says.'

'What sort of list, sir? Could be helpful.'

'Yes. Unfortunately, I didn't find out. The superintendent came through on the other line. He's complaining that we don't do enough to stamp out the local black market.'

'That's not fair. We're doing our best.'

'Quite. I said smashing that black market was our top priority. And I told Fowler you'd get over there sharpish and pick up the envelope. Have another chat with him while you're there. Find out what he thought of Webber. OK?'

Monk sighed. 'With respect, sir, couldn't Ernie Fairweather do that? I've got all these phone calls to make. And there's a lot of paperwork piled up.'

'Sorry, Arthur, it needs to be you. You know the Cavendish people, and they know you. You'll get the best out of Fowler. Do the phone calls first, and then get over to the Cavendish as soon as you can.'

'Very good, sir.' Monk allowed a hint of weariness to creep into his voice. He managed to restrain himself from saying, 'What did your last slave die of?'

And then Jessett had an afterthought. 'Talking of Sergeant Fairweather, if he hasn't got those biscuits from the Maypole yet, tell him to try and fiddle a packet of tea at the same time.'

*

It had been a bad day for the short man. It started with a shame-faced Garrett reporting last night's failure. By now it had dawned on Garrett that, since it was only Paynter the police wanted, he himself had no need to run. He should have stayed and followed the girl as instructed. It had been an instinctive reaction. Since childhood, a cry of 'It's the law!' had always caused instant flight.

Needing to hide his mistake, Garrett had told a story that varied greatly from the truth. In his account, there'd been a dozen police in Archer Street, questioning everyone at the scene. With his criminal record, Garrett had feared he might be detained. So he'd run, believing that, as a free man, he'd be more use to the short man in the future.

The short man had questioned Garrett's use to man or beast at any time. But Garrett had admitted he had no idea what had happened to Paynter: so, with a temporary lack of manpower, Garrett had been told to go back to the Windmill tonight.

After dismissing Garrett, the short man worried. Why so many police at the Windmill stage door? Perhaps they'd realized, as he had, that the best route to Webber was via Jane Hart. But why so many police to do a routine tailing job? Were they beginning to get an inkling of the bigger picture?

There was a lot of paperwork for him to do that day, and he busied himself with that. He was a perfectionist: both in his vision of the way society should be ruthlessly organized and in his detailed planning of the forthcoming action. He achieved some satisfaction from checking and re-checking arrangements and finding them all in order.

But anxiety and wrath returned when, soon after midday, a phone call informed him that Paynter was in custody at Tilfleet police station. He cursed the incompetence of the underworld characters he was compelled to employ. And he tried to console himself with the belief that, as he understood it, the criminal code would compel the man to keep his mouth shut. He told the caller to keep him informed.

Then, at five o'clock, came the call that set alarm bells ringing in overdrive.

He barked at the phone in disbelief.

'What? ... What? ... Are you sure? ... I thought he was supposed to be tough! ... The notebook? My God!'

The short man's fist tightened around the ebony ruler on his desk, and his knuckles were white.

'Well, he can't be allowed to! It could be disastrous! He has to be stopped! ... Absolutely ... If that's the only way, that's what you have to do ... No, of course I'm not paying! This'll be for your sake too. If things go wrong, you'll be in very big trouble! ... All right, two hundred. But get it done! And quick!'

With that he hung up, and sat looking at the telephone as if it were an unexploded bomb.

Adam Webber surveyed the scene in the public bar of The Bull. He'd done his best to make his entrance unobtrusive and, having bought his pint, had moved swiftly to a table in a quiet corner. He was very aware that he was the only young man in the place not in uniform. He hoped that Jane's father's spectacles would make him look exempt on medical grounds.

Fortunately the bar was crowded and dimly lit. And visibility was much reduced by the thick cloud of cigarette smoke that filled the air.

The Bull, like everywhere else, was suffering from wartime shortages. A chalked notice on a blackboard by the bar recorded today's restrictions: 'MILD ALE ONLY. WHISKY ONE SINGLE PER CUSTOMER. NO CREDIT.'

But the traditional activities of the British pub were carrying on as usual. Four soldiers in battle-dress were playing a noisy game of darts. There were more soldiers in the ribald crowd by the bar. Two elderly men were locked in fierce competition at a shove-ha'penny board.

At tables, and on benches round the walls, a varied collection of locals were taking their ease. The customers ranged from three rowdy middle-aged couples at one table, obviously having a celebration, to two old ladies at another, sipping their drinks in silence. The sextet were laughing and chatting and knocking back their beer at a rapid rate. The old ladies would make their glasses – one a half of mild and the other a port and lemon – last all evening.

The place certainly didn't look as rough and dangerous as Jane's report from Fowler had led Adam to expect: except, perhaps, for the two hefty and unsmiling barmen, whose rolled-up sleeves revealed bulging muscles and aggressive tattoos. And Adam could see, in the adjoining saloon bar, a bunch of sturdy men conversing in low voices. They looked like people one wouldn't want to aggravate.

Ten minutes' study had given Adam no ideas and no information. He would have to stick his neck out and start asking questions. He didn't fancy tangling with the barmen, both of whom had faces like granite tombstones. But at the far end of the bar, customers were served by a cheerful barmaid. With bleached blonde hair, large hoop ear-rings and a mass of scarlet lipstick, she didn't look like a charm school graduate, but she had smiled briefly when Adam caught her eye. He thought he might be able to establish some sort of liaison with her.

He went to the bar, gave her a big grin, and asked for another pint of mild. As she pulled the pump, he said, 'Busy tonight!'

'Yeah,' she said. 'Busy every night. Bloody Hitler's made everyone thirsty.'

'Have one yourself?'

'Oh. Ta. It has to be gin for me. I can't drink that rubbish.' She was looking at Adam's beer.

'That's OK. You're welcome,' said Adam.

The barmaid put a glass under an optic beneath an inverted gin bottle and poured herself a drink of water. This bottle was kept for the use of staff, enabling them to pocket the price of the gin and avoid getting drunk.

'Two and threepence,' said the barmaid, adding a dash of lime to her drink.

Adam paid and then raised his glass. 'Cheers!'

'Cheers!' said the barmaid.

Adam drank some beer and then looked at his glass. 'It's not that bad,' he said. 'But what's happened to the bitter?'

'Ran out last night. We don't get no more till Monday.'

Adam sighed. 'Friend of mine always liked the bitter here. Name of Maurice Cooper. Did you know him?'

The barmaid pursed her shining lips. 'Cooper? That's the bloke who got topped, innit?'

'That's what I hear. I'm merchant navy, I've been away. When I got back they told me Maurice had been done in.'

'Yeah. Someone beat his brains out. I didn't know him myself, I only started here last month.'

'He was going to do some business for me. He was a fixer, you know. Could get hold of anything you wanted. Did he have a mate here I could talk to?'

Now the barmaid had another customer. As she turned away, she said, 'You could try Sniffer Dean over there. By the window. He knows everyone.'

She indicated a man at a table in the corner, sitting alone and occasionally glancing at a newspaper.

'Thanks,' said Adam. He picked up his glass, and made his way over to Sniffer Dean's table.

Sniffer Dean was a small, gloomy man, with a small, gloomy moustache, wearing a large flat cap and an old blue raincoat. But his eyes were sharp and quick. He spotted Adam approaching and watched him intently.

'Mr Dean?' said Adam.

'Yeah,' said Dean. 'Somebody want me?'

'You might be able to help me. I was a friend of Maurice Cooper. Mind if I sit down?'

'Creeper Cooper? He went off owing me a drink. If you're his mate, you could put things right.'

'Yes, I'd be glad to. What'll you have?'

'Large Scotch.'

'That board says they'll only do singles.'

'Tell 'em it's for me.'

'Right,' said Adam, and went back to the bar. Here he found

the barmaid had already poured a double whisky as soon as she saw him returning.

'Looks like you're in,' she said.

Adam smiled ruefully. 'Yes. In with Dean, and out of pocket.' He paid, and took the drink back to Dean's table.

'Ta,' said Dean. 'Here's to Creeper.'

They both raised their glasses and drank.

'My name's Craig,' said Adam. 'I'm Merchant Navy, just got back from Malta. I was due to meet Cooper this week, and now I hear he's dead.'

'Yeah. The word is he got the wrong side of some of the local villains.'

'Really?' Adam strove to contain his excitement. Could he be about to get the sort of information he wanted? 'What happened?'

'I dunno. It's just a rumour. I dunno nothing about it really. How come you knew Creeper?'

Adam swallowed his disappointment. He had his story ready. 'He was living in a boarding house where I stayed a couple of nights. When he heard I was a seaman, he seemed to want to get friendly. He was some sort of dealer, wasn't he? I think he thought I might bring some stuff in on the boat for him.'

'Did you?'

'No. He hadn't come up with a real offer. It was one of the things we were going to talk about this week.'

'What runs do you do?' It seemed that Sniffer Dean himself saw Adam as a possible courier. They talked for a while about his imaginary travels, with Adam straining to recall all he'd learned about a seaman's life from films and books. An altercation broke out among the group in the saloon bar. Voices were raised, and Adam could see one man lean across the table, grab hold of another man's jacket and shout in his face. Then the rumpus died down.

'Silly buggers,' said Dean. 'They'll get themselves on Harry Paynter's blacklist. He won't stand no trouble on the premises.'

'D'you know those men?' asked Adam hopefully.

'Yeah. Bunch of roughnecks. They work at the oil refinery.'

Adam hoped Dean would go on to reveal that the men were involved in local rackets, but he said no more. Instead, he began talking about the war, which he thought was being mismanaged. Adam realized that he would have to take some risks to get the conversation back on track. He cleared his throat and spoke cautiously. 'Cooper was going to do some business for me this week.'

'Oh yeah? What sort of business?'

'I want a dozen bottles of whisky.'

'Yeah? Heavy drinker, are you?'

'Mate of mine runs a club down in Westcliff. His supplier got nicked last month. I said I'd try and help him.'

'Pity old Creeper's gone. He'd have fixed that for you all right.'

There was a pause. Then Adam tried again.

'Is there anyone else round here who can get hold of things?'

Dean stared at Adam in silence. Then he said, 'There could be. How much can you pay?'

'My mate's been paying four quid a bottle.'

Dean sniffed. 'There's a chance I might know a man who might be able to help. I'll ask if you like and get back to you. What's your number?'

'I haven't got one. I don't know where I'm staying.'

'That makes it difficult, dunnit?'

'I'm hoping to doss down with a girl I know. If not, I'll go back to the boat.'

'So how do I get hold of you?'

'Give me your number and I'll ring you tomorrow.'

Dean thought for a moment. Then he wrote a number on a corner of the *Evening News*, tore it off, and gave it to Adam. 'Don't ring tomorrow,' he said. 'I shan't see this bloke till tomorrow night. Ring me Thursday morning.'

'OK,' said Adam, putting the piece of paper in his pocket.

Dean downed the last of his whisky. 'Don't get no wrong ideas. I don't do no dodgy dealing. I'm just putting two punters in touch with each other.'

'Of course,' said Adam. 'Thanks.'

Dean wiped some whisky from his moustache with a finger, then licked the finger and looked thoughtful. 'I just remembered. Creeper had forgot his cash last time we met. It was two drinks he owed me.'

The weather was still mild and, once again, Bert Bailey had the stage door open, as he did whenever possible. But it had turned damp, and his rheumatism was troubling him. To take his mind off the discomfort, he sat in his cubby hole, listening to the intercom which relayed what was happening onstage.

In fact, he was listening to Vic Dudley trying out a new routine, though Bert would sooner die than admit that. Anyone who asked would be told that he was monitoring the show, in order to be prepared when the final curtain fell.

Bert's legendary contempt for all comedians, except the great Max Miller, was an affectation he'd established many years ago and now felt obliged to maintain. But, privately, he'd been surprised to find himself warming to Vic Dudley recently. This may have had something to do with the pound note Vic had slipped him, just for delivering a parcel to his dressing room. Now, as Vic finished his act, Bert was almost smiling.

'I'm afraid we've reached the point in the show you've all been dreading,' said Vic. 'Yes, I have to leave the stage. Now there's no one to entertain you but the girls. Sorry, fellers. Grin and bear it, and the girls will do the same. Good night.'

There was modest applause as the piano went into Vic's playoff, and then segued into the music for the finale.

Bert turned down the volume, stood up cautiously, winced, stretched, and then went to the open door, where he carried out his usual survey of the scene.

He saw the familiar faces of regular boyfriends and camp followers. And then he thought he recognized one of last night's newcomers, who'd been involved in the scuffle.

Bert began to feel a little uneasy.

Constable Thompson was savouring a rare bout of plain-clothes duty. Surprisingly, Sergeant Monk had asked to be excused tonight's mission, due to a pile-up of paperwork in his office. And Sergeant Fairweather was on desk duty. So now it was Jim Thompson beside Jessett in the Archer Street doorway.

Like Monk the previous night, he'd followed the Windmill show with close attention, making a special effort to study their quarry, Jane Hart. Now he waited patiently to see her with her clothes on. But he wished the inspector wouldn't smoke those wretched cigarillos.

Jessett was watching a man who stood on his own across the street. In the poor light, it had taken the inspector a while to remember where he'd seen the man before. But now it came to him, and he spoke quietly to the constable.

'See that chap over there, Thompson? By the litter bin?'

'The bloke in the grey raincoat, sir?'

'Yes. D'you know him?'

'Can't say I do, sir. Should I?'

'I don't know. He was here last night with Reggie Paynter.'

'Sorry, sir. Never seen him before.'

'Well, take a good look at him now. You need to get to know the local villains, Thompson. They're your stock in trade.'

'He's a villain, is he?'

'If he hangs around with Reggie Paynter, he has to be. And he did a runner when we nabbed Reggie.'

'So do we nick this bloke then?'

'We can't, we've got nothing on him yet, have we? Just note the face for your memory-book. There'll be no arrests tonight, Thompson. Tonight we definitely follow Jane Hart.'

But Jane Hart never appeared.

At 10.30 the pianist emerged from the stage door, and for the next twenty minutes people were leaving: but not the girl they were looking for.

Across the road, Sid Garrett was becoming frustrated and

restless, looking at his watch and starting to pace up and down.

By eleven o'clock, activity had ceased, and Bert was starting to close down for the night. Inspector Jessett gave an impatient snort, and made a decision.

'I've had enough of this,' he said. 'I'm not going to mess around a third night. Come on.'

He strode across the road, with Thompson at his side, and reached the stage door just as Bert had it half shut.

'Just a minute,' said Jessett. 'We're police.' He showed his warrant card. 'I need a word with you.'

A few yards away, Garrett heard Jessett's commanding voice and walked briskly off into the night, already planning his excuses for tomorrow.

Bert reluctantly opened the door. 'Blimey, so you're a copper! And you was one of the blokes making trouble last night!'

'That's what coppers are for,' said Jessett. 'Has Miss Hart come out yet?'

'I haven't seen her, but she must have done. I just checked, and all the dressing rooms are empty. I'm locking up.'

'Well, hold on a moment. Is there another way she could have come out?'

'Yeah, of course. Some of them go out through the front of the theatre. It's the quickest way to the tube.'

Jessett sighed, cursed quietly, and growled at the constable. 'You should have thought of that, Thompson. So we're back tomorrow night, and next time we split up.' He turned back to Bert. 'Two things, my friend. First off, don't tell Miss Hart we've been enquiring. It's for her own good. Right?'

'All right. If you say so.'

'The other thing is, I have to change my plans for the morning. Mind if I use your phone? Police business.'

Bert sniffed. 'I suppose you'll have to. Only be quick about it. My last train goes at 11.30.'

Jessett picked up the receiver and dialled Tilfleet Police Station.

'Leave your tuppence in the saucer,' said Bert, putting on his coat.

'Put tuppence in the saucer, Thompson,' said the inspector, and then the phone was picked up at the other end.

'Hello, Sergeant, Jessett here. I have to ... What? ... *What?!*' As the voice continued at the other end, Jessett stood rigid, listening with a mixture of astonishment and dismay.

Thompson hadn't got two pennies, so he put a threepenny bit in the saucer, and made a note for his next expenses claim.

At St Christopher's School, the academic day had ended two hours ago, the last of the staff and pupils had departed, and the building had reverted to its evening function as the headquarters of the local Home Guard.

In the playground, a row of sacks filled with straw stood ready for bayonet practice. Crude drawings of Hitler had been chalked on the sacks, to increase motivation. From the gym came the sound of men being drilled.

In the room reserved for the commanding officer, Tilfleet Unit, Cedric Dean was about to embark on a tricky conversation. Dean was not in the Home Guard, and therefore not subject to the commanding officer's authority. But, as he stood in front of the desk behind which the short man sat staring at him, he could not help being somewhat intimidated. He felt like a private charged with an offence, or a schoolboy up before his headmaster.

It was a feeling he fought hard to resist. He had something he knew the short man wanted, and he was here to get himself the best possible deal. It wasn't a good idea to let himself feel inferior.

Captain Brigden spoke briskly. 'My sergeant tells me you claim to have important information.'

'More than information, Squire,' said Dean. 'Mind if I sit down?'

'If you wish. But get to the point quickly. This is a training night. I'm short of time.' Brigden resented having to deal with people like Dean. But if what the man had told the sergeant was true, he couldn't afford not to.

'Ta,' said Dean. He pulled a chair from the side of the room and sat facing Brigden across the desk. 'That's more friendly, eh?'

There was no reply from Brigden, who continued to stare at Dean, like a doctor inspecting an unpleasant specimen.

Dean shifted on his seat, in a vain attempt to get more comfortable. Then he made his bid. 'Yeah … well … the word in the street is, you're after this bloke Webber, who's been in all the papers. Right?'

'Yes. We believe he has some property that was stolen from this office. Do you know where he is?'

'Not exactly. But I know how to get hold of him.'

'What does that mean?'

'He was at the pub, asking questions about Creeper Cooper. Someone put him on to me. He said his name was Craig and he wanted a load of whisky. He was wearing bins and a lot of stubble, but right off I knew it was Webber.'

Brigden's stare intensified. 'Are you sure?'

'Yeah, I'm good on faces. It was Webber all right and, whatever he's really after, it's not booze. I reckon he's looking to pin the Cooper job on someone else, and get himself off the hook.'

'Never mind all that,' snapped Brigden. 'Did you find out where he's hiding?'

'I tried, but he wasn't having any. Still, the point is, he wants something from me. He pretended it's Scotch, so I went along with that. I said I'd get some stuff together and if he rings me tomorrow, I'll tell him where to come.'

'I see. So you'll bring him somewhere where we can arrest him?'

'That's the idea, Squire. At a very reasonable price.'

Brigden frowned. 'There should be no question of money. Webber's a wanted criminal. It's your duty to hand him over to the authorities.'

'Yeah, well, that would be the police, wouldn't it? And I heard you want to get to him before the coppers do.'

'As it happens, that is correct. The stolen item concerns an army operation. It's not to be seen by any civilians, even the police.'

'That's up to you, Squire. None of my business. I'm just offering to give you Webber on a plate for five hundred quid. Cash down.'

'What? Don't be ridiculous! I'm not giving you five hundred pounds!'

Dean waited in silence for a moment. Then he half rose, as if to leave. 'Oh well ... I heard you was offering five hundred. If I got it wrong, perhaps I should go to the police after all.'

'Sit down!' barked Brigden. 'You realize that in half-a-minute I could have two men in here who'd beat the information out of you?'

'I haven't got any information, have I? Except what I already told you. And beating me up's no good to you. You need me OK to take Webber's call tomorrow and set him up for you.'

Brigden scowled. 'I'll give you two hundred and fifty.'

'Sorry, Squire, it has to be five hundred. Now.'

'I'll give you two hundred now, and three hundred when we've got Webber.'

'No thanks. Once you get your hands on Webber, I got no protection. My life won't be worth nothing. I could end up in a road accident, like that other bloke.'

Inwardly, Brigden was shaken, but his manner remained stern. 'What the hell are you talking about?'

'Some of us can put two and two together, Squire.'

'Well, don't,' said Brigden. 'It could be dangerous.'

'Yeah, that's what I reckon. I'm planning to make myself scarce for a bit. So there it is. You give me the five hundred and tell me where you want Webber delivered. I set him up tomorrow when he rings. Then I'm off to Cornwall. Stay with a pal of mine. Are we on?'

There was fury on Brigden's face as he stood up and, for a moment, it seemed he might strike the other man. Instead, he went to the wall behind him and began turning a dial. There'd been recriminations after the theft from his locked drawer and a safe had been installed, in keeping with the traditional British stable-door policy.

Brigden opened the door and took out the large brown envelope, in which he kept the cash to pay professional criminals. Rubber bands held five-pound notes together in wads of ten. He extracted ten of these, and threw them on the desk in front of Sniffer Dean.

'If we haven't got Webber in our hands in twenty-four hours,' he said, 'you will be dead. We have friends in Cornwall, and anywhere else you go.'

And then he told Dean what to say to Webber when he phoned.

8

WESTLEY'S DEMEANOUR WAS authoritative and quietly confident, as if he already felt he held the reins of power.

'Well, gentlemen, our day of action is imminent, and I think all our major plans are safely in place. Details that have yet to be filled in or changed will need to be dealt with today. Are there any matters that require clarification?'

Ernest Cox raised a hand. 'Can we take it that the top brass are not moving out of London?'

'Yes. The Cabinet have now rejected that proposal. And, if they changed their minds, it would be too late. The necessary arrangements couldn't be made before our takeover. So that's one adjustment we don't need to think about.'

'Have the orders for extra supplies gone through?' asked Denby.

'Yes. All approved and delivered. There were hold-ups, as you know. But Neville Straker managed to clear away all the obstacles. So, thus far at least, he seems to be up to his job.'

Westley cast a dark glance at Collis, who continued to study his notes.

'Right,' said Westley. 'I take it each of you has brought final action plans from every unit commander in your area.'

There were murmurs of assent, and rustling of papers.

'Good. We'll be going through them in detail shortly with our military commander, Major Fry. But, first, are there any other queries?'

Charles Bell spoke. 'I have a rather delicate point to make.

And I do so only because I'm concerned for the reputation and image of our movement.'

This sounded interesting. Eyes were raised from notes and focussed on Bell, who was suddenly the centre of attention.

'I'm sure that concerns us all,' said Westley. 'You'd better tell us.'

Bell's quiet voice conveyed regret at a painful necessity. 'I'd like to stress I make no moral judgments. I'm concerned only with the facts, and the effect they may have on our standing.'

Westley's voice was impatient. 'Quite. And what are the facts?'

'I learned yesterday from my contact in Fleet Street that the Sunday Pictorial is to run a scandal story on our friend Alfred Jupp here.'

Jupp looked startled. He'd had no warning of this. But then Bell had never forgiven him for beating him to the presidency of the college Fabian Society. Jupp decided he'd better ask the question before somebody else did. He tried to sound casual.

'What scandal is this?'

'I don't know how many scandals you're involved in, Alfie,' said Bell. 'The one the paper's on to is your mistress in Maida Vale. "Top MP Romps with Chorus Girl", that sort of thing.'

Westley was stern. 'Is this really something we should spend our time on?'

'I think so,' said Bell. 'I'm afraid a scandal like this could lose us public support just when we need it most. Alfie's supposed to play a very public role, both in our takeover, and in our new administration. But, in these circumstances, it might be better for him to keep a low profile for a while.'

Hugh Denby was angry. 'I don't know if this allegation is true or false, and I don't care! Either way it's nonsense! Many politicians have mistresses. Always have done. All French ministers keep young women, as a matter of course, except those who keep young men.'

'That's France,' said Bell. 'That's why they crumbled in 1940.'

'Let's be practical,' Westley commanded. 'Does your contact expect the Pictorial to print the story this Sunday?'

'No. Apparently they're still gathering material.'

'Then it doesn't matter, does it? By Sunday week we'll have control of the press. This article will never see the light of day. There'll be no room in the new Britain for the smut and scandal of the capitalist press. Now let's move on.'

Jupp breathed a sigh of relief. 'Thank you, Robert,' he said quietly.

'Now then,' said Westley, 'are there any serious matters unresolved?'

'I take it the missing Tilfleet logbook might still be regarded as serious?' Bill Ford was not letting this one go. 'Has there been any progress?'

Westley smiled. 'As it happens, I do have some good news to report on that matter. Our people on the ground are confident of apprehending the thief within the next twenty-four hours. Offering a reward to the underworld has borne fruit.'

Vic Dudley was fretting. The morning newspaper was a vital part of his normal brunch routine, and today it hadn't arrived. Vic was missing it. He always studied the *Daily Mirror* avidly at this time of day. Apart from the delights of Jane, Garth and the other comic strips, there was the fun of trawling through the news pages for items that could produce topical gags for his act. The great thing about topical gags was that they didn't actually have to be very funny. It was better if they were, of course, but in fact audiences were so impressed by up-to-the-minute references that they applauded anyway.

Jane, ever eager to help, had gone out to buy a paper at the newsagent's round the corner. But in the meantime, Vic was short of reading matter. Luckily, both his guests ate cereals so that, as a last resort, Vic was able to peruse the information on the packets.

Adam was knocking back his third mug of tea, and hoping it would finally wake him up.

'Hey, Adam,' said Vic, with sudden enthusiasm, 'd'you know how they get Puffed Wheat to blow up that big?'

'No,' said Adam. 'I can't say I've ever thought about it.'

'Well, you should,' said Vic. 'It's very interesting. Modern technology. According to this, the wheat germs are put under enormous pressure, and then they're fired from guns!' He pondered briefly on this oddity, and then added, 'I suppose that means conscientious objectors can't eat them.'

Adam rose from the table. 'I think it's time I rang this black market villain and got my instructions.'

On his return from The Bull he had told Vic and Jane his story, over late-night coffee. Jane remained apprehensive, but accepted that this was a lead that had to be followed up. Vic had agreed, and was still hoping to reap some alcoholic benefit from the project.

'Good luck, mate,' he said, and read on.

Adam left the kitchen and shut himself in the sitting room, to make his important call without interruption.

Vic settled down to read several endorsements by leading sportsmen who attributed their success to regular intake of Puffed Wheat.

And then Jane came rushing in, full of excitement. She thrust the *Daily Mirror* in front of Vic. 'Look!' she said. 'Here on page three!'

The headline leaped up at him. 'East End Gangster Dies in Police Cell.'

As Vic stared at the paper, words came bursting forth from Jane. 'It's Tilfleet again! What on earth's going on? That's three deaths! First poor Mark. Then Cooper. Now this!'

Vic read the story with astonishment. A man called Reginald Paynter, who'd been arrested on a charge of robbery with violence, had indeed died in Tilfleet Police Station. He'd been found hanged in his cell, and was pronounced dead at the local hospital.

Jane was unstoppable. 'It's incredible! I know about this man Paynter. George Fowler said he was involved in the Tilfleet black market. I told the police to go after him!'

'Looks like they took your advice,' Vic observed. He read

aloud. 'An enquiry will be started immediately. Unofficial sources say that Paynter, who had a long criminal record, is believed to have committed suicide.'

'How could that happen in a police cell?'

'Beats me,' said Vic. 'I thought when they locked people up, the rozzers took away their ties and belts and braces, anything they could use to top themselves.' He thought for a moment. 'Perhaps they forgot his bootlaces.'

Adam came back from the sitting room. 'I've got my orders,' he announced.

'Adam!' cried Jane. 'There's been another death in Tilfleet! It's in the paper! One of the men George told me about! You know, involved in black market at The Bull! The police arrested him, and now he's been found dead in his cell!'

'Wow!' said Adam. 'Things are hotting up! The whole business must be about black market feuds, like we thought. And, from what I just heard, I reckon there's a Home Guard connection.'

'The Home Guard?' The new thought set Jane's mind racing. She was recalling Mark Jefferson's evening training sessions.

'So what did your contact say?' Vic asked.

'I'm to go to this shed on the Essex marshes at two o'clock this afternoon. It's near Chalksea station, just by a Home Guard firing range. That must be where they keep their dodgy goods.'

Jane had gone pale. 'Adam, this is getting too dangerous! I don't want you going there!'

'Nonsense, my darling,' said Adam. 'This is my chance to get in on the inside. I have to find out what happened to Cooper, remember? Clear myself of the murder charge. We agreed that's what I should do.'

'I've changed my mind. Go to the police and tell them everything!'

'And end up dead in a cell? Oh no, I'm not giving up now, after all we've been through. Not just when I look like getting a break.'

'As long as it's not your neck,' said Vic.

'Besides, if I went to the police at this stage, you two could be in trouble. And Maggie. They'd charge you as accessories, for helping me avoid arrest.'

'I don't care about that,' said Jane.

'I'd plead ignorance,' said Vic. 'I've a long history of that.'

'Jane, we decided I was going to get to the bottom of all this, and that's what I'm going to do. Nothing's changed.'

'Yes, it has! Vic and I don't believe Paynter killed himself! Someone's murdering witnesses!'

'Well, I'm not a witness, I'm a customer, and a very good one, for all they know. I've got the money Vic lent me. I'll pay them well for the whisky, and tell them my mate in Westcliff will be wanting lots more. They'll love me.'

Jane saw that Adam's mind was made up. She sighed. 'Daft bugger,' she said. 'And I'm in the show today – I'm going to feel so useless. Is there anything I can do?'

Adam grinned. 'Yes, please. Pour me another cup of tea. And make it two sugars this time. It looks like I'll need all my energy.'

'You still haven't fixed Miss Jane's sash window,' Emily Hart complained.

'No, well, I haven't had time, have I?' protested George. 'I done her shelf and her chest of drawers, and I was just going to get to the sash, only you wanted the porch painted. Right?'

'I suppose so,' Mrs Hart conceded. 'But make sure that window's your next job, will you. Miss Jane'll be back here soon.'

'Oh, you've heard from her, have you?'

'Yes, she rang yesterday afternoon, during one of her breaks. Just a quick chat, you know. They're working her very hard. The producer keeps them at it all the time.'

'Still, it's better than fixing windows. Has she let on where she's living yet?'

'Oh yes, it's no secret. It's just that she has to keep moving, according to who can put her up. Just now she's staying with her friend, Victoria.'

'Victoria?'

'That'll be one of the girls in the show. Vic's got her own flat, in Notting Hill.'

'That's nice,' said George.

'They start their new show next week, and then she says she'll have more free time. I expect she'll be back here.'

'Good,' said George. 'I hope she likes her chest of drawers.'

Mrs Hart sighed. 'It'll be a relief when she's sleeping here again. I worry when she's up in town all the time, with those wretched V2s coming down.'

'Trouble is, they're just as likely to hit you out here as they are in London. I read in the *Mirror*, more V2s have landed in the country than in the city.'

'So they say. But at least, if she's under this roof, we'll all go together.'

'That's a bit morbid, Mrs H,' said George.

Emily Hart was in a thoughtful mood. 'I don't know, it might not be a bad way to go. The thing about these V2s is, you'd never know anything about it. One minute you'd be sitting here, the next you'd be in the next world.'

'Well, I ain't finished with this one yet, thank you very much. I got things to do. I got plans.'

'Plans? What plans?'

'Soon as this war's over, I want to get back to sea-fishing. Once the beaches are open again. And Southend Pier. There should be a lot of fish about. We've left them alone for five years – they'll have been breeding like rabbits!'

Emily Hart hadn't finished her survey of enemy weapons. 'It was the doodle-bugs that gave me the creeps,' she recalled. 'The V1s.' She shuddered. 'Ooh, when you heard the engine cut out! And you had time to wonder whether it was going to land on you, or in the next street. It sort of made you think about mortality.' She sighed. 'My coffee's cold, how's yours?'

George took a sip. 'I could do with a bit more hot,' he observed. He got up and switched on the electric kettle. 'I'll give us both a top-up.'

'Have you heard anything from that policeman, the one who took the envelope from Mr Webber's room? Sergeant Monk, was it?'

'Yeah, it was Sergeant Monk, but no, he hasn't got back to me. Matter of fact, I rang the nick this morning. To ask about them bits and pieces they're still holding.'

'Oh, the things from Mr Jefferson's room.'

'And that page from the register. Also, I was going to suggest they do a litmus test on that envelope. I asked for Sergeant Monk but he couldn't come to the phone. I got a feeling he wasn't there.'

'What about that Inspector Jessett?'

'They said he was tied up. No one seemed to want to talk.'

'I suppose they're all in a lather about the man who hanged himself.'

'You bet they are. Not that he'll be missed. A right villain, that Reggie Paynter was.'

'Was he? D'you know anything about him?'

The kettle had boiled, and George poured boiling water into both mugs.

'I know all about Reggie Paynter,' said George. 'And his mates.' He tried to tap the side of his nose, but instead hit his forehead with the teaspoon he was holding. 'Only it's more than my life's worth to talk about them.' He thought for a moment. 'Mind you, now he's gone, I suppose I could tell you a few things that would interest you.'

Something in the newspaper had caught Mrs Hart's eye, and her attention was straying. 'It's all right, George,' she said vaguely. 'Don't say anything you might regret.'

George's resolve stiffened. 'No, I'm not going to let those thugs scare me. Mind, you'd have to promise not to repeat anything.'

But the lady's mind was now elsewhere, and she failed to reply.

'Right,' said George, undaunted. 'I'll tell you.' He launched into a long and lurid account of Paynter's exploits, and let his coffee get cold again.

'Rotten sod!' said Jane. 'And in a letter! He hadn't the nerve to tell you to your face!'

'Alfie's never liked scenes,' said Maggie. 'He's got less guts than a kipper.' The two girls were eating sandwiches in the Windmill canteen, while the Accordion Aces held the stage. 'Anyway, there it is, I've got the elbow. I've got to be out by Sunday night. And he says if ever I talk to a newspaper again, he's got some friends who'll give me a hard time.'

'The bastard!' said Jane. And then a thought struck her. 'Again? Does that mean you did talk to the paper?'

'Not exactly. At least, I never meant to.'

'But you did?'

'Well, it was this boy I met in the pub, you see. He thought I was very good in the show. Said he'd like to introduce me to a friend of his, who's a big agent.'

'You didn't fall for that one? It's so old, it's got whiskers.'

'Not really, I suppose. The thing was, he looks a bit like Errol Flynn. And Alfie was away. So I said he could come back to the flat for a drink. How was I to know he was a reporter?'

'Weren't you suspicious when he started asking questions?'

'He never did. He was all action. But it seems he spotted Alfie's name on some papers. Alfie's quite well known, you know.'

'Yes. I've heard him on the radio saying how we should all pull together.'

'Then it turns out this bloke was back the next day when I was out. He talked to the neighbours. Then he wrote a spicy story for the *Sunday Pictorial*. They're going to print the stuff, and somehow Alfie got to hear about it.'

'Oh well, it'll get you talked about. Can't be bad for your career.'

'That's what I thought. I told Sandy, "Make sure you spell my name right."'

'Sandy?'

'That's the reporter. "Randy Sandy" I called him. He didn't seem to mind. I said, "Put me down as nineteen, and say I'm fond of animals."'

'Hang on. So you did give this man an interview?'

'Only after he'd already got the story. Couldn't do any harm then, could it? I wish they'd put more marge in these sandwiches.'

Jane sighed. 'Oh dear. So you're out in the cold. And Adam and I are at Vic's place. Otherwise you could have gone there. Anyway, I'm sure we could squeeze you in.'

'That's all right. I wouldn't go back to Vic's. He's a lovely feller but I can't take all those jokes before lunch.'

'So what are you going to do now?'

'I think I've just got time for a doughnut.'

'A doughnut? D'you think VD would approve?'

'If he doesn't, he shouldn't have them on sale here, should he? It's all right, I'll work it off in the can-can.'

'Maggie, I meant, where are you going to live?'

'For starters, I'm going back to Mum and Dad's for a bit. Catch up on some sleep. Get made a fuss of. They're great.'

Maggie fetched a doughnut from the counter, picking up a packet of biscuits at the same time. Jane listened to the relay from the stage. When Maggie returned, she observed, 'They're into "The Isle Of Capri". We've got eight minutes.'

'That's OK,' said Maggie. 'We'll eat the biscuits later during the Nuns' Chorus.'

'Are you going to be dating this Sandy?'

'Shouldn't think so. Turns out he's got a steady girlfriend.'

'Hard luck. Are you still going out with Phil?'

'Yes. Just for laughs. You know he's as queer as a nine-bob note?'

'Well, that's the way he comes across.'

'It's genuine. Beneath that camp exterior there's a great big fairy queen. But he's sweet and he's funny and I like him.'

'But you want something more than that, don't you?'

'All in good time. Don't worry about me, sweetheart. Very

soon there's going to be thousands of big brawny blokes coming back from the Forces. I'm keeping myself available.' Maggie bit a large chunk from her doughnut. 'Talking of brawny blokes, how's your man? Coping all right?'

'Just about,' said Jane. 'It isn't easy. He's gone down to Essex today, still trying to find out what's been going on. Tell you the truth, I'm worried sick.'

'He'll be all right,' said Maggie. 'He can look after himself, I reckon.' She took another bite from her doughnut.

Even in wartime, commuter trains between London and Shoeburyness, via Southend-on-Sea, were crowded at both ends of the day. It seemed that half the male population of south-east Essex, if too old for the forces and too young to retire, chose to brave the bombs and continue to earn their living in the capital, while enjoying fresh air at home.

So mornings found the railway carriages packed with men in city suits on their way to London, reading their morning papers or playing cards. And the late afternoon saw the reverse process: this time they read evening papers or snoozed after a day at the office.

But in the middle of the day the service, now reduced to one train an hour, was little used. The attractions of a day trip to the seaside were much reduced in those years, with Southend Pier closed and the beaches lined with barbed wire and gun emplacements, inaccessible to the public.

At 1 p.m. Adam found little activity at Fenchurch Street Station, that most functional and least romantic of London's railway termini. He had a scarf casually covering much of his face, as he leaned into the booking-office window to buy his day-return ticket. He was sure the police must ask booking clerks to look out for wanted men.

However, the bespectacled little man in the booking office, who was wearing a patterned sleeveless pullover and listening to *Workers' Playtime* on the radio, showed no interest in Adam. And the same was true of the few porters pushing occasional trolleys on the platform. The 1.10 for Southend was already waiting, the engine letting off sporadic bursts of steam into the chilly air. Adam easily found an empty compartment, and made himself comfortable in a corner seat by the window.

Two minutes later a disembodied voice announced that the train was leaving, then a whistle was blown, the guard waved a green flag, and the train moved off.

Adam intended to use the fifty-minute journey to make plans, both immediate and long term. His priority was to decide what he should do at this rendezvous with the whisky merchant. His purpose was to try and penetrate the Essex underworld and find out who killed Maurice Cooper. But how should he proceed? Should he chum up with the fellow, order more Scotch, arrange further meetings, and hope that somewhere along the line some clue might turn up, something that would lead him to the truth? Or should he put the man in an arm lock and twist until he told all he knew?

The latter course would be morally justified, for black marketeers were criminals, but it depended on the man being unaccompanied, and less powerful than Adam. On the whole, Adam favoured the first option. But that could end in him simply going back to London with bottles of expensive whisky, and none the wiser. The thought produced a wry smile: at least Vic Dudley wouldn't feel his journey had been wasted.

Then there was the bigger question. He knew now that Jane Hart was the girl with whom he wanted to share his life. But how could it be possible? He felt he could prove himself not guilty of murder. But he couldn't deny charges of stealing Adam Webber's identity, false pretences at the Marine Research Unit, resisting arrest, and God knows what else.

He faced prison, or life on the run. Jane had said she couldn't tolerate the latter, though he still nursed a faint hope of enticing her to a new life in Canada. But would that be fair on either of them, with the time-bomb of possible exposure forever ticking away?

Should he heed Jane's plea and give himself up? That would

mean at least two or three years in jail. Jane had said she'd wait for him, but a lot could change in two years. And, anyway, could he face being locked up?

A third option had been growing in his mind, the darkest of all. He found he cared a great deal about Jane's welfare. Would it be better for her if he got out of her life? Perhaps he should never go back to Vic's flat. Maybe he should revert to his first plan: after all, a fugitive can travel faster on his own. Now that he had a few pounds in his pocket (which he'd somehow repay later), surely he could get to a port and smuggle himself onto a ship. Jane would be better off without him. She'd pine for a while, but she'd get over it. Eventually, she'd forget him. But would he ever forget her?

As he pondered these things, Adam peered listlessly through the carriage window at the changing scenery moving gently past for his inspection.

The bleak grey streets of London's East End had given way to rows of neat suburban houses, their gardens backing onto the railway line. Normal people were getting on with their normal lives, hanging out washing, feeding the birds, playing with small children, and tending flowerbeds or vegetable patches (the British public were still being urged to Dig for Victory, by growing things you could eat). Adam envied all these folk.

Then the train was out into open country. Here and there, the creeks and dykes of the Essex marshes were reflecting the light from a pale sun. A lot of mud banks were on view, for the tide was out in the Thames Estuary. There was little sign of human life. Sea-birds were stalking about in the low water and on the scrubland, or standing in statuesque stillness, apparently gazing into the far distance, as if awaiting some great event.

From time to time small boats were to be seen, some upside-down among the reeds and bulrushes, perhaps abandoned.

None of this did anything for Adam's problems. Eventually he began to doze, half recalling his first night with Jane, and half-dreaming they were together on a beach.

*

The changing rhythm of the wheels on the tracks eased Adam out of his slumber. The train was slowing down. Soon the engine stopped and let off steam, and the rural voice of a porter was heard shouting 'Chalksea! Chalksea! This is Chalksea!' in tones that carried a hint of pride.

This was fair enough, for it was quite a pretty little station. There were flowerbeds at each end of the platform, and hanging baskets dangled from a few vantage points. The overhead wooden canopy seemed freshly painted and the edge of the platform was newly whitewashed. Facing the train, on the outside wall of the waiting-room, neat posters reminded travellers that Careless Talk Costs Lives, and urged them to Know Your Fire Drill.

As Adam alighted from the train, he noticed two men getting out further along. They had long canvas sheaths slung over their shoulders, like golf bags, but these weren't full of golf clubs. The men seemed to be carrying fishing rods, and Adam recalled that the river was not far away.

The pair exchanged greetings with the porter, who by now was standing at the little wooden gate that led to the outside world. He waved them through: obviously they had season tickets.

It seemed these two and Adam were the only arrivals. The guard had got out and enjoyed a brief chat with an old man who was tending one of the flowerbeds. No one had got on the train. Now the guard looked at his watch, checked that the platform was clear, gave a superfluous shout of 'Stand clear of the doors!', blew his whistle and waved his flag. The train ground slowly into motion again.

As it began to move, a door at the rear of the train opened and a middle-aged man in a dark suit stepped lightly out, closing the door behind him. Ignoring an angry shout from the guard, he paused a moment to survey the scene, and then began to stroll along the platform, his rolled umbrella slanted over his shoulder like a soldier's rifle.

Adam didn't see him. He was already at the barrier, fumbling in a pocket for his ticket. When he produced it, the porter said 'I thank you' in an affable manner. It was obviously his catch-phrase, borrowed from the radio. But there was a hint of suspicion on his face. He was wondering what this young man, obviously of military age but not in uniform, was doing in Chalksea in the middle of the day without a fishing rod.

His unease deepened when the passenger asked the way to the Home Guard firing range. Adam had the directions Sniffer Dean had given over the phone but Sniffer wasn't that articulate and Adam thought it wise to get confirmation.

'Up the road and turn left,' said the porter. 'Then right at the crossroads. But that's a government place, you can't go in there.'

'It's all right,' said Adam. 'It's official business.'

He passed through the gate, and began to walk up the country lane.

It should have been a pleasant walk. The trees and bushes were still in leaf, and wild flowers lingered in the hedgerows. Birds were singing and from the meadow beyond the hedge came the occasional sound of cows mooing.

But, in fact, it was irksome. For one thing, it was uphill all the way. It had been a ten-minute trudge to the crossroads, and a further five since. For another thing, Adam was apprehensive and in no mood to enjoy the scenery. He was wondering what awaited him. And he still had no plan of action. He would have to improvize, and he mustn't waste this opportunity.

For the last hundred yards the roadside hedge had been replaced by a fence, and at last Adam came to a gate, beside which a notice proclaimed 'Ministry of Defence Property: Keep Out'. Over the gate Adam could see a footpath leading across a field to a timber shack, like a cricket pavilion. There were no sentries. Indeed, there was no sign of life at all. The gate was unlocked. Adam opened it and went through, reflecting that if Hitler still planned to invade, this was the place to choose. As he walked up the path, the only sound was the trill of a robin. By the shack was a sign saying 'Danger! Live Ammunition in

Use!' Next to it, a red flag hung from a white flagpole. The firing range must start behind the building but currently no ammunition of any sort was in use.

Approaching the shack, Adam saw yet another injunction on the door: 'Home Guard Personnel Only'. By now he was convinced that elements of the Home Guard must be involved in the black market. The government had kindly provided them with this lair in the wilderness to store illicit goods. Perhaps Mark Jefferson had found out, and had to be silenced. Maybe he'd actually been involved and was killed by rivals. Adam hadn't known Jefferson well enough to judge which was the more likely. But Jane had been fond of Jefferson, so he hoped it was the former.

The robin had packed up for the day, and now all was silence, but Adam had begun to feel he was being watched.

He mounted a step onto the verandah of planking, which increased the resemblance to a cricket pavilion. It occurred to him that the area must have been playing fields before the war. He hoped a sporting spirit still prevailed.

He was now in front of the door. It seemed sensible to knock, as he had no wish to surprise anyone. So he rapped firmly on the door with his knuckles. A voice shouted, 'Come in,' so he turned the handle and entered.

The place was almost bare: plain wooden floor, plain wooden walls, no guns to be seen. Presumably, soldiers brought their weapons with them when they used the range. There were several church-hall-type chairs and one table.

At this table, on the far side of the room, sat a man in unkempt khaki battle-dress, buttons of his tunic undone. He was a big man, and he didn't smile.

As instructed on the phone, Adam led off with 'I'm a friend of Sniffer Dean'.

'That's a novelty,' said the man. 'He doesn't have many of those.'

'He said we might be able to do some business,' said Adam.

'Yeah, I'm sure we can,' said the man. 'Come over here and sit down.' He still wasn't smiling.

The man's manner wasn't that of someone with something to sell. This was all wrong. And there was no sign of whisky anywhere.

Suddenly Adam felt a violent sense of danger: all his instincts screamed at him to run. He turned quickly but already there were two men behind him, between him and the door: tough-looking characters, not in khaki but in sweaters and dark trousers. One of them kicked the door shut.

'Bring him over here,' said the man in khaki, and the other two took an arm each, shoved Adam across the room, and pushed him down into a chair.

Adam didn't resist. Three against one was odds he didn't fancy. Not at the moment, anyway. For now, it would be better to use his brain. Were they simply after money? He'd led Sniffer Dean to think he had plenty of cash.

'What's the idea?' he asked, firmly but pleasantly. 'I'm here to buy some Scotch.'

'You're here to answer questions, Webber,' said the man in khaki. 'And you'd better have the right answers or you're in for a very hard time!'

Adam was shaken by the threat, but the use of his surname was an equal shock. He'd been careful to give Dean no hint of his identity. Things were turning nasty but he decided to ignore the name and try to keep up the façade. He did his best to speak calmly. 'What are you talking about? This is an odd way to treat a customer. I was going to put a lot of business your way.'

'Cut the crap!' The man spat out the words. 'You know what this is about. You and your mate Jefferson nicked something that belongs to a friend of ours. Or he nicked it and passed it on to you. Either way, we want it back. And you're going to tell us what the hell you and him were up to.'

'Jefferson wasn't my mate. I only met him a couple of times.' Now they were getting down to basics, Adam thought the man might let something slip. He said, almost casually, 'Jefferson was killed, wasn't he? Did you kill him?'

The man was getting angry. 'I'll ask the bloody questions!' he snarled. 'Don't waste time! Jefferson burgled the Tilfleet Home Guard and took a logbook, right? And then he gave it to you and your bird. So where is it?'

'Logbook? I don't know anything about a logbook.'

The man in khaki snorted with exasperation. Then he nodded to the other two. One of them yanked Adam to his feet and held his arms. The other hit him hard in the stomach and then in the face. The first man released his arms and rabbit-punched his neck. After that, the second man smashed his fist against Adam's head, knocking him to the ground. Then both men kicked him.

Dizzy with pain, Adam still judged it would be foolish to fight back. In a brawl tempers would flare, and they could easily kill him. As things were, they wanted him alive to answer questions. He'd let them play it their way for now; he might even learn something. He lay sprawled on the floor, breathing hard.

'That'll do for now,' said the leader. 'He can't talk if he's unconscious. Get him up.'

The two men dragged Adam to his feet.

'Search him,' said the leader. 'He's not likely to have it on him, but you might find something.'

One man held Adam's arms again while the other went through his pockets. He extracted a handkerchief, which he threw on the floor, then some change and a small piece of cardboard.

'What's that?' asked the man in khaki.

'Return ticket to London.'

The leader laughed for the first time: a short, sharp, very unpleasant sound. 'Well, he won't be needing that. Give it here. And he won't want the money either. I'll have it.'

'Hang on,' said his underling, with a hint of defiance.

'It's all right,' said the leader. 'I'll share it out later.'

Adam watched the money being handed over. 'You're supposed to give me whisky for that,' he ventured.

'Shut up about the bloody whisky!' barked the man in khaki. 'There isn't any bloody whisky! Sit him down again!'

The men dumped Adam back on the chair like a sack of potatoes. His interrogator leaned across the desk and brought his face up close to Adam's.

'Listen, you stupid bastard,' he said. 'You're alone. You're miles from anywhere. No one can help you. We can work on you all day if we have to.'

'I'll be missed,' said Adam. 'I've got friends who'll go to the police.'

'No, they won't. The police are after you too. They're all set to top you for murder.' He stared into Adam's eyes for several seconds. Then he continued. 'You'll talk in the end, that's for sure. The joker on your right can do some very painful things with a razor, without killing you. You won't be dead but you'll wish you were. Right, Sid?'

'Yeah, that's right.' Sid chuckled with pleasurable anticipation. 'I can arrange your face so your own mother wouldn't know you.'

The man in khaki resumed. 'You talk now, you'll save yourself a lot of grief. We might even let you go in a couple of days, when it doesn't matter.'

What did that mean? Adam wondered. What would change in a couple of days?

'OK, let's try again,' said the man. 'For a start, where's the logbook?'

Several areas of Adam were hurting badly. Should he admit that a logbook had fallen into his hands? It was probably just an account of black market dealings. What the hell did it matter? He could say he'd had it and lost it. But then, if they forced the whereabouts out of him, there'd be danger for Leo at the Marine Research Unit. And also for Jane. He rejected the idea of telling them anything. He'd try one more bluff.

'For God's sake!' he shouted. 'You've told me there's no bloody whisky! I'm telling you there's no bloody logbook! I came here to buy booze for my mate who runs the club!' A desperate idea came to him, and he continued more quietly, but urgently. 'He knew I was coming here. That's his money you've taken. If I don't get back with the Scotch, his men'll be coming after you!'

The man in khaki looked at him with contempt. 'Balls!' he said. He turned to the man on Adam's right. 'OK, Sid, he's all yours for half an hour. Just remember, I don't want him dead, and I don't want him unconscious.'

Sid was reassuring. 'Don't worry, he won't croak. I'll just take off a few bits he won't miss much.' He took out a thin leather pouch, from which he produced a cut-throat razor. He opened the razor out. 'Only he might go mad and start jerking about. Better cuff him.'

'Right,' said the leader. He spoke to the third man. 'Get the cuffs, Stan.'

There was a first-aid cabinet fixed to the wall. The ginger-haired thug on Adam's left went and opened it, and took out a pair of handcuffs.

As he did this, Adam's mind was racing. His passive policy would have to change. And fast. Once they had him hand-cuffed, all hope was gone. This was the moment he had to act.

He put both hands under the table, heaved, and tipped it over onto the man sitting opposite. At the same time he jumped up and threw a punch at Stan as he returned from the cabinet, then spun round and smashed his fist into Sid's face.

It should have been no more than a doomed act of defiance. But then the V2 struck.

There was a deafening explosion, accompanied by a crashing of wood and turf and other flying debris, and a scalding tornado of wind, as the giant rocket, launched at London from Holland minutes earlier, missed its target. It landed on the firing range twenty-five yards from the hut where Adam was being tormented, and detonated on impact.

The explosion blew out the nearest side of the shack and brought down most of the roof. A section fell on the man in khaki, pinning him to the floor. A large piece of the 'Danger: Live Ammunition' notice felled Sid. Adam's punch had already put the third man on the floor, and now he was covered with debris.

Demonstrating that there is sometimes a reward for virtue, the mighty blast left Adam dazed, but unhurt. He staggered briefly, and then the sight of the ginger-haired thug pushing off the debris and getting to his feet swiftly cleared his mind.

Ludicrously, Adam headed briefly for the door. Then he realized that escape would be much easier via the space where the wall used to be. He ran through the gap, and carried on running.

He had a twenty-yard start on the ginger-haired Stan, who was trying to pull something from his pocket. Sid and the chief thug were slower to move, but seemed to be conscious.

9

SITTING ON A bench at the edge of the field, the man in the dark suit had witnessed the effects of the explosion but, since it was on the other side of the shack, he'd stayed unruffled. He remained seated, pulled out a walkie-talkie radio, spoke into it with calm urgency, and then returned it to his inside pocket.

He saw two figures emerge from the shattered building and head towards him. One appeared to be chasing the other.

Adam hadn't looked back, so he wasn't aware that there was only one man following him. For all he knew, all three thugs could have recovered and might now be on his tail, perhaps with guns. So Adam just had to keep running and try to reach a place where there were people, ordinary people, whose presence should deter the villains. Here, in the open fields, he was at their mercy.

His thought was to get back to Chalksea station: there might be people there by now. Besides, it was downhill. So he was running back along the path that would take him past the bench on which the man in the dark suit was sitting.

Adam was a natural athlete but the beating he'd taken had temporarily sapped his strength. His limbs were heavy and sore, he was fighting for breath, and there was a burning pain in his side. His progress was getting slower as he drew level with the bench. And then his progress ceased altogether, as the man stretched out his rolled umbrella and hooked the handle neatly round one of Adam's flying ankles. Adam tumbled flat out onto the grass.

His pursuer drew up, registering both surprise and triumph. Then he stooped over Adam and put his hands round his throat. As he bent over, the man in the dark suit swung his umbrella in a wide arc and hit him hard on the back of his head. In itself, the wooden handle would not have enough weight to cause much damage but the lump of lead buried inside caused the man to drop like a stone.

Adam sat up, bruised and bewildered. He looked back and was relieved to see there were no more pursuers. He peered at the man on the bench, convinced he'd seen him before. It had been pretty unkind of this character to trip him up but, on the other hand, he had dealt with his enemy very effectively.

Adam looked the man in the eye and said, 'Why did you do that?'

'You looked as if you could do with a lie down,' the man replied. 'Besides, it's time you and I had a chat. I'm afraid you've been keeping bad company.'

Adam's defence mechanism was alerted. 'Are you police?'

'No,' said the man. 'What happened there? I mean, before the bomb?'

'This man and two others lured me to that Home Guard place. Then they started beating me up.'

The man clicked his tongue. 'Tch. People behave very badly these days.'

'Then the bomb knocked two of them out, and I was able to run.'

'It's an ill wind that blows nobody any good, as they say.' The man pondered. Then he produced a polite query. 'You say they lured you there? How exactly did they do that?'

Adam thought quickly: he was in danger of saying too much. 'I was thinking of joining the Home Guard.'

The man smiled tolerantly. 'Really? With the war almost over? A bit like joining the Swiss Navy.'

Adam sat on the grass, wondering what to do next. Common sense said he should get up and move off fast. His other two tormenters could still recover and come after him. There was no reason why he should stay here, answering this chap's questions. He should be getting back to London. But they'd taken his money and his return ticket. And the man on the bench had an air of confidence and authority that was somehow reassuring. Besides, Adam was exhausted. So he carried on sitting there.

By now, south-east Essex was reacting to the V2. Air-raid sirens were heard and then the urgent bell of a police car coming up the lane, followed by a Civil Defence van. From the opposite direction came an ambulance. All the vehicles stopped near the entrance, and people began getting out.

First through the gate were two policemen, one with sergeant's stripes on his arm. They saw the man on the bench, and came over to him. Now it was too late for Adam to run.

'Mr Hoskins?' asked the sergeant.

'Yes.' The man on the bench nodded genially, then produced a card and showed it to them. 'A good quick response, Sergeant. Well done!'

The sergeant beamed. 'Thank you, sir. What's the situation?'

'Big explosion on the firing range over there. Almost certainly a V2, falling short. Another of Adolf's triumphs. I doubt if anyone was out there, getting hurt. But two men were injured in that building when it collapsed – we don't know how seriously.'

'There's an ambulance standing by.'

'Well, try and get to them first. And be careful. I'm pretty sure they're professional criminals. If they can move, they'll have made themselves scarce. If they're still there, they could be dangerous.'

'We're armed, sir.'

'Good. If you catch them, nick 'em for GBH. Likewise this character.' He prodded Stan's inert body with his umbrella. 'All three were assaulting Mr Carr here.'

The penultimate word hit Adam like an electric shock. It had been bad enough when the man in khaki had thrown in his recent name, which he wasn't supposed to know. Now here was another stranger casually using the name he was born with, the name he'd tried to leave behind. Adam wondered how he should react. But his brain was too tired for policy decisions.

'Very good, sir,' said the sergeant. 'I've got back-up on the way. We'll just make sure this comedian doesn't go anywhere. Cuff him to the leg of the bench, Fletcher.' The unconscious thug was secured. 'Good. Now we'll go and sort out the other two. What about this gentleman, sir? Is he injured?'

'Possibly,' said Hoskins. 'He's coming with me. He's needed back in London as soon as possible. I'll commandeer that ambulance to take us to the railway station. The ambulancemen can clean him up on the way.' He turned to Adam. 'You never know, you might even get a nurse.'

'Right you are, sir,' said the sergeant, and the two policemen walked off towards the wrecked pavilion.

Adam mustered a bit of spirit. 'What if I don't want to come with you?'

Hoskins smiled. 'I'm afraid you don't have any option, old chap.' He opened his jacket to reveal not only a light blue waistcoat but also a shoulder holster, from which protruded the butt of a small hand-gun. 'Anyway,' he continued, 'you'll be better off with me. This place will soon be swarming with policemen, all in a position to charge you with a hundred different offences.'

'I'm not guilty,' said Adam.

'We'll see,' said Hoskins. 'At least I'll ensure you get a chance to prove that. On the run, you'd still be in danger from that lot.' He nodded towards the remains of the Home Guard shack. 'And another thing,' he added. 'Co-operate with me, and Miss Hart will be pleased.'

Oh God, thought Adam, is there nothing this man doesn't know?

Hoskins rose to his feet. 'Let's go, shall we? Get some iodine on those cuts. And then I think you and I can help each other.'

Adam stood up wearily and looked at his captor. 'You said you're not police,' he said. 'And yet they all do what you tell them. Who are you?'

'Forgive me,' said Hoskins. 'I should have introduced myself. James Hoskins, Commander, British Intelligence.' He advanced a hand. 'How do you do?'

As the train began to move, Adam sat back in his seat and felt it was time to make a statement. The other man's firm but friendly manner encouraged him to speak out. 'Can we get a couple of things straight?' he ventured.

'By all means,' said Hoskins affably. 'Go ahead.'

'I didn't murder Maurice Cooper.'

'No,' agreed Hoskins. 'I know that.'

'And I didn't kill those two men on the pier.'

'Of course you didn't. I did.'

'You did?! You killed two men?'

'Had to, old chap. To save your skin. One of them was about to shoot you.'

'Oh. Then I'm very grateful.'

'To be honest, I didn't actually kill the second blighter. I just scared him a bit, and he jumped. Hadn't studied his tide-tables.'

'Well, thanks anyway.'

'No need for thanks, dear boy, it was all in the line of duty. We're relying on you for vital information. Couldn't afford to let those scruffs rub you out.'

'Hm,' said Adam ruefully. 'Those three this afternoon nearly managed it.'

'No,' said Hoskins. 'They want information from you too. They weren't going to kill you in a hurry.'

'Never mind the hurry, they'd have killed me in the end.'

'They weren't going to get the chance. We'd have pulled you out after an hour. I had a commando unit standing by at Laindon Barracks.'

'Good God!' said Adam.

'You're a very lucky young man, a protected species. British Intelligence has been watching over you ever since the Jefferson inquest.'

'You mean you've been following me?'

'I, or one of my colleagues.'

'All the time?'

'We lost you twice, but we quickly got back on track by following Jane Hart.'

'Just a minute.' Adam's voice changed from surprise to resentment. 'If you had people standing by, you were ahead of me. You must have known I was coming to Chalksea today.'

'Yes, of course. We've been tapping the man Dudley's phone since we knew you were staying there. We had to put up with some awful jokes but we heard your conversation with Dean.'

'So you watched me walk into a trap! You let those bastards get me!'

'Steady on, old chap. We didn't know for sure it was a trap, did we? Any more than you did. It could have been just the whisky deal, like you thought.'

'So why the commandos?'

'We suspected things might turn nasty. There have been rumours of East End gangsters using that hideout to rough up the opposition.'

'But the place is supposed to be Home Guard property!'

'There's a link, I'm afraid. That's something we'll have to talk about in a minute. But first I have to ask some questions.'

'So do I!' protested Adam. 'And this one won't wait. When I didn't come out with the whisky after five minutes, you must have known I was in trouble!'

'That was a fair assumption, yes.'

'And you were going to let them beat the hell out of me for an hour?'

'It was necessary, dear boy. You might have picked up some useful gen. The interrogator often gives away more than his victim.'

Adam had to admit to himself that this had been his own line of reasoning. 'As long as the victim lives to tell the tale,' he said bitterly. He winced, and rubbed his side where a kick had landed.

Hoskins produced a silver flask from his pocket. 'You still

look rather the worse for wear,' he observed. 'Knock back some of this and you might feel better. Then we can both put our cards on the table.'

Adam leaned back, put the flask to his lips, and swallowed a couple of mouthfuls. The brandy burned his dry throat but it sent a reviving charge of energy surging through his body. He closed his eyes and reviewed the events of the last hour.

As planned, the ambulance crew had done a good job of cleaning him up and tending cuts and bruises. Then they put the two men off at the station before returning to the firing range to look for further casualties.

Mid-afternoon passengers were still scarce on the Shoebury to London line and Hoskins had found an empty compartment on the first train.

Adam took another swig of brandy, sighed deeply, and handed the flask back to his companion. The pause had brought big questions storming to the front of his mind. 'I don't under-stand,' he said. 'The police seem to be searching for me, with their wanted notices, radio appeals and so on. But you say you knew where I was all along. So they could have arrested me at any time.'

Hoskins demurred with a smile. 'Er, no. I said we in Intelligence knew where you were. I never said the police did.'

'You mean you don't tell the police what you know?'

'Only when absolutely necessary.'

'Is that fair? Those coppers were rushing to do everything you asked.'

'They might not always do so, if they knew what we were up to. Don't worry about the police, dear boy. We have an excellent relationship with the boys in blue, based on their doing a lot for us, and our not doing much for them.'

'So why didn't you want me arrested?'

'Because you'd accidentally stumbled into a big conspiracy, a dangerous plot that threatens everyone in this country. We thought if we let you stumble on, you might blunder onto the truth. You see, we know the essence of this plot but we don't have the details. We hoped the plotters might come after you, and then we could nab them.'

'So I was the goat in a tiger trap!'

'Something like that. Well, you owed the nation a favour after pulling that stolen-identity trick.'

'How did you know I wasn't who I said I was?'

'Easy. For you, getting away with it depended on no one bothering to ask questions. As soon as anyone took an interest in you, the truth was sure to come out. You couldn't have accepted the Nobel Prize for Science, for instance.'

Adam wasn't in the mood for flippancy. He said tersely, 'I don't think I was in the running.'

'Anyway, once you turned up on our radar, we only had to run a few checks and we had the whole story. The Marine Research Unit told us you'd come from London University, and gave us your photograph. We showed it to a few folks at your old college and they all recalled you as Adam Carr.'

'Oh well,' said Adam. 'It's nice to be remembered.'

'And there was no problem in finding out that you shared digs with the other Adam, and only one survived the bomb.'

'I suppose you think that was a lousy thing to do.'

'I don't know all the circumstances. It certainly didn't make any difference to the real Adam Webber. Or to the poor chap's family, since they'd all gone before him. You broke the law pretty seriously, of course.'

'I realize that.'

'Which is a pretty good reason for you to co-operate with us now. When all this gets sorted out, you're going to need friends.'

'I am co-operating, aren't I? Listen, this big conspiracy you're talking about. It's black market, isn't it? And I can tell you, the Home Guard are involved.'

Hoskins gave a brief laugh. 'A small faction of the Home Guard seems to be in on this. But it's a lot more serious than peddling booze and nylons.'

'What is it then?'

Hoskins hesitated. He looked out of the window for a moment and studied the countryside. The tide was coming in now, most of the mud-flats were covered, and many of the sea-birds were on the wing. He realized it would be best to tell the young man everything. He cleared his throat.

'The fact is,' said Hoskins, 'it's a plot to overthrow the government.'

Adam gasped. He struggled to find words, and then he said, 'You mean, a revolution?'

'More like a coup d'état. Grabbing the reins of power in one swift strike.'

Adam remained incredulous. 'And the Home Guard are behind it? The Home Guard?!'

'A small but powerful section within the Home Guard, yes.'

'That's incredible!'

'In my job, old chap, you find nothing's incredible. Or impossible. The vast majority of Home Guard are decent, law-abiding men who want to defend Britain. But they have their rotten apples, like every other barrel – malcontents, anarchists, perpetual rebels – you know, the bolshie bunch. Many of them with time on their hands. We began to suspect some months ago that such people were being organized into small solid groups within the larger movement.'

'Organized? Who by?'

'By extremists on the outer limits of the Socialist and Communist parties. And some even further left than that. Admirers of Soviet Russia, who'd like to have the same sort of system over here.'

'God forbid!' Adam shuddered. 'And they've latched onto the Home Guard?'

'On the lunatic fringe I described, yes.'

'And they think they can overthrow the government?'

'Yes. And in dire circumstances they possibly could. Remember, the Home Guard have large stocks of guns and other weapons, plus plenty of ammunition and explosives, all the things they'd need to seize key areas. Also remember that most of our regular forces are still abroad, fighting in Europe and the Far East. If someone wants to mount a coup, there'll never be a better opportunity.'

'But you say most of the Home Guard are loyal. Surely they could put down the traitors.'

'Not necessarily. A well-organized fanatical minority can sometimes defeat an easy-going complacent majority. Don't forget, when Hitler seized power in Germany, his Fascists were in the minority. But they had the organization, and they had the will and the energy and a clear-cut plan. It seems the Red Brigade, as we call them, have been manoeuvring their men into key positions while the good guys have been at home, working on their allotments. When they strike, the first thing the extremists will do is grab control of their Home Guard units and their weapons.'

'Good God!' Adam was still trying to come to terms with the whole astounding concept. 'All right, they've got the guns and stuff, as you say. They could cause a lot of trouble, maybe they could even storm 10 Downing Street. But what do they do then? The rabble you describe wouldn't have the brains to run the country.'

'Well, here's the really alarming part. I said these renegades are being organized by political extremists. We believe that some serving MPs are involved, possibly even a government minister, though we don't know which. Enough to set up some sort of ruling junta with experience of government.'

'Phew!' Adam exhaled forcefully. Then he reached out his hand. 'I could do with another swig of that brandy.'

Hoskins handed over the flask and delivered further bleak news. 'There's also a third element. The plotters don't want their members in the Home Guard to show their hands before the big day. Also, they like to think of themselves as idealists. So, if there's dirty work to be done, they simply employ the criminal underworld to do it. As you yourself have discovered.'

'You mean the sods who beat me up this afternoon.'

'Exactly. They'll have been East End gangsters paid by the Red Brigade.'

Adam fingered a bruise. 'They seemed to enjoy their work.'

'Always useful if you can get paid to do what you like doing.'

'Talking of pay, where would the money for all this be coming from?'

'Almost certainly from Russia.'

'But they're our allies!'

'For now, yes. But Joe Stalin would like to take over the whole of Europe in due course. Including Britain. The Russians have their men over here, paving the way. They'll fund anyone who helps the cause.'

Adam sat in dumb astonishment for a moment. Then he said, 'I don't know if I can believe it.'

'I'd have thought what happened this afternoon would convince you that something nasty was going on. Now then, I've told you what all this is about. It's time you told me what you know.'

'I don't know anything.'

'Not true. You know a great deal more than you think you do. You can tell us a lot.' Hoskins felt the train slowing, and glanced out of the window. 'But wait a minute. We're coming in to a station. Make sure no one gets in here.'

It was Tilfleet, Adam's regular station. He was used to seeing it crowded with commuters. But, like Chalksea, at this time of day it was almost deserted. One woman approached their door but Hoskins, who had already opened the window, now stood by it and sneezed loudly several times. The woman moved further along the train, holding a handkerchief to her face.

It was a brief stop, and after a minute they were on the move again, the wheels settling back to their steady rhythm. Hoskins closed the window.

Adam had been thinking. 'All right. Suppose it's all true. It seems you know everything already. You can raid the Home Guard centres and arrest the plotters, you can lock up the suspect politicians. Why do you need anything from me?'

Hoskins frowned. 'Good Lord, man, don't you understand? I've told you, we don't yet have enough to act on. We've good reason to suspect all this, we're sure we know the basic plot, but we haven't any firm details: names, places, plans, dates and so on. We can't just pile into every Home Guard HQ in the country. A lot of them probably aren't involved in any way.'

'You don't even know which units are in on this?'

'No, not entirely. We have a good idea, but we haven't got it a hundred per cent. Or even eighty per cent. Likewise, we think we know some of the rogue MPs, but nothing's certain. This is a democratic country, we aren't allowed to seize several hundred people on suspicion. There'd be a terrible reaction: charges of false arrest, threats to civil liberty! Can't you see that?'

Adam nodded. 'Yes. Yes, if you put it like that, I suppose I can.'

'Besides, when we swoop we've got to get it totally right. We have to catch the lot. We can't afford to have the round-up go off at half-cock, and leave some of the buggers free to cause trouble elsewhere.'

'I still don't see how I can help.'

'You will. We've had our agents join up in various units, where we think there's subversive activity. Several have confirmed there's something going on, but they've not yet come up with firm facts. Several have found nothing to report. One or two have met with fatal accidents. The plotters are very cunning – at least, their key people are. They can spot a mole a mile off.'

Adam suddenly saw the light. 'Was Mark Jefferson one of your men?'

'Yes, he was, one of the best. That's why we put him into Tilfleet which, we have reason to believe, may be a Red Brigade stronghold: possibly their command centre for southern England.

'What made you think that?'

'Several pointers. For a start, their CO's a man called Brigden. We know he used to be extremely left-wing, a member of the Communist Party, and a very active one. Strikes, demonstrations, riots, he'd be in the forefront, hurling abuse at the police, plus the occasional brick. Three years ago, he left the Communist Party, became a model citizen, joined the Home Guard, and started standing to attention for the National Anthem.'

'Is that significant?'

'It's routine for extremists who've been told by their bosses to put on a respectable facade and start working underground. Also Tilfleet's been ordering more weapons and ammunition than you'd expect them to need.'

'Did Jefferson find anything?'

'He strengthened our suspicions. He reported that there's an elite squad of soldiers in that unit. They do special training at weekends, from which the others are excluded. Jefferson said Brigden works eighteen hours a day, and is surrounded by a bunch of henchmen who keep the rest of the men away.'

'Like Mussolini.'

'Like any dictator. It seems Brigden's a bitter and twisted character, born with a big chip on his shoulder. We checked his background. Expelled from school for persistent bullying. Missed out on college because he was already known as a problem-boy.'

'So how did he get to be a Home Guard commander?'

Hoskins shrugged. 'Low cunning, I suppose. He knew what he wanted and he went for it. Probably there weren't many volunteers for the job. And apparently he had some management skills. He'd joined Woolworth's as an office boy and was climbing the executive ladder. Then he got the sack, because he was always off work, making trouble. He's just the type for a leading role in an insurrection.'

'But you've got no firm evidence?'

'Nothing that we can act on yet. But we reckon Jefferson was getting close.'

'Pity about the accident.'

Hoskins gave a short, humourless laugh. 'That was no accident. The day before he was found dead, Jefferson told us he was going to break into Brigden's office. Tilfleet Home Guard are based at a school. They have the run of the place at weekends and weekday evenings, except Tuesday. Tuesday night the school works late – sport, societies and so on – but they pack up at eight. Then the school is empty. Jefferson reckoned that was his opportunity.'

'So what happened?'

'We don't know, we never heard from him again. But we have a pretty shrewd idea. We had men call at local houses, posing as council officials and asking if residents had any complaints about noise from the Home Guard. We got several reports of a fracas in the street that Tuesday night. People thought it was horse-play. Our guess is that Captain Eighteen-Hours-a-Day Brigden came back to work unexpectedly, and Jefferson had to run for it. From the condition he was in next day, I fear he didn't run fast enough.'

'Poor bloke. Jane Hart says he was a good man.'

'He was. And a very brave one. We believe you're the man to see his work isn't wasted.'

'If you think I can help, I will.'

'Good. Now here's the crunch. One resident we questioned was a bright old boy who likes looking out of his window. He loves the night sky, apparently. He reported seeing a man come running down his road, stop, put something in the pillar box, and then carry on running. It struck this chap as an odd way to post a letter. There was no hurry – the last collection had gone hours earlier. So it stuck in the old boy's mind and he told our man about it.'

'And you think it was Jefferson he saw?'

'We do. He fitted the description our man tried on the resident. Jefferson always wore this duffle coat. And he was a resourceful man. If he'd taken something from the safe before they surprised him, he wouldn't want them to catch him with it on him. He'd want to get it to us. So he posted it.'

'Would he have had time, with people chasing him?'

'Obviously not enough to find an envelope and address it to us. Anyway, we didn't receive anything. But he might have had a letter that he'd received and stuffed in his pocket, like you do. It would have his name and address on it. He'd just have time to shove whatever he'd found into the envelope and put it in the pillar box. Posting it to himself.'

'Good grief! That must be the notebook!'

'Notebook?' Hoskins tensed, his eyes bright. 'There was a notebook?'

'Yes. Jane picked up the few bits of post that arrived for Jefferson, after he didn't come home.'

'Eureka! That's what we hoped! Jefferson told us about this girlfriend where he was living. He said she might be useful for messages in a real emergency, although she didn't know what he was up to.'

'The poor chap didn't seem to have any relatives, so Jane tidied up his things, and I helped her. There was this notebook which baffled us. It was full of writing, but all in some sort of code.'

'My God, Carr, I said you'd have answers! There had to be a reason why the Red Brigade put their thugs on to you! That notebook must be hot stuff! When it went missing, they'll have made the same guess as we did – that Jefferson had somehow got it to the Cavendish. That's what they were looking for when they wrecked Jefferson's room. And then yours.'

'I suppose they killed Maurice Cooper?'

'He must have got in the way. They'd have killed you, if you'd been in your own bed. But no doubt you'd made more agreeable arrangements.'

Hoskins paused and looked at Adam. Adam said nothing.

Hoskins continued. 'We were just hoping Jefferson might have grabbed a few papers. This notebook is a huge bonus! It must be vital to the Red Brigade, the way they've reacted.'

'The thugs on the pier were on about it. So were those bastards this afternoon. Only they kept calling it a logbook.'

'That's even better. It could have names and a record of activities.'

'But I'm still puzzled. You could have nabbed Jane and me and asked all these questions at the outset.'

'Like I said, you were bait. Not knowing about anything as positive as a full logbook, we hoped we could learn more about the Red Brigade by watching them following you. We thought one of their leaders might break cover. That hasn't happened. All we've encountered is their hired help. So this afternoon I decided it was time I intervened directly.'

'Pity you didn't decide that sooner,' said Adam. Most of his body felt as if it had been rubbed with sandpaper and there was still a sharp pain in his side.

'Never mind that,' said Hoskins briskly. 'Where is this logbook now?'

'It's in code, as I said. Code-breaking is a hobby of one of my colleagues on Southend Pier. When I went to work that day, I took it with me and left it with him. I imagine he's still got it.'

'Did you tell the thugs that?'

'Of course not. I didn't want them going after Leo.'

'Thank God for that. But it doesn't mean the Red Brigade won't go sniffing round your Marine Research place. When they didn't find the book at the Cavendish, and it wasn't on you when they searched you, they might start thinking about your workplace. We'd better get there pretty damn quick.'

'We?'

'You can save us time by leading us to the right place and the right man. And you'll get him on our side straightaway, without a lot of explanations.' Hoskins smiled. 'I take it you'd rather be getting fresh air on Southend Pier than sitting in a police cell while an inspector tots up the number of offences he can charge you with. Including several unsolved local burglaries.'

'You're right,' said Adam. 'I'll come with you.'

'Tell me more about this afternoon's unpleasantness. They asked you about the logbook, right? What else?'

'They thought Jefferson and I were partners. They were trying to find out what we'd been up to, and how much we knew. As I didn't know anything, I wasn't much help.'

'Did they offer you any inducement to make you talk?'

'Only that, if I did, they might refrain from cutting me up with a razor.'

'Nothing more?'

Adam pondered. 'Oh yes. They said they might even let me go in a few days, when it didn't matter any more.'

'What? Say that again!'

Adam repeated the words.

'My God!' Hoskins punched the palm of his left hand with his right fist. 'The bloody thing must be imminent! I thought we had more time to work it out but we haven't! We'll have to act at once!'

'What'll you do?'

'As soon as we get to Fenchurch Street, you find us a cab. I'll ring the office and have them issue a general alert.'

'So you're going to trust me not to run away?'

'Yes. I hope I've said enough to get your support. And remember, you're going to need our help. Also, you wouldn't get very far – you've no money.'

Adam sighed. 'You forgot to mention, I'm too knackered to run anywhere.'

'I'll tell my people to have a fast car ready to take us to Southend. This logbook might crack it for us.'

'If Leo's decoded it.'

'We'll pray on the way down there. If not, of course, we've got experts who'll do it, but that would mean delay. Who's in charge at Marine Research?'

'A dragon called Edith Bird, Dr Edith Bird. Very tough. Leo and I reckon she wears Harris-tweed knickers. She won't welcome the intrusion.'

'Right. I'll get High Command to ring in advance and straighten her out. And, just in case the Red Brigade get the same idea at the same time, we'll take a bobby along with us, with a gun.'

'You've got a gun yourself.'

'Never use it, dear boy. I can't stand the noise.'

'I got a bit emotional the other night,' said Vic Dudley. 'It's true. I got emotional. See, I'd been in the pub, and what I heard made me emotional. When I got home, I took the wife in my arms, I said, "Darling, I'm so proud of you." The fag dropped out of her mouth, she said, "Proud of me?" I said, "Yes, proud of you. I was in the pub just now, and our milkman was bragging to his mates. He said he'd made love to every housewife in this street. Had 'em all. Except one!" She said, "That'll be that snooty cow at number thirty-two."'

Maggie laughed. Jane smiled and said, 'But you're not married.'

'Of course not,' said Vic. 'This isn't real life. It's a new gag for the act.'

'Yes, but people are supposed to believe you while you're telling it, aren't they? And they know you haven't got a wife. It said so in that piece they did about you in the *Radio Times*.'

'It's a convention,' said Vic. 'All comics make jokes about their wives and mothers-in-law. Even if they're not married. And some of them never will be.'

'All right,' said Jane. 'But somehow it doesn't ring true. A lot of your other jokes are about being a bachelor and chasing girls. It's contradictory.'

Vic wrinkled his brow and paused for thought. 'Well, yeah, I see what you mean. Perhaps I shouldn't do both kinds of gag in the same routine.'

'Sorry,' said Jane. 'I didn't mean to cause a problem.'

'No, no, it's OK, I think you're on to something.' Vic pondered a moment, and then found the solution. 'I know. I'll tell it about someone else. Yeah, that's it. Ta.' He left the girls' dressing room, talking to himself as he went. 'Funny thing happened to a mate of mine the other night. He dropped into the pub....'

The closing door shut off the rest.

Maggie chuckled. 'You've got him worried now.'

177

Jane protested. 'I didn't intend to. I was trying to be helpful.'

The girls were relaxing between shows. At least, Maggie was. Jane was on edge, wondering what was happening down in Essex. Vic's jokes and the subsequent debate had been a welcome diversion. Now she started fretting again.

She began to apply fresh lipstick to lips she'd fixed five minutes ago. Almost immediately, she dropped the lipstick. She reached down to scrabble for it on the floor, and then knocked her head on the dressing table as she straightened up, causing various items to fall over and roll about.

'Blimey!' said Maggie. 'You're as jumpy as a kangaroo on heat!' At one time she'd had an Australian boyfriend.

'Sorry,' said Jane. 'I just wish I knew how Adam's getting on.'

'Calm down, love. I told you, he'll be all right. Let's have the wireless on. We might catch *Music While You Work*. Get some nice tunes.'

Maggie was proud of her radio, one of Alfie's gifts from the good days. It was a genuine portable that didn't have to be plugged in. And it didn't need big glass batteries either: just small packs, like you used for a torch. Sadly, *Music While You Work* had finished and Bruce Belfrage had already launched into a news bulletin.

'… later, British troops forced their way into the town of Bedrun and took up new positions,' he announced.

'I wish they'd do that in my bedroom,' said Maggie.

Bruce Belfrage gave a tiny professional pause, and his voice subtly changed gear, as he proceeded to the next item. 'Another German V2 rocket, aimed at London, has fallen short. The latest missile has landed in playing fields at Chalksea in Essex.'

'Oh God!' cried Jane.

The newsreader continued, unperturbed. 'Full details have not yet emerged but it seems a sports pavilion was demolished by the blast. It's thought the building was unoccupied, and so far there are no reports of any casualties.'

Jane grasped the radio and brought it close to her ear, as if to squeeze out further information. But Bruce Belfrage had already moved smoothly on. 'The Ministry of Food today announced minor alterations to the meat ration. The proportion that must be taken in corned beef is to be adjusted in the case of—'

Jane switched it off and turned to Maggie in panic. 'Chalksea! That's where Adam was going this afternoon!'

'Ouch!' said Maggie. 'Still, I don't suppose he was playing football. Anyway, the man said there were no casualties.'

'"So far," he said. What does that mean?'

'You can bet it means there aren't any,' Maggie reassured her. 'Only they have to check everywhere, in case there was an old tramp sleeping under a bush or something. Don't worry, pet.'

'That's easy to say. But I am worried. My throat's gone dry.'

'You'd better have a drink then,' said Maggie.

There was a glass on the shelf in front of them, with a little water in it. It stood in front of a notice which declared 'No alcohol in dressing rooms.' Maggie opened her drawer, took out a perfume bottle, and poured gin into the water glass. She handed it to Jane with a cheerful smile. 'I've been keeping this for an emergency.'

'Thanks,' said Jane. She drank a mouthful and instantly started coughing.

There was a knock at the door, and Andy Gooch popped his head round. 'Jane, Bert's got a phone call for you. Have you got time to take it?'

Jane leaped to her feet. 'I've got to take it. Maggie, will you cover for me?'

'It's all right,' said Maggie. 'You've got five minutes. And don't worry about the drink. I'll finish it for you.'

Jane said 'Thanks, Andy' as she brushed past him and raced down the stairs, with no idea what she was hoping for. If Adam had been killed, it would take them a long time to identify him. And there'd be nothing to make them get in touch with Jane Hart at the Windmill. So it couldn't be bad news. Could it? Perhaps he'd been injured and was sending a message.

Her heart was pounding as she reached the stage door, where Bert sat, solid and unconcerned. In fact, he seemed slightly disapproving. 'I think it's your young man,' he said, as he handed her the receiver. 'Make it quick. VD don't like boyfriends ringing up on this line.'

Jane gasped 'Hello' into the mouthpiece. And then relief flooded over her, as the voice at the other end said, 'Jane, it's Adam.'

'Adam, thank God! Are you all right?'

'Of course I'm all right. Why wouldn't I be?'

'We just heard about the bomb at Chalksea!'

'Bomb? Oh yes, the bomb. Bit of luck, that. Saved my life.'

'Saved your life? What are you talking about?'

'No time to explain. Big news. We think we know what's going on.'

'What? Who's "we"?'

'Me and this chap from British Intelligence. Jane, I seem to be back on the right side of the law!'

'Wow! How did that happen?'

'I'll tell you when I get back. I'm ringing to say I may be out late tonight. There's a fast car waiting to take us down to Southend Pier.'

'You're going to the pier? Last time, you nearly got killed!'

'Not this time, darling. This time I've got help. I don't know what time I'll be back at Vic's place. But I will be.'

A bell rang, to call the cast onstage for the start of the next show. 'I'll have to go.'

'Me too. Listen, Jane, be careful. We're up against some bad people. And there's more of them than we thought. Stay close to Vic. And wish me luck.'

The director of Joint Services Liaison had lunched well and lingered over his brandy until 3.15. so when he returned to his office, he should have been in a mellow mood. But he wasn't. Indigestion was troubling him again. He was irritable, and felt the need to stir things up.

As he sat down heavily in his chair, he was wondering which department he could pester, in order to gain a little vicarious excitement. Then he remembered a point made by his secretary: some sections were late with their financial estimates. He opened the folder she had placed on his desk that morning and aggressively studied the top sheet. Then he pressed a switch and spoke into the intercom. 'Miss Ingram?'

The reply was swift. 'Yes, sir?'

'Get me James Hoskins in National Security, C Department.'

'Very good, sir.'

While he waited, the Whitehall mandarin mopped perspiration from his brow. The five-minute walk from his club had been a mistake. His doctor's instructions to take more exercise were foolish and misguided. He reached down for the briefcase that was leaning against the leg of his desk.

It was the large leather sort, reinforced with steel and provided with a combination lock, as issued to senior civil servants for carrying confidential documents. He flipped the briefcase open: the lock hadn't been used for years. He groped around among the contents: various crumpled papers, cigarette packets and a copy of *The Times*. Then he found what he was seeking – a miniature bottle of expensive brandy. He brought it out, broke the seal, removed the cap, put the bottle to his lips, and took a hefty gulp.

Miss Ingram's voice came through the intercom. 'Mr Hoskins is out, sir. But I have Mr Faraday on the line.'

'Faraday? Who's he?'

'He's an executive in Mr Hoskins' department.'

'All right. Put him through on Phone A.'

The next voice he heard was young, slightly nervous, and eager to please. It was a voice that knew the director was an important man.

'Nigel Faraday here, sir. C Department. Can I help you?'

'I wanted Hoskins. Where is he?'

'He's on his way to Southend, sir. Something urgent came up.'

A memory stirred at the back of Straker's mind. 'Southend?'

Faraday's voice grew enthusiastic, as he saw a chance to impress a member of senior management. 'That's right, sir. There's good news. We've apprehended a man Mr Hoskins has been wanting to question. Adam Webber.'

Suddenly, the director was fully alert and tingling.

'Webber? You've caught Webber?'

'Yes. Except that's not his real name. But it's the chap the police have been looking for. Mr Hoskins arrested him this afternoon.'

'But the man's a common criminal! This should be a police matter. Why is Mr Hoskins involved?'

'Apparently Webber has information about a big security threat that Mr Hoskins has been investigating. Mr Hoskins is taking him down to Southend to pursue his enquiries. It seems there's evidence there they need to look for.'

Now the beads of sweat were back on Straker's forehead. 'Let me get this straight. Hoskins has taken Webber into custody. But instead of handing him over to the police, he's taken him down to Southend?'

'To the pier, that's right, sir. I understand Webber used to work there. I believe they're hoping to find some sort of note-book or something.'

'And they've already left?'

'Yes, sir. Ten minutes ago.'

Straker let out a deep breath. 'I see. Well, have Hoskins send me a full report.' Then he remembered. 'And tell him he's late with his estimates.'

With that, the director put down the receiver, took the hand-kerchief from his breast pocket to wipe his moist hands, and pressed the intercom switch.

'I have to make a top-security call,' he said. 'Scramble Phone A.'

'Very good, sir,' came the disembodied reply. 'What number do you want?'

'That's all right, Miss Ingram. I'll dial the number myself.'

Superintendent Nash was fuming. 'How did it happen?' he demanded. 'How the hell could it happen?'

Inspector Jessett, weary after missing most of his night's sleep, was rather more phlegmatic. 'Well, sir,' he said, 'it can happen and it does happen. Paynter's not the first customer to hang himself in a police cell.'

'He's the first man to do it in a Tilfleet police cell!' Nash thundered. 'The Chief Constable's blowing his top! He's demanding an explanation!'

'In my opinion,' Jessett ventured, 'they put cell windows too high. If a man stands on a chair and gets a rope round the bars, once he kicks the chair away he can hang with his feet off the ground. If windows were lower down—'

Nash cut in. 'Never mind the bloody architecture, man! Paynter didn't have a rope, did he? Did he? I presume you searched him when you brought him in?'

'Of course, sir.'

'And you took away tie, belt, bootlaces and so on.'

'Paynter wasn't much of a one for wearing ties, sir. We removed all the rest.'

'So how did he manage to hang himself?'

'He used his shirt-sleeves.'

'His shirt-sleeves?! For God's sake, how did he do that?'

'He tore off both sleeves, knotted them together at the end and rolled them up tightly enough to make a ligature.'

'That's incredible!'

'It was very effective, actually. The knot hit his throat when he jumped off the chair, and crushed his Adam's apple. Speeded things up for him.'

'Why would he want to kill himself?'

'I don't know, sir. I'm sorry he did. I was just starting to get some useful information out of him.'

'So perhaps it was remorse. He was ashamed of grassing on his mates.'

'That's possible, I suppose. He certainly wasn't too happy. He was having to decide between doing a long spell in jail or shopping a lot of serious villains. He'll have been scared.'

'All right, tell me exactly what happened last night. The Chief Constable's demanding a full report for Scotland Yard. He's called them in, by the way.'

'Yes, sir. I heard. Well, I wasn't here early on. I was in the West End, with Constable Thompson, keeping a suspect under observation.'

'So who was here?'

'Sergeant Fairweather was duty officer. He'll be able to tell you more than I can. Sergeant Monk was in his office, catching up on some paperwork. There were two constables sharing desk duty, and four out on patrol.'

'I gather you came back here just before midnight. What were you told?'

'Sergeant Fairweather said Paynter was given his supper at six and then left alone in his cell. He asked for comics, so they gave him the *Daily Mirror*. When Constable Logan went to see him at 10.30, he found him hanging from the bars. He tried artificial respiration, but Paynter was already dead.'

'And no one had looked in on him all evening?'

'Apparently not, sir. He was in cell three, which is round a corner at the back. A bit out of the way.'

'You say he was going to be a valuable informant. Why was he put somewhere out of the way?'

'I don't know, sir. When I left him in the afternoon, he was in cell one, near the front desk. He was transferred after I left.'

'Why?'

'I don't know. As I said, I wasn't here. I'd guess one of the constables must have brought in a drunk, or someone especially difficult: a prisoner they had to keep an eye on. I'm sure you'll get the answer from Sergeant Fairweather.'

'I certainly hope so. I've spoken to you first because you're the senior man and Paynter was your prisoner. Now I'll talk to Fairweather. I'll also need to speak to Sergeant Monk. Where is he?'

'Not here, sir. Monk rang in this morning, reporting sick, I'm afraid.'

'Did he indeed? Well, get hold of him fast and tell him to get well bloody fast. Unless he's at death's door and has a medical certificate to prove it, I want him here within the hour!' There was a knock at the door. 'Come!' barked the superintendent, and in came John Taylor, the Tilfleet police doctor, a thin elderly man with a keen sense of drama.

'You wanted to know my findings as soon as possible,' he announced.

'Yes please, Doctor. I was telling Jessett, this is the first suicide we've had in Tilfleet, and we want it tidied up quickly.'

'That would be easy if it were a suicide. But I'm afraid we do have to consider other explanations.'

'What? You're not suggesting the fellow hanged himself by accident?'

'No, I think we can rule that out. But I fear we can't exclude the possibility of murder.'

'Murder?' Nash was incredulous. 'Murder?! Paynter was a big man, an ex-boxer. You think someone could have strung him up against his will?'

Taylor spoke calmly. 'They could have done if they'd drugged him first. Knockout drops in his tea, for instance.'

'That's preposterous!'

'Not so,' said the doctor. 'I exceeded my brief on this occasion, as it's an unusual case. I decided to analyse the stomach contents. And I found traces of barbiturates.'

'Barbiturates? Good God!'

'I've informed the coroner, and he's ordered a post mortem.'

10

It was a bleak scene as the small group alighted from the train at the end of Southend Pier. The late afternoon was grey and chilly. No naval vessel was alongside at present, so admin and maintenance staff were staying in their quarters as far as possible, avoiding the cold east wind. Already the lights were on in the Marine Research Centre, where they were working late, and those lights stood out brightly against a darkening sky.

As Adam expected, Dr Edith Bird was not pleased at the interruption. But there'd been a phone call from a very high level, commanding her to co-operate, so she received the trio with cool tolerance.

'I was told to expect you, Mr Hoskins. How can I help?'

Hoskins had already shown his own identity papers, and he now introduced his companions. 'This is Superintendent Barron of the Metropolitan Police.' Barron had recently been seconded to the Intelligence Service. Hoskins had added him to the party, and warned him to come armed. 'And Mr Webber, of course, you know already.'

'Yes indeed.' Dr Bird frowned at Adam.

Adam smiled and said, 'Good afternoon, Dr Bird. Sorry I'm late back.'

'That was rather an extended tea break you took the other day.'

Adam sighed. 'Sorry. The service is getting a bit slow in the canteen.'

'I think we'd all like to know what you've been up to.'

'Well … I'm afraid it's rather a long story.'

'And one we don't have time for now,' said Hoskins briskly. 'This is a matter of national security, and it's very urgent. We need to speak to Mr Leo Newman.'

Newman had been sitting at a bench, warming dark fluid over a Bunsen burner. When the visitors arrived, he placed the test-tube in a rack, left his stool, and stood smiling uncertainly. Now he responded.

'Hello, I'm Leo Newman. What can I do for you?'

'That notebook I gave you last week,' said Adam. 'We're hoping it's here.'

'Yes,' said Leo. 'I've been keeping it in my desk.'

Hoskins let out a huge sigh of relief as Newman continued. 'You were right, it's all in code. I've been amusing myself with it during lunch breaks.'

'Have you cracked the code?' Hoskins asked.

'Oh yes,' said Newman, somewhat pleased with himself. 'It's a fairly simple one. Basically, a matter of using one letter instead of another, the substitute letter changing each time, according to an arithmetical progression.'

'My word,' said Hoskins, mildly. 'As simple as that?'

'Yes, I've been copying it into plain English, doing a little every day. In fact, the job's almost finished.'

The young man opened a drawer and took out the precious notebook, plus a Marine Research scribbling pad, on which he'd been writing the translation.

'May I see those?' Hoskins made no effort to conceal his eagerness.

'Yes, of course.' Newman handed them over. 'Bit disappointing, I'm afraid. No secret formula, no dramatic messages. It seems to be mainly lists of names and addresses, all male. They're grouped under headings, which are the names of British towns – Brighton, Bristol, Hull and so on. That's what helped me crack the code. But there are a few notes that didn't mean anything to me.'

Hoskins had been skimming through the pages with

mounting excitement. 'Well, they could mean a hell of a lot to me! And to this country!'

'What d'you make of it?' asked Barron.

'It's a breakthrough!' Hoskins exclaimed. 'The great big breakthrough we've been praying for! All these places have Home Guard units. If Tilfleet's the command centre for the Red Brigade, they'd have a list of all their rogue members, the ones who are preparing to go into action! And this has to be it!'

'No wonder those bastards wanted it back!' said Adam, who continued to feel aches and pains, and was starting to feel a fervent hatred of the plotters.

Hoskins was still effervescing. 'My God, look at the date – it's on top of us!' He paused to look again at the notes, which included timings and what must surely be targets.

'Are we allowed to know what you're talking about?' asked Dr Bird, with a hint of impatience.

'The little matter of a plot to overthrow the government,' said Hoskins. 'No time to say more at the moment. Newman, you say you've almost finished decoding. How far is there to go?'

'About ten pages.'

'Well, we need to know the lot. Could you explain the code to the rest of us?'

'I should think so. As I said, it's not difficult.'

'Right,' said Hoskins. 'Dr Bird, you won't mind if we use your chairs and table?' He didn't wait for an answer. 'Barron, Webber, Newman, everyone please help. We'll each take a page at a time. Once Newman's explained the code, we'll get on and finish the job.'

Barron scratched his head. 'Are you sure? Wouldn't it be easier to take the stuff back to London and have the experts do it?'

'It would be easier for us, yes,' said Hoskins. 'But we can't delay that long. If we can complete the picture here and now, I can phone my people and start things moving. So it's time for volunteers – you, you and you!'

'Give me two pages,' Dr Bird commanded. 'I'm in charge here, and I do *The Times* crossword in ten minutes.'

'Anyone lend me a pencil?' said Adam.

The sea was getting rougher in the rising wind, as the motor-boat smashed and barged its way through the steep grey waves.

Brigden bawled at the engineer, 'Can't you go any faster, Henshaw?'

The reply was terse. 'If she hits these waves any harder, she'll break her back! And yours too!'

Brigden grunted. He was not a good sailor. But he was aware that, after recent events, security at the pier entrance was massively increased. Fake passes and identity cards, however well forged, wouldn't get intruders in now. And Straker's call had made it clear that immediate direct action was essential. So an approach from the sea was the only option.

Brigden knew this was a mission he had to lead himself. He couldn't let underlings bungle this one. It was infuriating that he had to break cover early. But, he consoled himself, he was due to do so shortly anyway. And if things went smoothly, there'd be no survivors to identify him. He'd be able to go back underground till the big day.

It should have been a short run to Southend Pier from Eastwell Quay, on the Essex marshes, where the Home Guard patrol boat was moored. But the weather had not been kind and the tide was running against them. Brigden's temper was beginning to fray.

The three men with him were not much enjoying their sea trip either, but they were being well paid for this difficult and probably bloody operation. Brigden was once more employing professional criminals, holding back his Home Guard revolutionaries for the momentous action that was now imminent.

Sid Garrett was there. He'd escaped from the collapsed pavilion just before the police arrived, and was happy to go back into action, being keen to avenge the blow that Adam had delivered. Brigden had told him to find another experienced villain to complete the raiding party, and he'd enlisted Mick Chase, an occasional partner-in-crime.

Peering through the spray, Brigden noticed that Garrett was holding his revolver in his hand, and he bellowed at him, straining to be heard above the roaring sea. 'Put that gun away, man! All of you, keep your firearms dry!'

Another ten minutes, and they were approaching the seaward end of the pier, the great structure of timber and rusting iron towering over them like a cliff. Now they could see the metal ladder Henshaw had told them about, attached to one of the huge upright stanchions.

They all knew the plan. A grappling iron thrown from the boat would draw it close enough for three men to get onto the ladder. Henshaw, a Leigh fisherman who knew about boats, would stay aboard, using the engine's power to prevent the craft being driven against the ironwork. Thus the boat would be ready for a swift getaway. Now Henshaw had it standing a little way off the pier, waiting for a patch of relative calm that would enable him to make the final approach.

Fortunately, the decoding proved easier in practice than it had sounded in description. Hoskins clearly enjoyed the challenge, as did Newman and Edith Bird. Barron tackled the task with quiet efficiency. Only Adam, who'd never been good at maths, was finding it a slow and difficult process.

Leo Newman, having finished his own pages, came to his aid. 'Let me finish that for you, Adam. You've got a few mistakes there. I don't think anyone's address would be "3 Statiop Road".' He pushed aside the faulty pages Adam had produced, and quickly finished the job for him.

When the communal task was completed, Hoskins collated the pages with immense satisfaction, and put them in a large buff envelope. Then he spoke triumphantly. 'Thank you, all of you. This result is better than I dared hope. I think we're just in time to prevent anarchy.' Dr Bird's voice was polite but firm. 'Would you now kindly find time to tell Newman and myself what on earth is going on?'

'Sorry, no,' said Hoskins. 'I have to call London at once. But my colleagues are at liberty to tell you all they know.' He moved swiftly to the telephone, which stood on a shelf below the window.

The scientist fixed Adam with a steady look. 'Well,' she observed. 'You heard what your leader said.'

Adam gathered his thoughts and tried to be succinct. 'Basically, it seems there's a hostile group within the Home Guard who are planning to seize power in Britain, and turn us into a Communist state, like Soviet Russia.'

Edith Bird was aghast. 'What?! The Home Guard? The Home Guard?!'

'It's true,' said Barron. 'Only a small element among them, of course. But it seems they're being organized by some very cunning people. They have weapons, and they could have enough men to take control of key areas.'

'And make Britain like Russia?' Dr Bird's face expressed a mixture of horror and incredulity. 'What sort of men would want to do that?'

Hoskins was delivering some swift instructions into the phone. And then the door crashed open, and the three raiders came in, pointing guns.

Adam recognized Garrett. 'Men like that,' he replied.

'All of you, stand against the wall with your hands up!' shouted Brigden. Then he noticed what Hoskins was doing. 'You! Put that phone down!'

Hoskins hesitated briefly, and Garrett fired a shot into the ceiling, to show they meant business. Hoskins said, 'Sorry, Auntie, some guests have arrived,' and then put the phone down.

Brigden rebuked his man. 'Wasted shot! From now on, you only shoot to kill!' He glared at Hoskins and gestured with his revolver. 'Right. Now join the others against the wall! And quick!'

Hoskins seemed confused and nervous. He took the hand-kerchief from his breast pocket and mopped his brow.

'Drop that!' said Brigden. 'Get your hands up! And back to the wall! Now!'

Hoskins was trembling. He let the handkerchief fall from nervous hands, raised his arms above his head, and went to stand with his back to the wall, choosing his place very carefully. The handkerchief fell on the table, covering the buff envelope.

Brigden turned to Garrett. 'Which one is Webber?'

'That one!' said Garrett. 'That's the sod who's given us all the trouble! Bleedin' toe-rag!' He walked forward and punched Adam hard in the stomach. 'I've got my razor with me, Webber. So this time you'd better talk!'

'You heard him,' said Brigden. 'Where's the logbook?'

Was there any point in continuing to deny all knowledge of the notebook's existence? Adam decided to try one more bluff. 'What logbook?' he gasped, still breathless from Garrett's blow.

And then Brigden saw the blue notebook lying on the table. 'That logbook!' he said. He picked it up and looked inside. 'This is the logbook your friend stole from my desk.' He put it in the large inside pocket of his waterproof jacket.

So Brigden had very quickly found what he'd come for. But he still needed to know what had been going on, and how much of a threat there was to the big plan. He stared hard at Adam.

'What the hell did low-life thieves like you and Jefferson want with this logbook?' he demanded.

Adam couldn't think of the wisest thing to say. So he said nothing.

Garrett hit him again. 'Answer the officer!' he barked.

By now, Adam had worked out that the best thing would be to feign ignorance of the notebook's contents. It was a long shot, but Brigden and his men might just take the notebook and go. And the decoded version was in the envelope hidden under Hoskins' handkerchief.

Adam sighed, as if finally forced to tell the truth. 'I found it in Jefferson's room at the Cavendish,' he said. 'It seemed to be in some kind of code, so I thought it might be important. I always reckoned Jefferson had some money hidden away, and I thought there might be clues in the notebook.'

'So what's it doing here?' rasped Brigden.

'I brought it to work, to see if anyone had any ideas.'

'And had they?'

'No. It's all gobbledygook.'

Brigden peered into Adam's eyes. For a moment, it seemed that he might be deceived. But then, as he looked away, his glance took in the handwritten sheets on the desk – Adam's flawed pages which Newman had discarded, pages with names and addresses on them.

'You bloody liar!' he rasped. 'You're not as thick as you look! You know what this is all about, don't you? Someone's been decoding the logbook!' Brigden scooped up the loose sheets and stuffed them into his pocket. His mind was racing. Straker's message, passed on through intermediaries, had been urgent but limited: simply that the logbook was at the Research Centre on Southend Pier, that Webber was on his way to retrieve it, and that he must be stopped at all costs. Now Brigden had to consider the implications.

'Who are all these people?' he demanded. 'What are they doing here?'

'They work here,' said Adam. 'We're all engaged in marine research.'

'Like hell they are!' said Garrett. He pointed at Superintendent Barron. 'That bugger's a copper! I've seen him on the job!'

'Kindly stop using objectionable language!' snapped Edith Bird.

Brigden ignored her. Now he sensed the full picture.

'So that's it!' he roared. 'You're working for British Intelligence, aren't you? All of you! Capitalist scum! And you think you can stop the revolution! Well, you're wrong!' He spoke curtly to his men. 'They'll all have to go. I'll take Webber and the policeman. Garrett, you take the other two men.' He nodded to Mick Chase, Garrett's friend. 'You take the woman.'

Chase, the late recruit, was shaken. In truth, he wasn't an ideal conscript for this job. A career criminal, his line was theft and burglary, with a little Grievous Bodily Harm thrown in when necessary. Although in the pub he bragged of ruthless violence, he'd actually never been involved in murder. And he had a morbid fear of hanging.

He spoke nervously. 'Just a minute, guv. You got the book and that. Do we really need to top them?'

'Don't argue with me, man!' shouted Brigden. 'They know all the plans, and they've still got time to wreck them! Now get on with it!' He raised his own gun and pointed it at the young man's head.

Like Adam earlier, Hoskins knew it was now or never. And, once again, a rearrangement of furniture seemed the best answer. He'd positioned himself so that his raised left hand was near the light switch. And the daylight had finally gone. He flicked the switch off and shouted, 'Everyone down on the floor!'

As he went down, Hoskins pushed over the table, making a barrier between his group and the intruders.

Brigden and his men fired into the darkness as the table hit their legs, and all the shots missed, except one. Adam, still stiff with pain, had been slow to move, and one of Garrett's bullets hit him in the chest. He sank to the floor with a groan.

'Wait!' shouted Brigden. 'Switch the light on! And keep calm! We're the ones with the guns! Hold your fire till we can see them!'

Garrett tried to recall where the light switch was and then, as he lurched forward with a groping hand, he stumbled against the crouching Barron, who'd taken his gun from its shoulder-holster. Garrett swore loudly and Barron, recognizing his voice, fired upwards twice, killing him instantly. The man fell sideways against the workbench, knocking the Bunsen burner to the floor.

The noise of gunfire in the confined space was deafening, and Mick Chase felt he'd rather be elsewhere. He turned and dashed out through the door and across the pier-head platform towards the escape ladder. Now Brigden knew the odds had changed. He was on his own, and up against armed men. If they shot him, they could reclaim the vital logbook and the decoded pages. And he needed to stay alive for the day of action. It was time for retreat.

He fired another shot in the general direction of the foe, leaving three bullets in his gun. Then he spun round and fled through the still-open door and across the planking.

'Look after Adam!' Hoskins bellowed at Leo Newman and Dr Bird. Then he and Barron struggled to their feet, picked their way past Garrett's body and the upturned furniture, and emerged onto the deck.

The navy had fixed hooded working-lights to the perimeter of the pier and, by their pale light, the two men could just make out the figure of Brigden ahead of them. They set off in pursuit.

Suddenly, there were more voices everywhere. The sound of shots had brought startled people out of their offices and workshops. And then up went the cry most dreaded in a wooden structure: 'Fire!'

The fallen Bunsen burner had ignited the waste-paper basket, and the flames quickly spread to the plywood partitions.

Edith Bird ran to the door of the cabin and shouted, 'Help! There are wounded men in here!' Two workers in overalls ran to assist. Behind them, the duty fire crew were being called into action.

The fugitives had a good start on their pursuers and the deck had been clear when Chase and Brigden ran across it. Moments later, Hoskins and Barron were impeded by staff emerging from their workplaces.

So Chase was out of sight, and Brigden had half a minute to spare when he reached the top of the ladder. He swung his burly frame out onto the top rung, and began to climb down.

'Bring the boat close!' he bellowed at the top of his voice. He wasn't surprised when he heard no answering cry. He hadn't expected one and, anyway, the mighty roar of the sea and the wind would surely swallow any response from the boat. Brigden was concentrating on placing his descending feet squarely but speedily on the wet and rusty metal steps. But then, as he neared the foot of the ladder, he heard the sound of the boat's engine receding.

The shooting and the shouting had suggested to Henshaw that things had gone wrong. And when Chase appeared at the top of the ladder screaming, 'We've got to get out! They've got guns!', he'd decided that prompt action was called for. He was grateful for the warning but had felt no obligation to stay and thank the messenger. He'd revved up the engine and headed west. So the boat had been yards away when Chase made his despairing leap and landed in the water, bitterly regretting that he'd never learnt to swim.

Moving fast, the boat was almost out of sight when Brigden reached the bottom of the ladder and looked around him. Chase had already disappeared in the surging sea. The only things that met Brigden's startled eyes were angry waves and flying spray.

Thirty yards below the safe, wide public arena at the sea-end of Southend Pier, there's a lower platform, a criss-cross of metal struts which, at low and middle tides, is used by adventurous anglers to get closer to their prey. It's covered by a foot of water at high tide or in bad weather, so the base of its uprights and the iron grid of the floor are festooned with seaweed and barnacles.

At this stage, the sea was just starting to bubble up through the grilles which formed the base of the structure: soon the whole surface would be awash. A dismal place indeed but it was the only refuge open to the desperate Brigden. He swung out from the ladder and in towards the platform. He had to jump the last yard and landed awkwardly on the slippery floor, crashing his shoulder against an upright. The razor-sharp barnacles tore his sleeve and the flesh beneath.

Cursing, he steadied himself and moved into the inner

regions of the lower pier, thinking hard. With the boat gone, he had few options. Surrender was impossible: he'd hang for murder. There were two imperatives. He must survive, to play his part in the coup. And he must prevent the enemy regaining the logbook.

He saw two possibilities. At worst, he could take to the water. But the sea was cold and rough, and land was a mile away. It would be better if he could eliminate his pursuers. Then he could go back up the ladder and down the pier, unobserved in the darkness and confusion.

He was suddenly aware of a hubbub on the upper deck, and saw flames through cracks in the planking high above him. So the pier was on fire! That should help him. People would be too busy fighting the fire to bother about Brigden. Only those at the research centre were likely to come after him: Webber was dead or crippled, the couple in white overalls seemed non-combatant. That left the policeman and one other man: two opponents, and he had three bullets left.

Brigden knew his best shot at the policeman would come when the man reached the foot of the ladder and had to perform the same tricky manoeuvre that he himself had done. He'd have to pause and then swivel his body, presenting a good target. Brigden waited patiently, half-hidden behind a stanchion.

The whole scene was becoming like a medieval painting of hell: the petrified forest of slimy green pillars now glowing with angry red light from the flames overhead. In the fierce wind, the fire was surging rapidly through the ancient tarred timbers, the salt spitting and spluttering in protest. Bits of blazing debris were starting to fall with a hiss into the water around Brigden's feet.

Then the moment arrived. Barron stood at the bottom of the ladder, conveniently silhouetted against a slight residual glow in the western sky. He began to pivot in towards the platform. Brigden took careful aim and fired.

As he did so, Barron's right foot skidded on the last rung of the ladder and he plunged sideways. Brigden's bullet passed above his head, and harmlessly on into the night. The policeman fell halfway into the water, drenching his body from the waist down. But he kept his gun dry and fired back. The noise echoed shrilly through the cast-iron underworld, and Barron's bullet expired against an upright that was cushioned with seaweed.

With surprising agility, the bulky officer hauled his body clear of the waves and flattened himself on the watery platform, soaking wet, but no longer an easy target. Then he crawled forward to the cover of a broad pillar, before getting up and setting out to stalk Brigden. Now the two men fought a battle of wits, moving between pillars, always seeking cover. Each was saving his bullets till he got a clear view of the other. Then, suddenly, came Brigden's chance.

As Barron moved swiftly between two pillars, a piece of burning timber fell from the upper deck and hit his back, knocking him over and briefly illuminating the scene. His gun went sliding across the floor.

Brigden could scarcely believe his luck. One of his remaining bullets would despatch the helpless policeman. After that, he could re-arm himself with the other man's gun. He walked to the defenceless man and took careful aim.

And then his own gun fell from his hand, as the weighted end of Hoskins' umbrella smashed down on his wrist. Appearing now from the shadows, Hoskins had come down by an easier route. Separated from Barron in the hurly-burly on the upper deck, he had used a stairway on the eastern side of the pier-head, which he knew of from earlier visits. This time his blade had remained sheathed. He wanted this villain alive for interrogation.

As Brigden staggered backwards, clutching his shattered forearm, Barron rolled free from the fallen timber, retrieved his gun and pointed it at Brigden.

'All right, Bob, don't shoot!' Hoskins shouted. 'I need a chat with this cove!'

But Brigden had other ideas. His only remaining purpose

now was to prevent the enemy from getting the logbook back. He wrenched it from his pocket with his undamaged hand and hurled it into the sea. The wind carried it several yards before a wave caught it and it was submerged. Hoskins moved forward to grab Brigden, who formed the wild notion that the man was about to dive and try to rescue the prize. He pushed Hoskins away, reclaimed his own gun, and managed to fire a random shot with his left hand. Hitting one of the pillars above the seaweed level, the bullet ricocheted across to another before falling to the floor.

The shot Barron fired was more accurate. It thudded into Brigden's heart, knocking him backwards. For a moment the man tottered, and then he toppled off the platform into the sea.

Hoskins was not pleased. 'You silly idiot!' he cried. 'I told you not to fire!'

'I wasn't taking any risks,' said Barron. 'I knew a man in Stepney who could shoot with either hand.' He dragged himself to his feet. 'So we've lost that bloody notebook after all,' he observed. 'Still, I suppose it doesn't matter. We've got the decoded version.'

'Yes, thank God,' said Hoskins. And then his mouth went dry. 'You picked it up, did you?'

'No,' said Barron. 'Didn't you?'

'No,' said Hoskins.

11

In the News Studio, on the sixth floor of Broadcasting House, Alvar Lidell studied the printed sheets in front of him. The war news was all good: the Allies were advancing everywhere. The last German soldiers had been driven from France, large parts of Belgium and Holland were now liberated, and Germany itself was being invaded by British and American troops from the west, and by the Russian army from the east.

Lidell checked the unfamiliar foreign names in the forthcoming bulletin. After each word that might give trouble, the BBC Pronunciation Unit had written the correct delivery, spelled phonetically in capital letters. Guidance was required mainly with foreign towns and individuals. But occasionally help would be offered with British names, as in the fourth item in today's news, which he was studying with interest.

'The main structure of Southend Pier, ravaged by the fire which started on Tuesday night, has now been declared salvageable. Old timbers had continued to smoulder in some inaccessible areas until this morning, according to Southend's fire chief, Superintendent John Cowper (pronounced COOPER). But these sections have now been cut away, and emergency work has begun to construct temporary facilities for use by the Royal Navy.'

Lidell reflected that he did know how to pronounce Cowper. And, recalling pleasure trips before the war, he hoped they'd remember to restore permanent facilities for use by the public.

Jim Owen, the engineer, was checking all the sound equipment that would carry the newsreader's voice by landline to the Droitwich transmitter, which would broadcast it to the nation. For millions of listeners at home, the one o'clock news was a focal point in the day. After a moment, Owen was reassured. Everything was working.

He pressed a button to switch on the red light outside the studio that said 'Live Transmission: No Entry'. There were still eight minutes to go before they went on air, but Owen was a cautious man. He didn't want messengers barging in at the last moment.

And then an amazing thing happened.

The studio door was thrust open violently, and in came half a dozen men in khaki, carrying guns. Their leader, in an officer's uniform, walked over to Alvar Lidell and pointed a pistol at his head. 'The studio is commandeered,' he said. 'Move out of this chair.'

Lidell was too astonished to move, but managed to blurt out, 'What? Who the devil are you?', before a burly soldier grabbed his arms and pulled him up and out of the way.

Jim Owen reacted quickly, and was reaching for the telephone, when another intruder crashed a rifle butt down on his wrist and dragged him from his seat.

'Put these two over there,' barked the officer, 'and keep them covered.'

Lidell and Owen were hustled into a corner, where a man with a corporal's stripes waved a Sten-gun at them. Now another soldier entered, escorting a civilian, a broad young man with a flabby face. This man went to Owen's seat and took charge of the control panel.

Owen recognized him. 'Good God! Alex Price! What the hell are you doing here?' Price had been one of his engineer colleagues at the BBC, until his dismissal for drunkenness last year. Ignoring Owen, Price did his own technical check. He was soon satisfied. 'All set to go,' he declared.

The officer went to the door and called, 'We're ready for transmission, sir!' Then in came Robert Westley and another man, both in grey suits.

He then led Westley to the chair vacated by Alvar Lidell. His voice was very respectful. 'This is your mike, sir. Perhaps you'd like to test your voice level for the engineer.'

'Thank you, Major Fry,' said Westley.

While the mike test was going on, the BBC men could only watch in outraged bewilderment, Owen wincing with pain and nursing his wrist. Lidell noticed that each intruder wore a bright red band on the sleeve of his khaki battle-dress.

Soon the studio clock showed a minute to one. Westley moved out of his chair and spoke to his companion. 'Barrett, you'd better sit here first for the introduction.' Barrett slid into the seat and nodded to the engineer. Then, as the minute hand reached one o'clock precisely, Price pressed the switch for the time signal and, after the familiar six pips, Barrett addressed the microphone. He had been chosen for his voice: clear and authoritative, but not posh.

'This is the British Broadcasting Corporation in London,' he said. 'In place of the one o'clock news today, we are broadcasting an important message to the nation, from the Right Honourable Robert Westley, hitherto Minister of State for Internal Affairs.' Then Barrett moved out of the chair and Westley took over. He tried to convey a mixture of strength and friendliness.

'Good afternoon,' he began. 'I'm here to announce a radical change in the government of this country, which takes effect immediately and will concern us all.

'I have to tell you that, as the war in Europe draws to a close, I and many others who believe in democracy have become aware of a plot by top members of the Churchill government to thwart the will of the British people.

'They have been planning to expel from power all Labour and Liberal members of the coalition government, who have contributed so much to the war effort. They would replace them with right-wing extremists.

'There would then be a snap election, rigged to install in power the most reactionary government this country has ever known. That government would increase the power of the wealthy classes, and prevent the reforms and moves towards social justice which this country so sorely needs: reforms which you and your fellow citizens have been promised, as you worked and fought to win this bitter war.

'In the face of this threat to our democracy, it was necessary to take rapid and decisive action. My colleagues and I have therefore been working for many months on forming an alternative group to undertake the running of this country, and to implement the many changes you have all been hoping for. Our plans are now complete.

'Accordingly, from 1 p.m. today, the Democratic Socialist Party of Great Britain has taken over the reins of government. As a senior minister, with four years' experience of national affairs, I have accepted the post of president. And I have appointed many prominent parliamentary figures, whom you know and trust, to take important posts in my cabinet: among them are Ernest Cox, who takes over as prime minister, Gerald Collis, Charles Bell, Reginald Fox, and William Ford, who will serve as my vice president. Great Britain is now a republic. The former King and Queen, together with Winston Churchill and other leading members of the Tory Party, have been placed under house arrest.

'Countries which have fought alongside us in our struggle against Nazi Germany are expected to welcome Britain's change of regime. A message of congratulation has already been received from our greatest ally, Soviet Russia.

'Most senior figures in the police and the armed forces endorse our actions: though some obstruction may be expected from reactionary elements. There may also be opposition from members of the upper classes, who see their unearned wealth and privilege threatened: as indeed they will be. Therefore, until everyone's allegiance is clear, the decisions and policies of our new government will be enforced by volunteers from the Home Guard, that fine organization which has guarded our shores for the last five years. The large proportion of Home

Guard soldiers who actively support our radical movement are wearing red armbands on the sleeves of their uniforms. These soldiers with red arm-bands will be known as The People's Militia, and will be acting at all times with the authority of the state.

'Since this change of government reflects the wishes and aspirations of the British people, it is hoped that the transition will be made peacefully and without bloodshed. Let us act together as brothers. However, it is important to remember that orders issued by The People's Militia must be obeyed. And, for your security, a form of martial law has been put in place with immediate effect.

'I look forward to working with all of you to build a new and fairer Britain.'

Having finished his speech, Westley moved out of the chair, and Barrett slid in to deliver the tailpiece. 'That was the president of the Democratic Republic of Great Britain, Robert Westley,' he stated. 'This station will broadcast news and instructions every hour. It is important that all citizens should go about their normal business in the usual way.'

Alex Price turned off the microphone, and the soldiers in the studio applauded. Barrett rose and shook Westley's hand. 'Well done, sir. I think you made everything very clear.'

'Thank you,' said Westley, and then he turned to the Home Guard leader. 'And I thank you and your men, Major, for a very efficient operation.'

Barrett added his congratulations. 'I'd never have thought a big organization like the BBC could be taken over so easily.'

'We had the benefit of inside information, from our young friend here,' said the major. Price smirked. 'Plus the advantage of being completely unexpected. There were only half a dozen commissionaires to deal with, and a couple of rather dozy security men. They didn't give us much trouble.'

'Let's hope it's being as easy as that for our other units.'

'They'll have met much stiffer resistance at military sites, of course,' cautioned the major. 'But they all had surprise on their side. They're heavily armed, and each attack has been meticulously planned to the last detail.' The major was in buoyant mood.

'You did the midnight check-up, as planned?' asked Westley.

'Yes. Between 12 and 1 a.m. I spoke to every group leader in the country.'

'And there were no hitches?'

'Just one. Brigden, CO at Tilfleet, has disappeared.'

'Brigden's disappeared?'

'He went on a mission to Southend and didn't come back. They think he must have got caught up in the fire on Southend Pier.'

'Unfortunate. He's a key man, isn't he? Or was.'

'No one's indispensable, sir. All our people work as a team. His number two has taken over. Sergeant Crowe, he's a very good man – he won't let us down. Rest assured, sir, all our units were fully prepared, and ready to strike at noon plus fifty minutes.'

'Have you heard anything since?'

'No, I ordered complete telephone and radio silence between 1 a.m. and 1 p.m., to prevent any last-minute leaks. Price told me the direct number for this studio, and I told all local commanders to ring here as soon as their job's done. For the next few hours this is our national control centre.'

'Thank you, Major,' said Westley. 'Well done.'

Barrett addressed his president with some deference. 'Presumably, sir, you'll move into 10 Downing Street as soon as it's taken over?'

Westley was extremely positive. 'Yes, certainly. That's the vital location. Symbolic, plus a lot of good practical reasons.'

'It shouldn't be long,' said the major. 'I put one of our three crack units on that job.'

'And the other two?'

'One's gone into the Home Office, the other the Ministry of Defence.'

'Excellent. Fox and Collis will take up their duties as soon as

we hear those buildings are clear. When do the street demonstrations start?'

Barrett responded enthusiastically. 'Any minute now. They're
planned for ten past one, as a spontaneous reaction to your
broadcast.'

'Good,' said Westley. 'They're very important.'

'They are indeed. Something we've learned from our Russian
comrades. Our Intelligence people will have crowds of republi-
cans celebrating in Whitehall and Portland Place, and in all
major cities. Plus, of course, around Buckingham Palace. By the
end of the day, the coup should be a fait accompli.'

Amid all this exuberance, Westley was beginning to wish the
phone would ring and bring some reassuring news. There was
a hint of tension in his voice as he turned back to his military
commander. 'No doubt you're ready to defend this building
against any counter-attack by reactionary forces?'

'Most certainly.' The major exuded confidence. 'I have fifty
heavily armed men deployed around the ground floor, and
guarding all entrances. And there are two trucks full of rein-
forcements, with mortars and tear gas, parked round the corner
in Duchess Street. We're totally secure here.'

As he spoke, there was thunderous noise and an explosion of
activity, as twelve marine commandos came crashing in
through the windows, boots first. They'd landed their heli-
copter on the roof and then abseiled down the face of the
building. The News Studio's soundproofing had kept their
approach silent, but now all hell broke loose.

The People's Militia had no time to react as the commandos
surged in, some hurling smoke-bombs as they came, others
firing from the hip. By the time their feet hit the floor, they'd
identified the danger men, the ones brandishing guns; and
they'd put them all out of action before any of them could pull
a trigger. Three of the red-band soldiers were dead, and the rest
had dropped their weapons.

As the smoke began to clear the studio door opened again,
and in came the squad of uniformed police who'd been waiting

in the rehearsal room down the corridor. They were led by the commissioner of police and alongside him was James Hoskins, his umbrella as immaculately furled as ever.

The two men walked up to the little group by the microphone, and the commissioner spoke calmly. 'Robert Charles Westley, I am arresting you on charges of high treason and conspiracy to commit murder. Anything you say will be taken down and may be used in evidence against you.'

Westley, like all his men, had been stunned by events. But he'd recovered more quickly than most, and his voice was firm. 'All I have to say to you, Commissioner, is this. Make the most of the next few minutes: because after that, you're out of a job. Our forces are at this moment taking over Scotland Yard.'

The commissioner smiled. 'Are you sure about that, Mr Westley?'

Major Fry intervened. 'Don't make trouble for yourself, Commissioner. Your lot are out of power. Any minute now you'll see crowds in the streets, supporting the new regime!'

'We're a republic now!' Barrett affirmed. 'No more fascist police. In future the law will be in the hands of The People's Militia.'

The major was regaining his buoyancy. 'The British public are with us. That broadcast will cause them to rise up and overthrow their masters!'

Now Hoskins spoke for the first time. 'I don't think so, old chap. The thing is, none of the British public will have actually heard the broadcast.'

'Nonsense!' said Westley. 'Fifty per cent of the British public switch on for the one o'clock news.'

'And I'm sure they did today. They'll have heard the normal news bulletin, coming from our Birmingham studios.'

'What?'

'I'm afraid your little bit of nonsense went no further than the recording machine in the basement. The line from here to the transmitter was cut off at Droitwich.'

Barrett turned on Alex Price. 'I thought you said everything was working!'

'Don't blame him, old chap, he had no way of knowing. We thought we'd let you go ahead with your speech – the recording will be useful evidence at the trials.'

Westley was now lost for words. But the major was not yet crushed. 'Never mind the broadcast. The point is, The People's Militia are at this moment taking control of all areas of power.'

'Ah. Sorry. Wrong again. Five thousand members of the Home Guard, who were planning to take part in this insurrection, were arrested in their homes at dawn today. Well, four thousand, eight hundred and something, actually. Does the number ring a bell?'

Although shaken, the major still managed a little more bluster. 'I don't believe it! We've heard nothing of this.'

'That was our intention. We took trouble to ensure the news didn't reach you and your little gang here. We thought it best if you went ahead in this one location. Let the poison out of the system. So we all know where we stand.'

Fry now saw that his hopes were dashed. He would not be getting instant promotion to the rank of general, and the post of British army supremo. He fell as quiet as Westley and Barrett. For a brief moment there was silence after the turmoil. Then a resentful voice was heard from the sidelines.

'You mean you let these bastards come here and crack my arm when you could have stopped them?' protested Owen.

'Sorry, dear boy,' said Hoskins. 'Can't make omelettes without breaking eggs. You'll get compensation, of course. Think of it as a war wound.'

'I have first aiders with me,' said the commissioner. 'They'll look after you till the ambulances arrive.'

'Ambulances? I don't need an ambulance!'

'No, but these characters do.' The commissioner indicated several of the red-band soldiers who were nursing wounds. 'The Middlesex Hospital have four blood-wagons standing by.' He turned to one of his aides. 'Curtis, ring and tell them they're needed now, to tidy up after Operation Mike.'

As Curtis went to the phone, Hoskins spoke to the leader of

the commandos. 'Captain Cole, perhaps you and your chaps could go down and sort out the riff-raff who've taken over the ground floor here.'

Cole snapped to attention. 'With pleasure, sir.'

'They're a rabble, but they're well armed. So be ready for anything.'

Cole was reassuring. 'With respect, sir, we always are. That lot shouldn't detain us long.'

Westley raised a hand to halt the proceedings. 'Just a minute. No point in further bloodshed.' The phone hadn't rung, no supportive crowds had appeared outside. 'It seems the Establishment have won again. No doubt this place has loud-speakers. I'll tell our soldiers to lay down their arms.'

'Very wise, Mr Westley,' said Hoskins. 'And humane. I'll see it's taken into account when you appear in court.'

Westley sighed. 'How did you know our plans? I suppose someone ratted on us.'

'Not exactly,' said Hoskins. 'Let's just say, a little bird told us.'

12

THERE WAS A clink as something solid was put down on Adam's bedside cabinet. 'A cup of tea,' the nurse announced brightly.

Adam opened his eyes wide enough to confirm that she had identified the object correctly. 'Thanks,' he said, and then he closed them again while he made up his mind whether or not to wake up properly. The tea was always piping hot, so he had a couple of minutes to think things over.

He reviewed the last few days, which had been strangely calm and uneventful after all the preceding turbulence. Of the night he'd been involved in the pier affray, he remembered little that happened after Hoskins flicked the lights off. He'd felt a searing pain in his chest, and a blinding pain in his skull, as his head hit something on the way down. Then it had been black-ness, punctuated by vivid impressions of flames and frantic activity. There was a vague memory of being bumped along on a stretcher beneath a bewildered moon.

He'd first regained full consciousness in a hospital bed. Not the bed he was in now– this one was by a window. He'd been exhausted and in pain and attached to blood transfusion equipment. He'd instantly started worrying about Jane. There'd been a nurse in the room, and he'd managed to stay awake long enough to ask her if Mr Hoskins was all right. She'd seemed to know who he was talking about, and said he was. 'Please ask him to tell my girlfriend I'm OK,' he'd pleaded. And she'd replied, 'I think that's taken care of. But I'll check.'

Reassured, he'd switched off and slept for what seemed like a week, but was probably just ten or twelve hours.

Next time Adam woke, it was because a doctor was pulling off dressings in order to inspect the wounds in his chest and back. The doctor had been relaxed and cheerful, telling Adam that he was a fortunate fellow. The bullet had passed right through the flesh without hitting anything vital. The pain as the dressings came off was like being shot all over again. The doctor had revealed that, as well as the bullet wound, Adam had suffered substantial concussion, a cracked rib, severe bruising, and slight damage to the kidney area. He would make a full recovery but he'd have to rest in bed for several days, until his wounds were seen to be healing. The varied injuries had made the doctor wonder if the young man had been in a brawl, as well as a gunfight. But Adam had been too weary to explain.

'I think I fell in with the wrong crowd,' he said.

The doctor smiled indulgently, and made no further enquiries. He applied new dressings as gently as he could, and said that Adam's transfusion could now be terminated, and the line removed from his arm. Adam expressed his thanks, and then asked the doctor where he was.

'The Middlesex Hospital,' the doctor replied.

'In London?' Adam expressed surprise. 'I thought I was in Southend.'

'You were initially taken to Southend Hospital. But someone in authority intervened. A person called James Hoskins. He wanted you transferred here.'

'Why?' asked Adam.

'I don't know. I think he must like you. He's got one of his men on guard outside your door.'

That had brought a grunt from Adam. It was a reminder that he'd been wanted by the police. Was he still, he wondered? Why had nobody told him anything? He cleared his throat and said, 'Has anyone been asking about me?'

'Several people. They've all been told you're OK, but you have to rest in hospital for a few days. A Miss Hart sent her love.'

That was good news. 'Can I have visitors?' he asked.

'Not until Mr Hoskins says so. I don't know who this Mr Hoskins is, but it seems we all have to do as he tells us.'

'I think he's second-in-command to Winston Churchill,' said Adam.

'That's certainly how it looks,' said the doctor. 'In fact, Winston had better watch out he doesn't take over. That reminds me, I'm supposed to let Hoskins know as soon as you're sitting up and taking notice.'

'I notice they're only putting one lump of sugar in my tea,' complained Adam. 'D'you think you could persuade them to manage two?'

'Don't you know there's a war on?' said the doctor, falling back on the nation's favourite excuse. 'Still, the nurse likes the look of you, so you may be in luck. And now I'd better ring Hoskins' office.'

'Will you please remind him he owes me a favour? And tell him I'd like to know what the hell's going on.'

The doctor had left his bedside with a grin. 'I will convey the message,' he said. 'But perhaps not in quite those words. Anyway, I'll see that he knows you're becoming restless. Now try and get some sleep.'

Half an hour later a nurse had come in, wheeling a trolley with a telephone on it. Rather attractive, Adam thought, and realized he must be getting better. The nurse brought the trolley to Adam's bedside and announced, 'A phone call for you.' She spoke in tones that betrayed some interest. All the staff were intrigued by their mysterious patient, and his apparent importance to officialdom.

Someone had thought he looked like the man whose picture had been featured after the Tilfleet murder. But a senior consultant had ruled that out. Someone else had heard that he'd escaped from Germany after a failed attempt to assassinate Hitler. Staff had been told not to ask him questions. But there was nothing to stop them speculating.

Adam had lifted the receiver and heard the now-familiar

voice of James Hoskins, apparently in genial mood. 'How are you, dear boy?' he asked. 'Able to take a little nourishment?'

'I'm surviving, thanks, but I'm confused.'

'Confused?'

'No one's telling me anything. Why can't I have visitors? And there's a guard outside my door.'

'Ah yes. Arthur French, one of our best men. Very experienced. You'll be all right with him.'

'But why is he there? Am I under arrest?'

'You could put it like that if you wanted to.' Hoskins sounded amused. 'Or you could call it protective custody.'

'What's the difference?'

'None. They both mean you're not going anywhere. But then I don't suppose you feel like going anywhere. The thing is, at present I can't have you talking to anyone except hospital staff. And they have orders not to discuss anything except medical matters. It's just until I can give you a proper briefing.'

'Can't you do that now?'

'No, sorry, old chap. Unfinished business. But don't worry, Jane's all right, she knows you're all right, and everything's under control. With a bit of luck, I'll be in tomorrow. Till then, no chattering about recent goings-on. Understand?'

'I suppose so,' Adam had reluctantly conceded. By now he was tired. He wasn't sorry when Hoskins rang off and he was free to go back to sleep again.

That had been yesterday. Today Adam felt stronger. His recollections completed, he decided that he would definitely wake up and drink that cup of tea. It was now only lukewarm, but seemed to contain at least two sugars. He was further cheered by the presence of a couple of biscuits. Intravenous feeding was all very well, but he'd be glad to start using his teeth again.

There were headphones hanging over the bed-head. With these, Adam could listen to the BBC Home Service or the Forces' Programme. During these last few days he'd caught some news bulletins, but he'd always fallen asleep before the end. More alert today, he tuned in to an Agatha Christie whodunnit on *Afternoon Theatre*.

After fifty minutes, the detective had gathered all the suspects together in the drawing room, and was just about to denounce the culprit when the door of Adam's room opened and in came James Hoskins, wearing a neat dark suit and a cheery smile. There was a red carnation in his button-hole.

'Good afternoon, dear boy,' he said.

The nurse had followed him in, and she put a chair for him at Adam's bedside. Hoskins thanked her, and then politely indicated that he'd like to be left alone with her patient. The nurse left, a little disappointed, and Hoskins sat down, resting his furled umbrella on the floor.

'How are you feeling today?' he enquired.

'D'you mind hanging on a moment?' asked Adam. 'I'm listening to the end of an Agatha Christie.'

'Which Agatha Christie is it?' Hoskins demanded.

'It's about a chap called Ackroyd.'

'*The Murder of Roger Ackroyd*,' said Hoskins. 'The narrator did it. Now switch it off, there's a good chap. I've a lot to do today.'

Adam sighed and complied. This was no time to fall out with the man in charge. He removed the headphones.

'Well, dear boy,' said Hoskins, 'the quacks say you'll be out of here in four or five days, and fully fit in six weeks. Good news, eh?'

'Yes,' Adam agreed. 'I've been very lucky. But what happens then? And what's been going on while I've been lying here?'

'Let's take the second question first, shall we? You must have heard some of the news on that thing.' Hoskins indicated the radio.

'I heard about the fire on the pier. And then there was some sort of attack on Broadcasting House. A group of anarchists, they said. That's all I know.'

'That's all the public know. And it's all they'll ever know.'

'But what about Brigden and his gang? What about the Red Brigade?'

Hoskins blew out some air through pursed lips. 'I suppose, after all you've been through, you're entitled to know the full story. But this is for your ears only. Right?'

'All right. If that's the way it has to be.'

'It does,' said Hoskins. Then he told Adam all about Brigden's demise, the fire on the pier, the dawn arrest of all the potential insurgents, the foiled assault on Broadcasting House, the failure of the coup, and the arrest of the ringleaders.

'Phew!' said Adam. 'All thanks to that logbook! Lucky the decoded version wasn't lost in the fire!'

'It wasn't luck, actually. It was thanks to your boss, the formidable Dr Bird.'

'Old Bossy Bird? What did she do?'

'She was the heroine, took charge of everything. She organized Newman and others to get you ashore and into an ambulance. And she remembered to shove the vital documents down her Harris-tweed knickers.'

'Brilliant!' said Adam. 'They'd be safe enough down there.'

'Quite,' said Hoskins drily. 'Now then, I've had to neglect you for a few days, because there's been a fair amount of clearing up to do. I've also been involved in lengthy discussions about your future.'

'My future?'

'Oh yes, you do have one. It looked a touch bleak at first. Possibly a long spell in chokey on account of all the offences you committed. Including the capital crime of hitting a policeman.'

'That was a mistake,' said Adam. 'And I did help at the end, didn't I?'

'Yes, you did. And that's the point I've been making. Fortunately, I have a few fairly influential friends. I've been bending their ears on your behalf.'

'Thanks. Any luck?'

'A lot more than you deserve, dear boy. No charges will be brought. Adam Webber died in the Blitz. You're Adam Carr, and you're a free man.'

'Wow!' Adam attempted to raise his arms in jubilation, but they didn't get very high. He winced and sank back on his pillow, but there was a broad smile on his face.

'There is a condition.'

'Ah. I might have guessed. Oh well, as long as it's nothing illegal.'

'The one vital thing is that you have to keep your mouth shut. The government's imposed a total security clamp-down on this whole business. People must never know there was nearly a revolution. And the Home Guard's reputation must remain untarnished.'

'But surely everyone's heard about the attack on Broadcasting House!'

'An isolated incident. A bunch of left-wing students who'd dressed up in combat gear, obtainable at any army surplus store. Not connected with the accidental fire on Southend Pier.'

Something clicked in Adam's brain. 'So how did I manage to get shot?'

'You didn't,' said Hoskins, 'you were hit by flying debris while working at the Marine Research place. That's all that happened. And if you ever say anything different, you'll be locked up in the Tower of London for a hundred years. Have you got that?'

'Yes, I've got it,' said Adam. He was still euphoric over his escape. He relaxed and thought for a moment. 'I still can't get over the Oozlum Bird saving the nation. I shall look on her with new respect.'

'Ah. Sorry. The sad fact is, henceforth you won't be looking on her at all.'

'My God! You don't mean ...' Adam hesitated.

'No, I don't. But she's moving into government circles, which is almost as bad. She's been made assistant to the government's chief scientific officer.'

'Good for her!' said Adam. 'From what you say, she deserves it.'

'Also, you won't be doing any Marine Research for a long time. The unit on the pier was totally destroyed by the fire.'

'There are other Marine Research units.'

'True, but I'm afraid you won't be working in any of them. There's something else you need to know about your future. The fact is—'

At this moment the door was knocked on and opened and the security man put his head round.

'Excuse me, sir. Miss Hart is here. You said to tell you when she arrived.'

'Yes. Thank you, French. Just ask her to wait half a minute, would you?'

'Very good, sir. And there's a man with her,' said French.

'Right. The same goes for him. And check his identity, please.'

French withdrew, and Hoskins addressed the patient sternly. 'Adam, that embargo extends to what you say to Miss Hart. When I spoke to her on the phone, she thought the whole shenanigans was about some black market racket. She's to go on believing that. Otherwise she could face charges of obstructing the police. OK?'

Adam had been looking forward to explaining everything to Jane. However, there was no option but to agree, so he did. 'OK, if you insist.'

'I do. No doubt the man with her is that Dudley fellow you were living with. I assume he thinks the same as Miss Hart. He too must retain that illusion.'

Once more Adam nodded his assent. Then Hoskins went to the door and told French to let the visitors in.

It was indeed Vic Dudley who accompanied Jane into the room. He stood back, as she rushed to the bedside with a cry of, 'Adam, darling, are you all right?' Then she kissed and hugged her sweetheart, jarring his wounds. So there was a little pain mixed with his delight.

'I'm fine,' he said. 'I just got in the way of a stray bu— a stray bit of flying metal. When the oil tank blew up. Luckily it went straight through.'

'Like the first pint of beer on an empty stomach,' Vic Dudley observed.

The government man extended a hand towards Jane. 'I'm James Hoskins, Civil Service. How do you do, Miss Hart?'

Jane responded warmly. 'Hello, Mr Hoskins. I think it was you who phoned to tell me Adam was all right.'

'Yes. I tried to let you know as soon as possible.'

'Thanks a million. Oh, and this is my friend, Vic Dudley.'

Hoskins smiled. 'Ah yes. Mr Dudley. I recall seeing you at the Windmill.'

'Good man,' said Vic. 'Not many customers come out of the Mill thinking about the comic.'

'Well, there was something that struck me about your act,' said Hoskins.

The comedian prepared himself for a compliment. 'Oh yes?'

'Yes,' said Hoskins. 'You're obviously quite a young man. Why aren't you in the army?'

It wasn't the sort of remark Vic Dudley had expected. But he'd heard the question before, and he had his answer ready. 'Flat feet,' he said. 'The doctors said I'd wear out army boots too quickly.'

'Pity,' said Hoskins. 'You'd have been very useful in the front line.'

'You think so?'

'Yes. If you'd done your act at the enemy, most of them would have fled.'

'Ta,' said Vic. 'You must let me come and watch your act some time.' Then he turned to Adam. 'Sorry I can't stay, mate. I'm back on stage in twenty minutes. I brought you some bits and pieces.' He put two items on Adam's bedside cabinet.

One was a Lucozade bottle, containing a fluid rather browner than the usual contents. 'Take a dose three times a day, with water,' Vic prescribed. 'Not too much of the water – it can bring on rheumatism. And this might give you a laugh.' The second gift was a copy of *Blighty*, a pocket magazine which mixed pin-up pictures with slightly rude stories.

'Thanks,' said Adam. 'You're a pal.'

'I'll be off then,' said Vic. 'Nice to meet you, Mr Hoskins. I hope you do well in the Diplomatic Service. See you later, Jane. Don't get this lad too excited. Bye, Adam. Mind you don't take a turn for the nurse.' And with that Vic Dudley was gone.

'I must be off too,' said Hoskins. 'A lot of paperwork to do.' He rose from his chair. 'I'm sure you young people won't mind being left alone. Miss Hart, I've told Adam he's off the hook. Everything's been cleared up. There'll be no prosecution.'

'Mr Hoskins, you're wonderful!' Jane exclaimed. She grabbed his arm and kissed him on the cheek.

Hoskins seemed mildly pleased. 'Thank you, my dear. But now I think you should save your kisses for this young man. He's had a rough time.' He began to move off. 'Adam will give you all the details. But if you two decide to tie the knot, it's worth remembering you'll be Mrs Carr, not Mrs Webber.'

Jane was radiant. 'Thank you again, Mr Hoskins.'

Hoskins was halfway to the door. 'I'll call in again in the next few days,' he said. 'Tie up a few loose ends.'

'Just a minute,' said Adam. 'You've forgotten your umbrella. And you were going to tell me something more about my future.'

'Ah yes,' said Hoskins, returning. He picked up his umbrella. 'You'll recall that Adam Webber was exempt from military service because he passed his exams and qualified as a research scientist.'

'That's right, he was a bright chap.'

'Alas, Adam Carr didn't do either of those things. You'll be getting your army call-up in about six weeks.'

POSTSCRIPT

THE WAR IN Europe ended in May 1945 and the prime minister, Winston Churchill, immediately dissolved his wartime government and called a general election, as he had promised. The result was a landslide victory for the Socialist Party, and the formation of a Labour government, under Clement Attlee.

Attlee's regime peacefully implemented most of the things left-wing thinkers had long wanted: a National Health Service, wider Trade Union rights, and the nationalization of the commanding heights of the economy – mines, railways, public utilities and so on. Compensation was paid to dispossessed shareholders. The King and Queen remained in place. Democracy and the rule of law were maintained.

Now that they were no longer needed to guard Britain's shores, the Home Guard were honourably disbanded, and their weapons were transferred to the regular army.

The government succeeded in suppressing news of the attempted coup and the brief existence of the Red Brigade. Westley and his fellow conspirators were tried and convicted in a secret court, under wartime emergency legislation. Their sentences were limited to two or three years, in return for their co-operation in maintaining the veil of secrecy imposed on their activities.

They were also required to leave the country on their release from jail. Most made their new homes in Eastern Europe but Bill Ford went to the USA, having been recruited by the American Secret Service to help with countering Soviet espionage. Neville Straker died of a heart attack before he could be brought to trial.

Those among the Home Guard renegades who'd committed assault and other offences in the attack on Broadcasting House were charged individually, as civilians, and received appropriate sentences, again reduced on a promise of silence about the planned coup.

The potential insurgents who'd been arrested before they could go into action were not charged but they were watched by British Intelligence for the rest of their lives. Almost all abandoned thoughts of revolutionary action, many of their socialist goals having been peacefully and democratically achieved. The extreme malcontents found new causes to espouse, and new ways to promote them, less violent than the Red Brigade's plans. They favoured civil disobedience, sit-ins, demonstrations and marches, which did nothing worse than disrupt the traffic.

Adam and Jane were married shortly after his release from hospital, and just before his conscription. Adam served for two years in the British Army of Occupation in Germany and then, after demobilization, re-took his course at London University. This time he passed his exams, and began his career as a marine biologist. During those early years, Jane continued at the Windmill, to support them both. In 1951 she retired and they started their family.

Vic Dudley's career blossomed, as long as variety theatres flourished throughout Britain. In the late forties he starred in his own radio series, *Dudley's Doings*, and appeared in a Royal Command Variety Performance. When the variety theatres began to close, he started a new career as a character actor on stage and TV, and in films. In 1980, he became a contract actor at the National Theatre.

Maggie Rayner remained a chorus girl for another five years, graduating from the Windmill to the London Coliseum and the Palladium, where she had a brief spell of glory as feed to the comedian Tommy Trinder. In 1950 she married a local lad in the building trade. He put all his energy and savings into renovating and developing property, and became a millionaire. They had five children.

Inspector Jessett stayed in his post at Tilfleet Police Station until his retirement, after which he devoted his time to gardening and writing his memoirs which, alas, were never published.

Sergeant Monk managed to get a transfer to the Metropolitan Police, where he reached the rank of detective inspector, and was involved in the dismantling of the Krays' criminal empire.

Sergeant Ernest Fairweather was convicted of the murder of Reginald Paynter, having confessed after barbiturates were traced to him, and his fingerprints were found on Paynter's shirt-buttons. His death sentence was commuted to life imprisonment after he supplied information on criminal activity in south Essex and east London. Several arrests were made at The Bull public house, and a quantity of black market merchandise was seized.

Sniffer Dean continued to operate as police informer and underworld fixer until 1954. Then his life changed after he was inadvertently caught up in a gangland fight, during which a London gangster was killed. The publicity engendered by this, plus his colourful nickname, made him a minor celebrity and, after serving a two-year sentence, he became resident rogue on one of ITV's first real-life crime series. Later, he served on the government's advisory committee on prison reform.

No one was charged with the assassination of Martin Hunter. The investigation pointed to Thomas Henry Crick, one of the rebels killed by commandos at Broadcasting House. It was established that he had committed other crimes on behalf of the Red Brigade, and he was known as a top marksman with a rifle. But there was insufficient evidence, and the inquest returned a verdict of murder by a person or persons unknown.

Emily Hart married George Fowler. Friends said that this was just so that she could cease paying him wages but in fact they'd become quite fond of each other. They ran the Cavendish together for ten years, and then retired to Eastbourne, where

George was able to continue his sea-fishing, and Emily revived her theatrical interests with the local amateur dramatic club.

James Hoskins, whose unorthodox approach and lack of respect for his superiors had long irritated the Establishment, was encouraged to take early retirement in the fifties. He had earned particular disfavour by demanding, unsuccessfully, an investigation into Kim Philby, a highly regarded figure in British Intelligence, whom he suspected of being a traitor. Hoskins retired to Buckinghamshire, where he grew roses and became a successful author of books for young children. His wife did the illustrations. Hoskins consistently declined to disclose information about the activities of British Intelligence, preferring to honour the oath he had taken when he joined. Back in 1945, Hoskins had traced Mark Jefferson's widowed mother, and arranged for her to receive a pension from British Intelligence, plus a letter from the King, commending her son's courage in the service of his country.